VALIS

PHILIP K. DICK

VALIS

VINTAGE BOOKS

A Division of Random House, Inc.

New York

To Russell Galen,
Who showed me the right way.

First Vintage Books Edition, July 1991

Library of Congress Cataloging-in-Publication Data
Dick, Philip K.
Valis/Philip Dick. —1st Vintage Books ed.
p. cm.
ISBN 0-679-73446-5
I. Title.
[PS3554.I3V35   1991]
813'.54—dc20   90-55676
CIP

Manufactured in the United States of America
10 9 8 7 6 5 4 3 2

VALIS (acronym of Vast Active Living Intelligence System from an American film): A perturbation in the reality field in which a spontaneous self-monitoring negentropic vortex is formed, tending progressively to subsume and incorporate its environment into arrangements of information. Characterized by quasi-consciousness, purpose, intelligence, growth and an armillary coherence.

—*Great Soviet Dictionary*
Sixth Edition, 1992

1

Horselover Fat's nervous breakdown began the day he got the phonecall from Gloria asking if he had any Nembutals. He asked her why she wanted them and she said that she intended to kill herself. She was calling everyone she knew. By now she had fifty of them, but she needed thirty or forty more to be on the safe side.

At once Horselover Fat leaped to the conclusion that this was her way of asking for help. It had been Fat's delusion for years that he could help people. His psychiatrist once told him that to get well he would have to do two things; get off dope (which he hadn't done) and to stop trying to help people (he still tried to help people).

As a matter of fact, he had no Nembutals. He had no sleeping pills of any sort. He never did sleeping pills. He did uppers. So giving Gloria sleeping pills by which she could kill herself was beyond his power. Anyhow, he wouldn't have done it if he could.

"I have ten," he said. Because if he told her the truth she would hang up.

"Then I'll drive up to your place," Gloria said in a rational, calm voice, the same tone in which she had asked for the pills.

He realized then that she was not asking for help. She was trying to die. She was completely crazy. If she were sane she would realize that it was necessary to veil her purpose, because this way she made him guilty of complicity. For him to agree, he would need to want her dead. No motive existed for him—or anyone—to want that. Gloria was gentle and civilized, but she dropped a lot of acid. It was obvious that the acid, since he had last heard from her six months ago, had wrecked her mind.

"What've you been doing?" Fat asked.

"I've been in Mount Zion Hospital in San Francisco. I tried suicide and my mother committed me. They discharged me last week."

"Are you cured?" he said.

"Yes," she said.

That's when Fat began to go nuts. At the time he didn't know it, but he had been drawn into an unspeakable psychological game. There was no way out. Gloria Knudson had wrecked him, her friend, along with her own brain. Probably she had wrecked six or seven other people, all friends who loved her, along the way, with similar phone conversations. She had undoubtedly destroyed her mother and father as well. Fat heard in her rational tone the harp of nihilism, the twang of the void. He was not dealing with a person; he had a reflex-arc thing at the other end of the phone line.

What he did not know then is that it is sometimes an appropriate response to reality to go insane. To listen to Gloria rationally ask to die was to inhale the contagion. It was a Chinese finger trap, where the harder you pull to get out, the tighter the trap gets.

"Where are you now?" he asked.

"Modesto. At my parents' home."

Since he lived in Marin County, she was several hours' drive away. Few inducements would have gotten him to make such a drive. This was another serving-up of lunacy: three hours' drive each way for ten Nembutals. Why not just total the car? Gloria was not even committing her irrational act rationally. Thank you, Tim Leary, Fat thought. You and your promotion of the joy of expanded consciousness through dope.

He did not know his own life was on the line. This was 1971. In 1972 he would be up north in Vancouver, British Columbia, involved in trying to kill himself, alone, poor and scared, in a foreign city. Right now he was spared that knowledge. All he wanted to do was coax Gloria up to Marin County so he could help her. One of God's greatest mercies is that he keeps us perpetually occluded. In 1976, totally crazy with grief, Horselover Fat would slit his wrist (the Vancouver suicide attempt having failed), take forty-nine tablets of high-grade

10

digitalis, and sit in a closed garage with his car motor running—and fail there, too. Well, the body has powers unknown to the mind, Gloria's mind had total control over her body; she was *rationally* insane.

Most insanity can be identified with the bizarre and the theatrical. You put a pan on your head and a towel around your waist, paint yourself purple and go outdoors. Gloria was as calm as she had ever been; polite and civilized. If she had lived in ancient Rome or Japan, she would have gone unnoticed. Her driving skills probably remained unimpaired. She would stop at every red light and not exceed the speed limit—on her trip to pick up the ten Nembutals.

I am Horselover Fat, and I am writing this in the third person to gain much-needed objectivity. I did not love Gloria Knudson, but I liked her. In Berkeley, she and her husband had given elegant parties, and my wife and I always got invited. Gloria spent hours fixing little sandwiches and served different wines, and she dressed up and looked lovely, with her sandy-colored short-cut curly hair.

Anyhow, Horselover Fat had no Nembutal to give her, and a week later Gloria threw herself out of a tenth floor window of the Synanon Building in Oakland, California, and smashed herself to bits on the pavement along MacArthur Boulevard, and Horselover Fat continued his insidious, long decline into misery and illness, the sort of chaos that astrophysicists say is the fate in store for the whole universe. Fat was ahead of his time, ahead of the universe. Eventually he forgot what event had started off his decline into entropy; God mercifully occludes us to the past as well as the future. For two months, after he learned of Gloria's suicide, he cried and watched TV and took more dope—his brain was going too, but he didn't know it. Infinite are the mercies of God.

As a matter of fact, Fat had lost his own wife, the year before, to mental illness. It was like a plague. No one could discern how much was due to drugs. This time in America—1960 to 1970—and this place, the Bay Area of Northern California, was totally fucked. I'm sorry to tell you this, but that's the truth. Fancy terms and ornate theories cannot cover this fact up. The authorities became as psychotic as those they

11

hunted. They wanted to put all persons who were not clones of the establishment away. The authorities were filled with hate. Fat had seen police glower at him with the ferocity of dogs. The day they moved Angela Davis, the black Marxist, out of the Marin County jail, the authorities dismantled the whole civic center. This was to baffle radicals who might intend trouble. The elevators got unwired; doors got relabeled with spurious information; the district attorney hid. Fat saw all this. He had gone to the civic center that day to return a library book. At the electronic hoop at the civic center entrance, two cops had ripped open the book and papers that Fat carried. He was perplexed. The whole day perplexed him. In the cafeteria, an armed cop watched everyone eat. Fat returned home by cab, afraid of his own car and wondering if he was nuts. He was, but so was everyone else.

I am by profession, a science fiction writer. I deal in fantasies. My life is a fantasy. Nonetheless, Gloria Knudson lies in a box in Modesto, California. There's a photo of her funeral wreaths in my photo album. It's a color photo so you can see how lovely the wreaths are. In the background a VW is parked. I can be seen crawling into the VW, in the midst of the service. I am not able to take any more.

After the graveside service Gloria's former husband Bob and I and some tearful friend of his—and hers—had a late lunch at a fancy restaurant in Modesto near the cemetery. The waitress seated us in the rear because the three of us looked like hippies even though we had suits and ties on. We didn't give a shit. I don't remember what we talked about. The night before, Bob and I—I mean, Bob and Horselover Fat—drove to Oakland to see the movie *Patton*. Just before the graveside service Fat met Gloria's parents for the first time. Like their deceased daughter, they treated him with utmost civility. A number of Gloria's friends stood around the corny California ranch-style living room recalling the person who linked them together. Naturally, Mrs. Knudson wore too much makeup; women always put on too much makeup when someone dies. Fat petted the dead girl's cat, Chairman Mao. He remembered the few days Gloria had spent with him upon her futile trip to his house for the Nembutal which he did not have. She greeted the disclosure of his lie with aplomb, even a neutrality. When you are going to die you do not care about small things.

"I took them," Far had told her, lie upon lie.

They decided to drive to the beach, the great ocean beach of the Point Reyes Peninsula. In Gloria's VW, with Gloria driving (it never entered his mind that she might, on impulse, wipe out him, herself and the car) and, an hour later, sat together on the sand smoking dope.

What Fat wanted to know most of all was why she intended to kill herself.

Gloria had on many-times-washed-jeans and a T-shirt with Mick Jagger's leering face across the front of it. Because the sand felt nice she took off her shoes. Fat noticed that she had pink-painted toenails and that they were perfectly pedicured. To himself he thought, she died as she lived.

"They stole my bank account," Gloria said.

After a time he realized, from her measured, lucidly stated narration, that no "they" existed. Gloria unfolded a panorama of total and relentless madness, lapidary in construction. She had filled in all the details with tools as precise as dental tools. No vacuum existed anywhere in her account. He could find no error, except of course for the premise, which was that everyone hated her, was out to get her, and she was worthless in every respect. As she talked she began to disappear. He watched her go; it was amazing. Gloria, in her measured way, talked herself out of existence word by word. It was rationality at the service of—well, he thought, at the service of nonbeing. Her mind had become one great, expert eraser. All that really remained now was her husk; which is to say, her uninhabited corpse.

She is dead now, he realized that day on the beach.

After they had smoked up all their dope, they walked along and commented on seaweed and the height of waves. Seagulls croaked by overhead, sailing themselves like frisbies. A few people sat or walked here and there, but mostly the beach was deserted. Signs warned of undertow. Fat, for the life of him, could not figure out why Gloria didn't simply walk out into the surf. He simply could not get into her head. All she could think of was the Nembutal she still needed, or imagined she needed.

"My favourite Dead album is *Workingman's Dead*," Gloria

13

said at one point. "But I don't think they should advocate taking cocaine. A lot of kids listen to rock."

"They don't advocate it. The song's just about someone taking it. And it killed him, indirectly; he smashed up his train."

"But that's why I started on drugs," Gloria said.

"Because of the Grateful Dead?"

"Because," Gloria said, "everyone wanted me to do it. I'm tired of doing what other people want me to do."

"Don't kill yourself," Fat said. "Move in with me. I'm all alone. I really like you. Try it for a while, at least. We'll move your stuff up, me and my friends. There's lots of things we can do, like go places, like to the beach today. Isn't it nice here?"

To that, Gloria said nothing.

"It would really make me feel terrible," Fat said. "For the rest of my life, if you did away with yourself." Thereby, as he later realized, he presented her with all the wrong reasons for living. She would be doing it as a favor to others. He could not have found a worse reason to give had he looked for years. Better to back the VW over her. This is why suicide hotlines are not manned by nitwits; Fat learned this later in Vancouver, when, suicidal himself, he phoned the British Columbia Crisis Center and got expert advice. There was no correlation between this and what he told Gloria on the beach that day.

Pausing to rub a small stone loose from her foot, Gloria said, "I'd like to stay overnight at your place tonight."

Hearing this, Fat experienced involuntary visions of sex.

"Far out," he said, which was the way he talked in those days. The counterculture possessed a whole book of phrases which bordered on meaning nothing. Fat used to string a bunch of them together. He did so now, deluded by his own carnality into imagining that he had saved his friend's life. His judgment, which wasn't worth much anyhow, dropped to a new nadir of acuity. The existence of a good person hung in the balance, hung in a balance which Fat held, and all he could think of now was the prospect of scoring. "I can dig it," he prattled away as they walked. "Out of sight."

A few days later she was dead. They spent that night together, sleeping fully dressed; they did not make love; the

14

next afternoon Gloria drove off, ostensibly to get her stuff from her parents' house in Modesto. He never saw her again. For several days he waited for her to show up and then one night the phone rang and it was her ex-husband Bob.

"Where are you right now?" Bob asked.

The question bewildered him; he was at home, where his phone was, in the kitchen, Bob sounded calm. "I'm here," Fat said.

"Gloria killed herself today," Bob said.

*

I have a photo of Gloria holding Chairman Mao in her arms; Gloria is kneeling and smiling and her eyes shine. Chairman Mao is trying to get down. To their left, part of a Christmas tree can be seen. On the back, Mrs. Knudson has written in tidy letters:

How we made her feel gratitude for our love.

I've never been able to fathom whether Mrs. Knudson wrote that after Gloria's death or before. The Knudsons mailed me the photo a month—mailed Horselover Fat the photo a month—after Gloria's funeral. Fat had written asking for a photo of her. Initially he had asked Bob, who replied in a savage tone, "What do you want a picture of Gloria for?" To which Fat could give no answer. When Fat got me started writing this, he asked me why I thought Bob Langley got so mad at this request. I don't know. I don't care. Maybe Bob knew that Gloria and Fat had spent a night together and he was jealous. Fat used to say Bob Langley was a schizoid; he claimed that Bob himself told him that. A schizoid lacks proper affect to go with his thinking; he's got what's called "flattening of affect." A schizoid would see no reason not to tell you that about himself. On the other hand, Bob bent down after the graveside service and put a rose on Gloria's coffin. That was about when Fat had gone crawling off to the VW. Which reaction is more appropriate? Fat weeping in the parked car by himself, or the ex-husband bending down with the rose, saying

15

nothing, showing nothing, but doing something . . . Fat contributed nothing to the funeral except a bundle of flowers which he had belatedly bought on the trip down to Modesto. He had given them to Mrs. Knudson, who remarked that they were lovely. Bob had picked them out.

After the funeral, at the fancy restaurant where the waitress had moved the three of them out of view, Fat asked Bob what Gloria had been doing at Synanon, since she was supposed to be getting her possessions together and driving back up to Marin County to live with him—he had thought.

"Carmina talked her into going to Synanon," Bob said. That was Mrs. Knudson. "Because of her history of drug involvement."

Timothy, the friend Fat didn't know, said, "They sure didn't help her very much."

What had happened was that Gloria walked in the front door of Synanon and they had gamed her right off. Someone, on purpose, had walked past her as she sat waiting to be interviewed and had remarked on how ugly she was. The next person to parade past her informed her that her hair looked like something a rat slept in. Gloria had always been sensitive about her curly hair. She wished it was long like all the other hair in the world. What the third Synanon member would have said was moot, because by then Gloria had gone upstairs to the tenth floor.

"Is that how Synanon works?" Fat asked.

Bob said, "It's a technique to break down the personality. It's a fascist therapy that makes the person totally outer-directed and dependent on the group. Then they can build up a new personality that isn't drug-oriented."

"Didn't they realize she was suicidal?" Timothy asked.

"Of course," Bob said. "She phoned in and talked to them; they knew her name and why she was there."

"Did you talk to them after her death?" Fat asked.

Bob said, "I phoned them up and asked to talk to someone high up and told him they had killed my wife, and the man said that they wanted me to come down there and teach them how to handle suicidal people. He was super upset. I felt sorry for him."

At that, hearing that, Fat decided that Bob himself was not right in the head. Bob felt sorry for Synanon. Bob was all fucked up. Everyone was fucked up, including Carmina Knudson. There wasn't a sane person left in Northern California. It was time to move somewhere else. He sat eating his salad and wondering where he could go. Out of the country. Flee to Canada, like the draft protesters. He personally knew ten guys who had slipped across into Canada rather than fight in Vietnam. Probably in Vancouver he would run into half a dozen people he knew. Vancouver was supposed to be one of the most beautiful cities in the world. Like San Francisco, it was a major port. He could start life all over and forget the past.

It entered his head as he sat fooling with his salad that when Bob phoned he hadn't said, "Gloria killed herself" but rather "Gloria killed herself today," as if it had been inevitable that she would do it one day or another. Perhaps this had done it, this assumption. Gloria had been timed, as if she were taking a math test. Who really was the insane one? Gloria or himself (probably himself) or her ex-husband or all of them, the Bay Area, not insane in the loose sense of the term but in the strict technical sense? Let it be said that one of the first symptoms of psychosis is that the person feels perhaps he is becoming psychotic. It is another Chinese fingertrap. You cannot think about it without becoming part of it. By thinking about madness, Horselover Fat slipped by degrees into madness.

I wish I could have helped him.

2

Although there was nothing I could do to help Horselover Fat, he did escape death. The first thing that came along to save him took the form of an eighteen-year-old highschool girl living down the street from him and the second was God. Of the two of them the girl did better.

I'm not sure God did anything at all for him; in fact in some ways God made him sicker. This was a subject on which Fat and I could not agree. Fat was certain that God had healed him completely. That is not possible. There is a line in the *I Ching* reading, "Always ill but never dies." That fits my friend.

Stephanie entered Fat's life as a dope dealer. After Gloria's death he did so much dope that he had to buy from every source available to him. Buying dope from highschool kids is not a smart move. It has nothing to do with dope itself but with the law and morality. Once you begin to buy dope from kids you are a marked man. I'm sure it's obvious why. But the thing I knew—which the authorities did not—is this: Horselover Fat really wasn't interested in the dope that Stephanie had for sale. She dealt hash and grass but never uppers. She did not approve of uppers. Stephanie never sold anything she did not approve of. She never sold psychedelics no matter what pressure was put on her. Now and then she sold cocaine. Nobody could quite figure out her reasoning, but it was a form of reasoning. In the normal sense, Stephanie did not think at all. But she did arrive at decisions, and once she arrived at them no one could budge her. Fat liked her.

There lay the gist of it; he liked her and not the dope, but to maintain a relationship with her he had to be a buyer, which meant he had to do hash. For Stephanie, hash was the beginning and end of life—life worth living, anyhow.

If God came in a poor second, at least he wasn't doing anything illegal, as Stephanie was. Fat was convinced that Stephanie would wind up in jail; he expected her to be arrested any day. All Fat's friends expected him to be arrested any day. We worried about that and about his slow decline into depression and psychosis and isolation. Fat worried about Stephanie. Stephanie worried about the price of hash. More so, she worried about the price of cocaine. We used to imagine her suddenly sitting bolt upright in the middle of the night and exclaiming, "Coke has gone up to a hundred dollars a gram!" She worried about the price of dope the way normal women worry about the price of coffee.

We used to argue that Stephanie could not have existed before the Sixties. Dope had brought her into being, summoned her out of the very ground. She was a coefficient of dope, part of an equation. And yet it was through her that Fat made his way eventually to God. Not through her dope; it has nothing to do with dope. There is no door to God through dope; that is a lie peddled by the unscrupulous. The means by which Stephanie brought Horselover Fat to God was by means of a little clay pot which she threw on her kickwheel, a kickwheel which Fat had helped pay for, as a present on her eighteenth birthday. When he fled to Canada he took the pot with him, wrapped up in shorts, socks and shirts, in his single suitcase.

It looked like an ordinary pot: squat and light brown, with a small amount of blue glaze as trim. Stephanie was not an expert potter. This pot was one of the first she threw, at least outside of her ceramics class in high school. Naturally, one of her first pots would go to Fat. She and he had a close relationship. When he'd get upset, Stephanie would quiet him down by supercharging him with her hashpipe. The pot was unusual in one way, however. In it slumbered God. He slumbered in the pot for a long time, for almost too long. There is a theory among some religions that God intervenes at the eleventh hour. Maybe that is so; I couldn't say. In Horselover Fat's case God waited until three minutes before twelve, and even then what he did was barely enough: barely enough and virtually too late. You can't hold Stephanie responsible for that; she threw the pot, glazed it and fired it as soon as she had the

19

kickwheel. She did her best to help her friend Fat, who, like Gloria before him, was beginning to die. She helped her friend the way Fat had tried to help his friend, only Stephanie did a better job. But that was the difference between her and Fat. In a crisis she knew what to do. Fat did not. Therefore Fat is alive today and Gloria is not. Fat had a better friend that Gloria had had. Perhaps he would have wanted it the other way around but the option was not his. We do not serve up people to ourselves; the universe does. The universe makes certain decisions and on the basis of these decisions some people live and some people die. This is a harsh law. But every creature yields to it out of necessity. Fat got God, and Gloria Knudson got death. It is unfair and Fat would be the first person to say so. Give him credit for that.

After he had encountered God, Fat developed a love for him which was not normal. It is not what is usually meant in saying that someone "loves God." With Fat it was an actual hunger. And stranger still, he explained to us that God had injured him and still he yearned for him, like a drunk yearns for booze. God, he told us, had fired a beam of pink light directly at him, at his head, his eyes; Fat had been temporarily blinded and his head had ached for days. It was easy, he said, to describe the beam of pink light; it's exactly what you get as a phosphene after-image when a flashbulb has gone off in your face. Fat was spiritually haunted by that color. Sometimes it showed up on a TV screen. He lived for that light, that one particular color.

However, he could never really find it again. Nothing could generate that color for light but God. In other words, normal light did not contain that color. One time Fat studied a color chart, a chart of the visible spectrum. The color was absent. He had seen a color which no one can see; it lay off the end.

What comes after light in terms of frequency? Heat? Radio waves? I should know but I don't. Fat told me (I don't know how true this is) that in the solar spectrum what he saw was above seven hundred millimicrons; in terms of Fraunhofer Lines, past B in the direction of A. Make of that what you will. I deem it a symptom of Fat's breakdown. People suffering nervous breakdowns often do a lot of research, to find explanations for what they are undergoing. The research, of course, fails.

It fails as far as we are concerned, but the unhappy fact is that it sometimes provides a spurious rationalization to the disintegrating mind—like Gloria's "they." I looked up the Fraunhofer Lines one time, and there is no "A." The earliest letter-indication that I could find is B. It goes from G to B, from ultraviolet to infrared. That's it. There is no more. What Fat saw, or thought he saw, was not light.

After he returned from Canada—after he got God—Fat and I spent a lot of time together, and in the course of our going out at night, a regular event with us, cruising for action, seeing what was happening, we one time were in the process of parking my car when all at once a spot of pink light showed up on my left arm. I knew what it was, although I had never seen such a thing before; someone had turned a laser beam on us.

"That's a laser," I said to Fat, who had seen it, too, since the spot was moving all around, onto telephone poles and the cement wall of the garage.

Two teenagers stood at the far end of the street holding a square object between them.

"They built the goddam thing," I said.

The kids walked up to us, grinning. They had built it, they told us, from a kit. We told them how impressed we were, and they walked off to spook someone else.

"That color pink?" I asked Fat.

He said nothing. But I had the impression that he was not being up front with me. I had the feeling that I had seen his color. Why he would not say so, if such it was, I do not know. Maybe the notion spoiled a more elegant theory. The mentally disturbed do not employ the Principle of Scientific Parsimony: the most simple theory to explain a given set of facts. They shoot for the baroque.

The cardinal point which Fat had made to us regarding his experience with the pink beam which had injured and blinded him was this: he claimed that instantly—as soon as the beam struck him—he knew things he had never known. He knew, specifically, that his five-year-old son had an undiagnosed birth defect and he knew what that birth defect consisted of, down to the anatomical details. Down, in fact, to the medical specifics to relate to the doctor.

I wanted to see how he told it to the doctor. How he explained knowing the medical details. His brain had trapped all the information the beam of pink light had nailed him with, but how would he account for it?

Fat later developed a theory that the universe is made out of information. He started keeping a journal—had been, in fact, secretly doing so for some time: the furtive act of a deranged person. His encounter with God was all there on the pages in his—Fat's, not God's—handwriting.

The term "journal" is mine, not Fat's. His term was "exegesis," a theological term meaning a piece of writing that explains or interprets a portion of scripture. Fat believed that the information fired at him and progressively crammed into his head in successive waves had a holy origin and hence should be regarded as a form of scripture, even if it just applied to his son's undiagnosed right inguinal hernia which had popped the hydrocele and gone down into the scrotal sack. This was the news Fat had for the doctor. The news turned out to be correct, as was confirmed when Fat's ex-wife took Christopher in to be examined. Surgery was scheduled for the next day, which is to say as soon as possible. The surgeon cheerfully informed Fat and his ex-wife that Christopher's life had been in danger for years. He could have died during the night from a strangulated piece of his own gut. It was fortunate, the surgeon said, that they had found out about it. Thus again Gloria's "they," except that in this instance the "they" actually existed.

The surgery came off a success, and Christopher stopped being such a complaining child. He had been in pain since birth. After that, Fat and his ex-wife took their son to another GP, one who had eyes.

One of the paragraphs in Fat's journal impressed me enough to copy it out and include it here. It does not deal with right inguinal hernias but is more general in nature, expressing Fat's growing opinion that the nature of the universe is information. He had begun to believe this because for him the universe—his universe—was indeed fast turning into information. Once God

22

started talking to him he never seemed to stop. I don't think they report that in the Bible.

Journal entry 37. **Thoughts of the Brain are experienced by us as arrangements and rearrangements—change—in a physical universe; but in fact it is really information and information-processing which we substantialize. We do not merely see its thoughts as objects, but rather as the movement, or, more precisely, the placement of objects: how they become linked to one another. But we cannot read the patterns of arrangement; we cannot extract the information in it—i.e. it as information, which is what it is. The linking and relinking of objects by the Brain is actually a language, but not a language like ours (since it is addressing itself and not someone or something outside itself).**

Fat kept working this particular theme over and over again, both in this journal and in his oral discourse to his friends. He felt sure the universe had begun to talk to him. Another entry in his journal reads:

36. We should be able to hear this information, or rather narrative, as a neutral voice inside us. But something has gone wrong. All creation is a language and nothing but a language, which for some inexplicable reason we can't read outside and can't hear inside. So I say, we have become idiots. Something has happened to our intelligence. My reasoning is this: arrangement of parts of the Brain is a language. We are parts of the Brain; therefore we are language. Why, then, do we not know this? We do not even know what we are, let alone what the outer reality is of which we are parts. The origin of the word "idiot" is the word "private." Each of us has become private, and no longer shares the common thought of the Brain, except at a subliminal level. Thus our real life and purpose are conducted below our threshold of consciousness.

To which I personally am tempted to say, Speak for yourself, Fat.

Over a long period of time (or "Deserts of vast Eternity," as he would have put it) Fat developed a lot of unusual theories to account for his contact with God, and the information derived therefrom. One in particular struck me as interesting, being different from the others. It amounted to a kind of mental capitulation by Fat to what he was undergoing. This

23

theory held that in actuality he wasn't experiencing anything at all. Sites of his brain were being selectively stimulated by tight energy beams emanating from far off, perhaps millions of miles away. These selective brain-site stimulations generated in his head the *impression*—for him—that he was in fact seeing and hearing words, pictures, figures of people, printed pages, in short God and God's Message, or, as Fat liked to call it, the Logos. But (this particular theory held) he really only imagined he experienced these things. They resembled holograms. What struck me was the oddity of a lunatic discounting his hallucinations in this sophisticated manner; Fat had intellectually dealt himself out of the game of madness while still enjoying its sights and sounds. In effect, he no longer claimed that what he experienced was actually there. Did this indicate he had begun to get better? Hardly. Now he held the view that "they" or God or someone owned a long-range very tight information-rich beam of energy focussed on Fat's head. In this I saw no improvement, but it did represent a change. Fat could now honestly discount his hallucinations, which meant he recognized them as such. But, like Gloria, he now had a "they." It seemed to me a Pyrrhic victory. Fat's life struck me as a litany of exactly that, as, for example, the way he had rescued Gloria.

The exegesis Fat labored on month after month struck me as a Pyrrhic victory if there ever was one—in this case an attempt by a beleaguered mind to make sense out of the inscrutable. Perhaps this is the bottom line to mental illness: incomprehensible events occur; your life becomes a bin for hoax-like fluctuations of what used to be reality. And not only that—as if that weren't enough—but you, like Fat, ponder forever over these fluctuations in an effort to order them into a coherency, when in fact the only sense they make is the sense you impose on them, out of the necessity to restore everything into shapes and processes you can recognize. The first thing to depart in mental illness is the familiar. And what takes its place is bad news because not only can you not understand it, you also cannot communicate it to other people. The madman experiences something, but what it is or where it comes from he does not know.

24

In the midst of his shattered landscape, which one can trace back to Gloria Knudson's death, Fat imagined God had cured him. Once you notice Pyrrhic victories they seem to abound. It reminds me of a girl I once knew who was dying of cancer. I visited her in the hospital and did not recognize her; sitting up in her bed she looked like a little old hairless man. From the chemotherapy she had swollen up like a great grape. From the cancer and the therapy she had become virtually blind, nearly deaf, underwent constant seizures, and when I bent close to her to ask her how she felt she answered, when she could understand my question, "I feel that God is healing me." She had been religiously inclined and had planned to go into a religious order. On the metal stand beside her bed she had, or someone had, laid out her rosary. In my opinion a FUCK YOU, GOD sign would have been appropriate; the rosary was not.

Yet in all fairness, I have to admit that God—or someone calling himself God, a distinction of mere semantics—had fired precious information at Horselover Fat's head by which their son Christopher's life had been saved. Some people God cures and some he slays. Fat denies that God slays anyone. Fat says, God never harms anyone. Illness, pain and undeserved suffering arise not from God but from elsewhere, to which I say, How did this elsewhere arise? Are there two gods? Or is part of the universe out from under God's control? Fat used to quote Plato. In Plato's cosmology, noös or Mind is persuading ananke or blind necessity—or blind chance, according to some experts—into submission. Noös happened to come along and to its surprise discovered blind chance: chaos, in other words, onto which noös imposes order (although how this "persuading" is done Plato nowhere says). According to Fat, my friend's cancer consisted of disorder not yet persuaded into sentient shape. Noös or God had not yet gotten around to her, to which I said, "Well, when he did get around to her it was too late." Fat had no answer for that, at least in terms of oral rebuttal. Probably he sneaked off and wrote about it in his journal. He stayed up to four A.M. every night scratching away in his journal. I suppose all the secrets of the universe lay in it somewhere amid the rubble.

25

We enjoyed baiting Fat into theological disputation because he always got angry, taking the point of view that what we said on the topic mattered—that the topic itself mattered. By now he had become totally whacked out. We enjoyed introducing the discussion by way of some careless comment: "Well, God gave me a ticket on the freeway today" or something like that. Ensnared, Fat would leap into action. We whiled away the time pleasantly in this fashion, torturing Fat in a benign way. After we left his place we had the added satisfaction of knowing he was writing it all down in in the journal. Of course, in the journal his view always prevailed.

No need existed to bait Fat with idle questions, such as, "If God can do anything can he create a ditch so wide he can't jump over it?" We had plenty of real questions that Fat couldn't field. Our friend Kevin always began his attack one way. "What about my dead cat?" Kevin would ask. Several years ago, Kevin had been out walking his cat in the early evening. Kevin, the fool, had not put the cat on a leash, and the cat had dashed into the street and right into the front wheel of a passing car. When he picked up the remains of the cat it was still alive, breathing in bloody foam and staring at him in horror. Kevin liked to say, "On judgement day when I'm brought up before the great judge I'm going to say, 'Hold on a second,' and then I'm going to whip out my dead cat from inside my coat. 'How do you explain *this?*' I'm going to ask." By then, Kevin used to say, the cat would be as stiff as a frying pan; he would hold out the cat by its handle, its tail, and wait for a satisfactory answer.

Fat said, "No answer would satisfy you."

"No answer you could give," Kevin sneered. "Okay, so God saved your son's life; why didn't he have my cat run out into the street five seconds later? *Three* seconds later? Would that have been too much trouble? Of course, I suppose a cat doesn't matter."

"You know, Kevin," I pointed out one time, "you could have put the cat on a leash."

"No," Fat said. "He has a point. It's been bothering me. For him the cat is a symbol of everything about the universe he doesn't understand."

26

"I understand fine," Kevin said bitterly. "I just think it's fucked. God is either powerless, stupid or he doesn't give a shit. Or all three. He's evil, dumb and weak. I think I'll start my own exegesis."

"But God doesn't talk to you," I said.

"You know who talks to Horse?" Kevin said. "Who really talks to Horse in the middle of the night? People from the planet Stupid. Horse, what's the wisdom of God called again? Saint what?"

"Hagia Sophia," Horse said cautiously.

Kevin said, "How do you say Hagia Stupid? St. Stupid?"

"Hagia Moron," Horse said. He always defended himself by giving in. "Moron is a Greek word like Hagia. I came across it when I was looking up the spelling of oxymoron."

"Except that the -on suffix is the neuter ending," I said.

That gives you an idea of where our theological arguments tended to wind up. Three malinformed people disagreeing with one another. We also had David our Roman Catholic friend and the girl who had been dying of cancer, Sherri. She had gone into remission and the hospital had discharged her. To some extent her hearing and vision were permanently impaired, but otherwise she seemed to be fine.

Fat, of course, used this as an argument for God and God's healing love, as did David and of course Sherri herself. Kevin saw her remission as a miracle of radiation therapy and chemotherapy and luck. Also, he confided to us, the remission was temporary. At any time, Sherri could get sick again. Kevin hinted darkly that the next time she got sick there wouldn't be a remission. We sometimes thought that he hoped so, since it would confirm his view of the universe.

It was a mainstay of Kevin's bag of verbal tricks that the universe consisted of misery and hostility and would get you in the end. He looked at the universe the way most people regard an unpaid bill; eventually they will force payment. The universe reeled you out, let you flop and thrash and then reeled you in. Kevin waited constantly for this to begin with him, with me, with David and especially with Sherri. As to Horselover Fat, Kevin believed that the line hadn't been payed out in years; Fat had long been in the part of the cycle where they reel

27

you back in. He considered Fat not just potentially doomed but doomed in fact.

Fat had the good sense not to discuss Gloria Knudson and her death in front of Kevin. Had he done so, Kevin would add her to his dead cat. He would be talking about whipping her out from under his coat on judgement day, along with the cat.

Being a Catholic, David always traced everything wrong back to man's free will. This used to annoy even me. I once asked him if Sherri getting cancer consisted of an instance of free will, knowing as I did that David kept up with all the latest news in the field of psychology and would make the mistake of claiming that Sherri had subconsciously wanted to get cancer and so had shut down her immune system, a view floating around in advanced psychological circles at that time. Sure enough, David fell for it and said so.

"Then why did she get well?" I asked. "Did she subconsciously want to get well?"

David looked perplexed. If he consigned her illness to her own mind he was stuck with having to consign her remission to mundane and not supernatural causes. God had nothing to do with it.

"What C. S. Lewis would say," David began, which at once angered Fat, who was present. It maddened him when David turned to C. S. Lewis to bolster his straight-down-the-pipe orthodoxy.

"Maybe Sherri overrode God," I said. "God wanted her sick and she fought to get well." The thrust of David's impending argument would of course be that Sherri had neurotically gotten cancer due to being fucked up, but God had stepped in and saved her; I had turned it around in anticipation.

"No," Fat said. "It's the other way around. Like when he cured me."

Fortunately, Kevin was not present. He did not consider Fat cured (nor did anyone else) and anyway God didn't do it. That is a logic which Freud attacks, by the way, the two-proposition self-cancelling structure. Freud considered this structure a revelation of rationalization. Someone is accused of stealing a horse, to which he replies, "I don't steal horses and anyhow you have a crummy horse." If you ponder the reasoning in this you can see the actual thought-process behind it. The second statement does not reinforce the first. It only looks like it does. In terms of our perpetual theological disputations—brought on by Fat's supposed encounter with the divine—the two-proposition self-cancelling structure would appear like this:

1) God does not exist.
2) And anyhow he's stupid.

A careful study of Kevin's cynical rantings reveals this structure at every turn. David continually quoted C. S. Lewis; Kevin contradicted himself logically in his zeal to defame God; Fat made obscure references to information fired into his head by a beam of pink light; Sherri, who had suffered dreadfully, wheezed out pious mummeries: I switched my position according to who I was talking to at the time. None of us had a grip on the situation, but we did have a lot of free time to waste in this fashion. By now the epoch of drug-taking had ended, and everyone had begun casting about for a new obsession. For us the new obsession, thanks to Fat, was theology.

A favourite antique quotation of Fat's goes:

"And can I think the great Jehovah sleeps,
Like Shemosh, and such fabled deities?
Ah! no; heav'n heard my thoughts, and wrote them down—
It must be so."

Fat doesn't like to quote the rest of it.

" 'Tis this that racks my brain,
And pours into my breast a thousand pangs,
That lash me into madness . . ."

It's from an aria by Handel. Fat and I used to listen to my Seraphim LP of Richard Lewis singing it. *Deeper, and deeper still.*

Once I told Fat that another aria on the record described his mind perfectly.

"Which aria?" Fat said guardedly.

"Total eclipse," I answered.

> "Total eclipse! no sun, no moon,
> All dark amidst the blaze of noon!
> Oh, glorious light! no cheering ray
> To glad my eyes with welcome day!
> Why thus deprived Thy prime decree?
> Sun, moon and stars are dark to me!"

To which Fat said, "The opposite is true in my case. I am illuminated by holy light fired at me from another world. I see what no other man sees."

He had a point there.

3

A question we had to learn to deal with during the dope decade was, How do you break the news to someone that his brains are fried? This issue had now passed over into Horselover Fat's theological world as a problem for us—his friends—to field.

It would have been simple to tie the two together in Fat's case: the dope he did during the Sixties had pickled his head on into the Seventies. If I could have arranged it so that I could think so I would have; I like solutions that answer a variety of problems simultaneously. But I really couldn't think so. Fat hadn't done psychedelics, at least not to any real extent. Once, in 1964, when Sandox LSD-25 could still be acquired—especially in Berkeley—Fat had dropped one huge hit of it and had abreacted back in time or had shot forward in time or up outside of time; anyhow he had spoken in Latin and believed that the *Dies Irae*, the Day of Wrath, had come. He could hear God thumping tremendously, in fury. For eight hours Fat had prayed and whined in Latin. Later he claimed that during his trip he could only think in Latin and talk in Latin; he had found a book with a Latin quotation in it, and could read it as easily as he normally read English. Well, perhaps the etiology of his later God-madness lay there. His brain, in 1964, liked the acid trip and taped it, for future replay.

On the other hand, this line of reasoning merely relegates the question back to 1964. As far as I can determine, the ability to read, think and speak in Latin is not normal for an acid trip. Fat knows no Latin. He can't speak it now. He couldn't speak it before he dropped the huge hit of Sandoz LSD-25. Later, when his religious experiences began, he found himself thinking in a foreign language which he did *not* understand (he

31

had understood his own Latin in '64). Phonetically, he had written down some of the words, remembered at random. To him they constituted no language at all, and he hesitated to show anyone what he had put on paper. His wife—his later wife Beth—had taken a year of Greek in college and she recognized what Fat had written down, inaccurately, as *koine* Greek. Or at least Greek of some sort, Attic or *koine*.

The Greek word *koine* simply means *common*. By the time of the New Testament, the *koine* had become the *lingua franca* of the Middle East, replacing Aramaic which had previously supplanted Akkadian (I know these things because I am a professional writer and it is essential that I possess a scholarly knowledge about languages). The New Testament manuscripts survived in *koine* Greek, although probably Q, the source of the synoptics, had been written in Aramaic, which is in fact, a form of Hebrew. Jesus spoke Aramaic. Thus, when Horselover Fat began to think in *koine* Greek, he was thinking in the language which St. Luke and St. Paul—who were close friends—had used, at least to write with. The *koine* looks funny when written down because the scribes left no spaces between the words. This can lead to a lot of peculiar translations, since the translator gets to put the spaces wherever he feels is appropriate or in fact wherever he wants. Take this English instance:

GOD IS NO WHERE
GOD IS NOW HERE

Actually, these matters were pointed out to me by Beth, who never took Fat's religious experiences seriously until she saw him write down phonetically several words of the *koine*, which she knew he had no experience with and could not recognize even as a genuine language. What Fat claimed was—well, Fat claimed plenty. I must not start any sentence with, "What Fat claimed was." During the years—outright years!—that he labored on his exegesis, Fat must have come up with more theories than there are stars in the universe. Every day he developed a new one, more cunning, more exciting and more fucked. God, however, remained a constant theme. Fat

32

ventured away from belief in God the way a timid dog I once owned had ventured off its front lawn. He—both of them— would go first one step, then another, then perhaps a third and then turn tail and run frantically back to familiar territory. God, to Fat, constituted a territory which he had staked out. Unfortunately for him, following the initial experience, Fat could not find his way back to that territory.

They ought to make it a binding clause that if you find God you get to keep him. For Fat, finding God (if indeed he did find God) became, ultimately, a bummer, a constantly diminishing supply of joy, sinking lower and lower like the contents of a bag of uppers. Who deals God? Fat knew that the churches couldn't help, although he did consult with one of David's priests. It didn't work. Nothing worked. Kevin suggested dope. Being involved with literature, I recommended he read the English seventeenth century minor metaphysical poets such as Vaughan and Herbert:

> "He knows he hath a home, but scarce knows where,
>   He sayes it is so far
> That he hath quite forgot how to go there."

Which is from Vaughan's poem "Man." As nearly as I could make out, Fat had devolved to the level of those poets, and had, for these times, become an anachronism. The universe has a habit of deleting anachronisms. I saw this coming for Fat if he didn't get his shit together.

Of all the suggestions given to Fat, the one that seemed most promising came from Sherri, who still lingered on with us in a state of remission. "What you should do," she told Fat during one of his darker hours, "is get into studying the characteristics of the T-34."

Fat asked what that was. It turned out that Sherri had read a book on Russian armor during World War Two. The T-34 tank had been the Soviet Union's salvation and thereby the salvation of all the Allied Powers—and, by extension, Horse-lover Fat's, since without the T-34 he would be speaking—not English or Latin or the *koine*—but German.

"The T-34," Sherri explained, "moved very rapidly. At

33

Kursk they knocked out even Porsche Elefants. You have no idea what they did to the Fourth Panzer Army." She then started drawing sketches of the situation at Kursk in 1943, giving figures. Fat and the rest of us were mystified. This was a side of Sherri we hadn't known. "It took Zhukov himself to turn the tide against the Panzers," Sherri wheezed on. "Vatutin screwed up. He was later murdered by pro-Nazi partisans. Now, consider the Tiger tank the Germans had and their Panthers." She showed us photographs of various tanks and related with relish how General Koniev had successfully crossed the Dniester and Prut Rivers by March twenty-sixth.

Basically, Sherri's idea had to do with bringing Fat's mind down from the cosmic and the abstract to the particular. She had hatched out the practical notion that nothing is more real than a large World War Two Soviet tank. She wanted to provide an antitoxin to Fat's madness. However, her recitation, complete with maps and photographs, only served to remind him of the night he and Bob had seen the movie *Patton* before attending Gloria's graveside service. Naturally, Sherri had not known about that.

"I think he should take up sewing," Kevin said. "Don't you have a sewing machine, Sherri? Teach him to use it."

Sherri, showing a high degree of stubbornness, continued, "The tank battles at Kursk involved over four thousand armored vehicles. It was the greatest battle of armor in history. Everyone knows about Stalingrad, but nobody knows about Kursk. The real victory by the Soviet Union took place at Kursk. When you consider—"

"Kevin," David interrupted, "what the Germans should have done was show the Russians a dead cat and ask them to explain it."

"That would have stopped the Soviet offensive right there," I said. "Zhukov would still be trying to account for the cat's death."

To Kevin, Sherri said, "In view of the stunning victory by the good side at Kursk, how can you complain about one cat?"

"There's something in the Bible about falling sparrows," Kevin said. "About his eye being on them. That's what's wrong with God; he only has one eye."

34

"Did God win the battle at Kursk?" I said to Sherri. "That must be news to the Russians, especially the ones who built the tanks and drove them and got killed."

Sherri said patiently, "God uses us as instruments through which he works."

"Well," Kevin said, "regarding Horse, God has a defective instrument. Or maybe they're both defective, like an eighty-year-old lady driving a Pinto with a drop-in gas tank."

"The Germans would have had to hold up Kevin's dead cat," Fat said. "Not just any dead cat. All Kevin cares about is that one cat."

"That cat," Kevin said, "did not exist during World War Two."

"Did you grieve over him then?" Fat said.

"How could I?" Kevin said. "He didn't exist."

"Then his condition was the same as now," Fat said.

"Wrong," Kevin said.

"Wrong in what way?" Fat said. "How did his nonexistence then differ from his nonexistence now?"

"Kevin's got the corpse now," David said. "To hold up. That was the whole point of the cat's existence. He lived to become a corpse by which Kevin could refute the goodness of God."

"Kevin," Fat said, "who created your cat?"

"God did," Kevin said.

"So God created a refutation of his own goodness," Sherri said. "By your logic."

"God is stupid," Kevin said. "We have a stupid deity. I've said that before."

Sherri said, "Does it take much skill to create a cat?"

"You just need two cats," Kevin said. "One male and one female." But he could obviously see where she was leading him. "It takes—" He paused, grinning. "Okay, it takes skill, if you presume purpose in the universe."

"You don't see any purpose?" Sherri said.

Hesitating, Kevin said, "Living creatures have purpose."

"Who puts the purpose in them?" Sherri said.

"They—" Again Kevin hesitated. "They are their purpose. They and their purpose can't be separated."

35

"So an animal is an expression of purpose," Sherri said. "So there is purpose in the universe."

"In small parts of it."

"And unpurpose gives rise to purpose."

Kevin eyed her. "Eat shit," he said.

*

In my opinion, Kevin's cynical stance had done more to ratify Fat's madness than any other single factor—any other, that is, than the original cause, whatever that might have been. Kevin had become the unintentional instrument of that original cause, a realization which had not escaped Fat. In no way, shape or form did Kevin represent a viable alternative to mental illness. His cynical grin had about it the grin of death; he grinned like a triumphant skull. Kevin lived to defeat life. It originally amazed me that Fat would put up with Kevin, but later I could see why. Every time Kevin tore down Fat's system of delusions—mocked them and lampooned them—Fat gained strength. If mockery were the only antidote to his malady, he was palpably better off as he stood. Whacked out as he was, Fat could see this. Actually, were the truth known, Kevin could see it too. But he evidently had a feedback loop in his head that caused him to step up the attacks rather than abandon them. His failure reinforced his efforts. So the attacks grew and Fat's strength grew. It resembled a Greek myth.

In Horselover Fat's exegesis the theme of this issue is put forth over and over again. Fat believed that a streak of the irrational permeated the entire universe, all the way up to God or the Ultimate Mind, which lay behind it. He wrote:

38. From loss and grief the Mind has become deranged. Therefore we, as parts of the universe, the Brain, are partly deranged.

Obviously he had extrapolated into cosmic proportions from his own loss of Gloria.

35. The Mind is not talking to us but by means of us. Its narrative passes through us and its sorrow infuses us irrationally. As Plato discerned, there is a streak of the irrational in the World Soul.

Entry 32 gives more on this:

The changing information which we experience as World is an unfolding narrative. *It tells about the death of a woman* (italics mine). **This woman, who died long ago, was one of the primordial twins. She was one half of the divine syzygy. The purpose of the narrative is the recollection of her and of her death. The Mind does not wish to forget her. Thus the ratiocination of the Brain consists of a permanent record of her existence, and, if read, will be understood this way. All the information processed by the Brain—experienced by us as the arranging and rearranging of physical objects—is an attempt at this preservation of her; stones and rocks and sticks and amoebae are traces of her. The record of her existence and passing is ordered onto the meanest level of reality by the suffering Mind which is now alone.**

If, in reading this, you cannot see that Fat is writing about himself, then you understand nothing.

On the other hand, I am not denying that Fat was totally whacked out. He began to decline when Gloria phoned him and he continued to decline forever and ever. Unlike Sherri and her cancer, Fat experienced no remission. Encountering God was not a remission. But probably it wasn't a worsening, despite Kevin's cynical views. You cannot say that an encounter with God is to mental illness what death is to cancer: the logical outcome of a deteriorating illness process. The technical term—theological technical term, not psychiatric—is theophany. A theophany consists of a self-disclosure by the divine. It does not consist of something the percipient does; it consists of something the divine—the God or gods, the high power—does. Moses did not create the burning bush. Elijah, on Mount Horeb, did not generate the low, murmuring voice. How are we to distinguish a genuine theophany from a mere hallucination on the part of the percipient? If the voice tells him something he does not know *and could not know*, then perhaps we are dealing with the genuine thing and not the spurious. Fat knew no *koine* Greek. Does this prove anything? He did not know about his son's birth defect—at least not consciously. Perhaps he knew about the near-strangulated hernia unconsciously, and simply did not want to face it. There exists, too, a mechanism by which he might have known the *koine*; it has to

37

do with phylogenic memory, the experience of which has been reported by Jung: he terms it the collective or racial unconscious. The ontogeny—that is, the individual—recapitulates the phylogeny—that is, the species—and since this is generally accepted, then maybe here lies a basis for Fat's mind serving up a language spoken two thousand years ago. If there were phylogenic memories buried in the individual human mind, this is what you might expect to find. But Jung's concept is speculative. No one, really, has been able to verify it.

If you grant the possibility of a divine entity, you cannot deny it the power of self-disclosure; obviously any entity or being worthy of the term "god" would possess, without effort, that ability. The real question (as I see it) is not, Why theophanies? but, Why aren't there more? The key concept to account for this is the idea of the *deus absconditus*, the hidden, concealed, secret or unknown god. For some reason Jung regards this as a notorious idea. But if God exists, he must be a *deus absconditus*—with the exception of his rare theopanies, or else he does not exist at all. The latter view makes more sense, except for the theophanies, rare though they be. All that is required is one absolutely verified theophany and the latter view is voided.

The vividness of the impression which a supposed theophany makes on the percipient is no proof of authenticity. Nor, really, is group perception (as Spinoza supposed, the entire universe may be one theophany, but then, again, the universe may not exist at all, as the Buddhist idealists decided). Any given alleged theophany may be a fake because anything may be a fake, from stamps to fossil skulls to black holes in space.

That the entire universe—as we experience it—could be a forgery is an idea best expressed by Heraclitus. Once you have taken his notion, or doubt into your head, you are ready to deal with the issue of God.

"It is necessary to have understanding (*noös*) in order to be able to interpret the evidence of eyes and ears. The step from the obvious to the latent truth is like the translation of utterances in a language which is foreign to most men. Heraclitus . . . in *Fragment 56* says that men, in regard to knowledge of perceptible things, 'are the victims of illusion much as Homer was.' To reach the truth from the appearances, it is necessary to interpret, to guess the riddle . . . but though this seems to be within the capacity of men, it is something most men never do. Heraclitus is very vehement in his attacks on the foolishness of ordinary men, and of what passes for knowledge among them. They are compared to sleepers in private worlds of their own."

Thus says Edward Hussey, Lecturer in Ancient Philosophy at the University of Oxford and a Fellow of All Souls College, in his book *The Presocratics*, published by Charles Scribner's Sons, New York, 1972, pages 37-38. In all my reading I have—I mean, Horselover Fat has—never found anything more significant as an insight into the nature of reality. In *Fragment 123*, Heraclitus says, "The nature of things is in the habit of concealing itself." And in *Fragment 54* he says, "Latent structure is master of obvious structure," to which Edward Hussey adds, "Consequently, he (Heraclitus) necessarily agreed . . . that reality was to some extent 'hidden.' " So if reality "[is] to some extent 'hidden,' " then what is meant by "theophany"? Because a theophany is an in-breaking of God, an in-breaking which amounts to an invasion of our world; and yet our world is only seeming; it is only "obvious structure," which is under the mastery of unseen "latent structure." Horselover Fat would like you to consider this above all other things. Because if Heraclitus is correct, there is in fact no reality but that of theophanies; the rest is illusion; in which case Fat alone among us comprehends the truth, and Fat, starting with - Gloria's phonecall, is insane.

Insane people—psychologically defined, not legally defined —are not in touch with reality. Horselover Fat is insane; therefore he is not in touch with reality. Entry no. 30 from his exegesis:

The phenomenal world does not exist; it is a hypostasis of the information processed by the Mind.

35. The Mind is not talking to us but by means of us. Its narrative passes through us and its sorrow infuses us irrationally.

As Plato discerned, there is a streak of the irrational in the World Soul.

In other words, the universe itself—and the Mind behind it—is insane. Therefore someone in touch with reality is, by definition, in touch with the insane: infused by the irrational.

In essence, Fat monitored his own mind and found it defective. He then, by the use of that mind, monitored outer reality, that which is called the macrocosm. He found it defective as well. As the Hermetic philosophers stipulated, the macrocosm and the microcosm mirror each other faithfully. Fat, using a defective instrument, swept out a defective subject, and from this sweep got back the report that everything was wrong.

And in addition, there was no way out. The interlocking between the defective instrument and the defective subject produced another perfect Chinese finger-trap. Caught in his own maze, like Daedalus, who built the labyrinth for King Minos of Crete and then fell into it and couldn't get out. Presumably Daedalus is still there, and so are we. The only difference between us and Horselover Fat is that Fat knows his situation and we do not; therefore Fat is insane and we are normal. "They are compared to sleepers in private worlds of their own," as Hussey put it, and he would know; he is the foremost living authority on ancient Greek thought, with the possible exception of Francis Cornford. And it is Cornford who says that Plato believed that there was an element of the irrational in the World Soul.[1]

There is no route out of the maze. The maze shifts as you move through it, because it is alive.

> PARSIFAL: I move only a little, yet already I seem to have gone far.
> GURNEMANZ: You see, my son, here time turns into space.

(The whole landscape becomes indistinct. A forest ebbs out and a wall of rough rock ebbs in, through which can be seen a

[1] *Plato's Cosmology, The Timaeus of Plato*, Library of Liberal Arts, New York, 1937.

40

gateway. The two men pass through the gateway. What happened to the forest? The two men did not really move; they did not go anywhere, and yet they are not now where they originally were. *Here time turns into space.* Wagner began *Parsifal* in 1845. He died in 1873, long before Hermann Minkowski postulated four-dimensional space-time (1908). The source-basis for *Parsifal* consisted of Celtic legends, and Wagner's research into Buddhism for his never-written opera about the Buddha to be called *The Victors (Die Sieger)*. Where did Richard Wagner get the notion that time could turn into space?)

And if time can turn into space, can space turn into time? In Mircea Eliade's book *Myth and Reality* one chapter is titled "Time Can Be Overcome." It is a basic purpose of mythic ritual and sacrament to overcome time. Horselover Fat found himself thinking in a language used two thousand years ago, the language in which St. Paul wrote. *Here time turns into space.* Fat told me another feature of his encounter with God: all of a sudden the landscape of California, USA, 1974 ebbed out and the landscape of Rome of the first century C.E. ebbed in. He experienced a superimposition of the two for a while, like techniques familiar in movies. In photography. Why? How? God explained many things to Fat but he never explained that, except for this cryptic statement: it is journal listing 3. **He causes things to look different so it would appear time has passed.** Who is "he"? Are we to infer that time has *not* in fact passed? And did it ever pass? Was there once a real time, and for that matter a real world, and now there is counterfeit time and a counterfeit world, like a sort of bubble growing and looking different but actually static?

Horselover Fat saw fit to list this statement early in his journal or exegesis or whatever he calls it. Journal listing 4, the next entry, goes:

Matter is plastic in the face of Mind.

Is any world out there at all? For all intents and purposes Gurnemanz and Parsifal stand still, and the landscape changes; so they become located in another space—a space which formerly had been experienced as time. Fat thought in a language of two thousand years ago and saw the ancient world

41

appropriate to that language; the inner contents of his mind matched his perceptions of the outer world. Some kind of logic seems involved, here. Perhaps a time dysfunction took place. But why didn't his wife Beth experience it, too? She was living with him when he had his encounter with the divine. For her nothing changed, except (as she told me) she heard strange popping sounds, like something overloaded: objects pushed to the point where they exploded, as if jammed, jammed with too much energy.

Both Fat and his wife told me another aspect of those days, in March 1974. Their pet animals underwent a peculiar metamorphosis. The animals looked more intelligent and more peaceful. That is, until both animals died of massive malignant tumors.

Both Fat and his wife told me one thing about their pets which has stuck in my mind ever since. During that time the animals seemed to be trying to communicate with them, trying to use language. That cannot be written off as part of Fat's psychosis—that, and the animals' death.

The first thing that went wrong, according to Fat, had to do with the radio. Listening to it one night—he had not been able to sleep for a long time—he heard the radio saying hideous words, sentences which it could not be saying. Beth, being asleep, missed that. So that could have been Fat's mind breaking down; by then his psyche was disintegrating at a terrible velocity.

Mental illness is not funny.

4

Following his spectacular suicide attempt with the pills, the razor sharp blade and the car engine, all this due to Beth taking their son Christopher and leaving him, Fat found himself locked up in the Orange County mental hospital. An armed cop had pushed him in a wheelchair from the cardiac intensive care ward through the underground corridor which connected with the psychiatric wing.

Fat had never been locked up before. From the forty-nine tablets of digitalis he had suffered several days of PAT arrhythmia, since his efforts had yielded maximum dig toxicity, listed on the scale as Three. Digitalis had been prescribed for him to counter an hereditary PAT arrhythmia, but nothing such as he experienced while dig toxic. It's ironic than an overdose of digitalis induces the very arrhythmia it is used to counteract. At one point, while Fat lay on his back gazing up at the cathode-tube screen over his head, a straight line showed; his heart had stopped beating. He continued to watch, and finally the trace dot resumed its wave-form. The mercies of God are infinite.

So in a weakened condition he arrived under armed guard at the psychiatric lock-up, where he soon found himself sitting in a corridor breathing vast amounts of cigarette smoke and shaking, both from fatigue and fear. That night he slept on a cot—six cots to a room—and discovered that his cot came equipped with leather manacles. The door had been propped open to the corridor so the psych techs could keep watch over the patients. Fat could see the commercial TV set, which remained on. Johnny Carson's guest turned out to be Sammy Davis, Jr. Fat lay watching, wondering how it felt to have one

43

glass eye. At that point he had no insight into his situation. He understood that he had survived the dig toxicity; he understood that for all intents and purposes he was now under arrest for his suicide attempt; he had no idea what Beth had been doing during the time he lay in the cardiac intensive care ward. She had neither called nor come to visit him. Sherri had come first, then David. No one else knew. Fat particularly did not want Kevin to know because Kevin would show up and be cynical at his—Fat's—expense. And he wasn't in any condition to receive cynicism, even if it were well meant.

The chief cardiologist at the Orange County Medical Center had exhibited Fat to a whole group of student doctors from U.C. Irvine. OCMC was a teaching hospital. They all wanted to listen to a heart labouring under forty-nine tabs of high-grade digitalis.

Also, he had lost blood from the slash on his left wrist. What had saved his life initially emanated from a defect in the choke of his car; the choke hadn't opened properly as the engine warmed, and finally the engine had stalled. Fat had made his way unsteadily back into the house and lain down on his bed to die. The next morning he woke up, still alive, and had begun to vomit up the digitalis. That was the second thing which saved him. The third thing came in the form of all the paramedics in the world removing the glass and aluminum sliding door at the rear of Fat's house. Fat had phoned his pharmacy somewhere along the line to get a refill on his Librium prescription; he had taken thirty Librium just before taking the digitalis. The pharmacist had contacted the paramedics. A lot can be said for the infinite mercies of God, but the smarts of a good pharmacist, when you get down to it, is worth more.

After one night in the receiving ward of the psychiatric wing of the county medical hospital, Fat underwent his automatic evaluation. A whole host of well-dressed men and women confronted him; each held a clipboard and all of them scrutinized him intently.

Fat put on the trappings of sanity, as best he could. He did everything possible to convince them that he had regained his senses. As he spoke he realized that nobody believed him. He could have delivered his monolog in Swahili with equal effect.

All he managed to do was abase himself and thereby divest himself of his last remnant of dignity. He had stripped away his self-respect by his own earnest efforts. Another Chinese finger-trap.

Fuck it, Fat said to himself finally, and ceased talking.

"Go outside," one of the psych techs said, "and we'll let you know our decision."

"I really have learned my lesson," Fat said as he rose and started out of the room. "Suicide represents the introjection of hostility which should better be directed outward at the person who has frustrated you. I had a lot of time to meditate during the intensive cardiac care unit or ward and I realized that years of self-abnegation and denial manifested itself in my destructive act. But what amazed me the most was the wisdom of my body, which knew not only to defend itself from my mind but specifically how to defend itself. I realize now that Yeats's statement, 'I am an immortal soul tied to the body of a dying animal' is diametrically opposite to the actual state of affairs *vis-à-vis* the human condition."

The psych tech said, "We'll talk to you outside after we've made our decision."

Fat said, "I miss my son."

No one looked at him.

"I thought Beth might hurt Christopher," Fat said. That was the only true statement he had made since entering the room. He had tried to kill himself not so much because Beth had left him but because with her living elsewhere he could not look after his little son.

Presently, he sat outside in the corridor, on a plastic and chrome couch, listening to a fat old woman tell how her husband had plotted to kill her by pumping poison gas under the door of her bedroom. Fat thought back over his life. He did not think about God, who he had seen. He did not say to himself, I am one of the few human beings who has actually seen God. Instead he thought back to Stephanie who had made him the little clay pot which he called Oh Ho because it seemed like a Chinese pot to him. He wondered if Stephanie had become a heroin addict by now or had been locked up in jail, as he was now locked up, or was dead, or married, or living in the

45

snow in Washington like she had always talked about, the state of Washington, which she had never seen but dreamed about. Maybe all of those things or none of them. Maybe she had been crippled in an auto accident. He wondered what Stephanie would say to him if she could see him now, locked up, his wife and child gone, the choke on his car not working, his mind fried.

Were his mind not fried he probably would have thought about how lucky he was to be alive—not in the philosophical sense of lucky but in the statistical sense. Nobody survives forty-nine tabs of high grade pure digitalis. As a general rule, twice the prescribed dose of digitalis will off you. Fat's prescribed dose had been fixed at *q.i.d.*: four a day. He had swallowed 12.25 times his prescribed daily dose and survived. The infinite mercies of God make no sense whatsoever, in terms of practical considerations. In addition he had downed all his Librium, twenty Quide and sixty Apresoline, plus half a bottle of wine. All that remained of his medication was a bottle of Miles Nervine. Fat was technically dead.

Spiritually, he was dead, too.

Either he had seen God too soon or he had seen him too late. In any case, it had done him no good at all in terms of survival. Encountering the living God had not helped to equip him for the tasks of ordinary endurance, which ordinary men, not so favored, handle.

But it could also be pointed out—and Kevin had done so—that Fat had accomplished something else in addition to seeing God. Kevin had phoned him up one day in excitement, having in his possession another book by Mircea Eliade.

"Listen!" Kevin said. "You know what Eliade says about the dream-time of the Australian bushmen? He says that anthropologists are wrong in assuming that the dream-time is time in the past. Eliade says that it's another kind of time going on right now, which the bushmen break through and into, the age of the heroes and their deeds. Wait: I'll read you the part." An interval of silence. "Fuck," Kevin then said. "I can't find it. But the way they prepare for it is to undergo dreadful pain; it's their ritual of initiation. You were in a lot of pain when you had your experience; you had that impacted wisdom tooth and you were—" On the phone Kevin lowered his voice; he had been shouting. "You remember. Afraid about the authorities getting you."

"I was nuts," Fat had answered. "They weren't after me."

"But you thought they were and you were so scared you fucking couldn't sleep at night, night after night. And you underwent sensory deprivation."

"Well, I lay in bed unable to sleep."

"You started seeing colors, Floating colors." Kevin had begun to shout again in excitement; when his cynicism vanished he became manic. "That's described in *The Tibetan Book of the Dead*; that's the trip across to the next world. You were mentally dying! From stress and fear! That's how it's done—reaching into the next reality! The dream-time!"

Right now Fat sat on the plastic and chrome couch mentally dying; in fact he was already mentally dead, and in the room he had left, the experts were deciding his fate, passing sentence and judgment on what remained of him. It is proper that technically qualified non-lunatics should sit in judgment on lunatics. How could things be otherwise?

"If they could just get across to the dream-time!" Kevin shouted. "That's the only *real* time; all the real events happen in the dream-time! The actions of the gods!"

Beside Fat the huge old lady held up a plastic pan; for hours she had been trying to throw up the Thorazine they had forced on her; she believed, she rasped at Fat, that the Thorazine had poison in it, by which her husband—who had penetrated the top levels of the hospital staff under a variety of names—intended to finish killing her.

"You found your way into the upper realm," Kevin declared. "Isn't that how you put it in your journal?"

48. Two realms there are, upper and lower. The upper derived from hyperuniverse I or Yang, Form I of Parmenides, is sentient and volitional. The lower realm, or Yin, Form II of Parmenides, is mechanical, driven by blind, efficient cause, deterministic and without intelligence, since it emanates from a dead source. In ancient times it was termed "astral determinism." We are trapped, by and large, in the lower realm, but are, through the sacraments, by means of the plasmate, extricated. Until

astral determinism is broken, we are not even aware of it, so occluded are we. "The Empire never ended."

A small, pretty, dark-haired girl walked silently past Fat and the huge old woman, carrying her shoes. At breakfast time she had tried to smash a window using her shoes and then, having failed, knocked down a six-foot-high black technician. Now the girl had about her the presence of absolute calm.

"The Empire never ended," Fat quoted to himself. That one sentence appeared over and over again in his exegesis; it had become his tag line. Originally the sentence had been revealed to him in a great dream. In the dream he again was a child, searching dusty used-book stores for rare old science fiction magazines, in particular *Astoundings*. In the dream he had looked through countless tattered issues, stacks upon stacks, for the priceless serial entitled "The Empire Never Ended." If he could find it and read it he would know everything; that had been the burden of the dream.

Prior to that, during the interval in which he had experienced the two-world superimposition, he had seen not only California, USA, of the year 1974 but also ancient Rome, he had discerned within the superimposition a Gestalt shared by both space-time continua, their common element: a Black Iron Prison. This is what the dream referred to as "the Empire." He knew it because, upon seeing the Black Iron Prison, he had recognized it. Everyone dwelt in it without realizing it. The Black Iron Prison was their world.

Who had built the prison—and why—he could not say. But he could discern one good thing: the prison lay under attack. An organization of Christians, not regular Christians such as those who attended church every Sunday and prayed, but secret early Christians wearing light gray-colored robes, had started an assault on the prison, and with success. The secret, early Christians were filled with joy.

Fat, in his madness, understood the reason for their joy. This time the early, secret, gray-robed Christians would get the prison, *rather than the other way around*. The deeds of the heroes, in the sacred dream-time . . . the only time, according to the bushmen, that was real.

Once, in a cheap science fiction novel, Fat had come across

a perfect description of the Black Iron Prison but set in the far future. So if you superimposed the past (ancient Rome) over the present (California in the twentieth century) and superimposed the far future world of *The Android Cried Me a River* over that, you got the Empire, the Black Iron Prison, as the supra- or trans-temporal constant. Everyone who had ever lived was literally surrounded by the iron walls of the prison; they were all inside it and none of them knew it—except for the gray-robed secret Christians.

That made the early, secret Christians supra- or trans-temporal, too, which is to say present at all times, a situation which Fat could not fathom. How could they be early but in the present and the future? And if they existed in the present, why couldn't anyone see them. On the other hand, why couldn't anyone see the walls of the Black Iron Prison which enclosed everyone, including himself, on all sides? Why did these antithetical forces emerge into palpability only when the past, present and future somehow—for whatever reason—got superimposed?

Maybe in the bushmen's dream-time no time existed. But if no time existed, how could the early, secret Christians be scampering away in glee from the Black Iron Prison which they had just succeeded in blowing up? And how could they blow it up back in Rome circa 70 C.E., since no explosives existed in those days? And how, if no time passed in the dream-time, could the prison come to an end? It reminded Fat of the peculiar statement in *Parsifal:* "You see, my son, here time turns into space." During his religious experience in March of 1974, Fat had seen an augmentation of space: yards and yards of space, extending all the way to the stars; space opened up around him as if a confining box had been removed. He had felt like a tomcat which had been carried inside a box on a car drive, and then they'd reached their destination and he had been let out of the box, let free. And at night in sleep he had dreamed of a measureless void, yet a void which was alive. The void extended and drifted and seemed totally empty and yet it possessed personality. The void expressed delight in seeing Fat, who, in the dreams, had no body; he, like the boundless void, merely drifted, very slowly; and he could, in addition, hear a

49

faint humming, like music. Apparently the void communicated through this echo, this humming.

"You of all people," the void communicated. "Out of everyone, it is you I love the most."

The void had been waiting to be reunited with Horselover Fat, of all the humans who had ever existed. Like its extension into space, the love in the void lay boundless; it and its love floated forever. Fat had never been so happy in all his life.

The psych tech walked up to him and said, "We are holding you for fourteen days."

"I can't go home?" Fat said.

"No, we feel you need treatment. You're not ready to go home yet."

"Read me my rights," Fat said, feeling numb and afraid.

"We can hold you fourteen days without a court hearing. After that with court approval we can, if we feel it's necessary, hold you another ninety days."

Fat knew that if he said anything, anything at all, they would hold him the ninety days. So he said nothing. When you are crazy you learn to keep quiet.

Being crazy and getting caught at it, out in the open, turns out to be a way to wind up in jail. Fat now knew this. Besides having a county drunk tank, the County of Orange had a county lunatic tank. He was in it. He could stay in it for a long time. Meanwhile, back at home, Beth undoubtedly was taking everything she wanted from their house to the apartment she had rented—she had refused to tell him where the apartment was; she wouldn't even tell him the city.

Actually, although Fat didn't know it at the time, due to his own folly he had allowed payment on his house to lapse, as well as on his car; he had not paid the electric bill nor the phone bill. Beth, distraught over Fat's mental and physical state, could not be expected to take on the crushing problems Fat had created. So when Fat got out of the hospital and returned home he found a notice of foreclosure, his car gone, the refrigerator leaking water, and when he tried to phone for help the phone was dreadfully silent. This had the effect of wiping out what little morale he had left, and he knew it was all his own fault. It was his karma.

Right now, Fat did not know these things. All he knew was that he had been thrown in the lock-up for a minimum of two weeks. Also, he had found out one other thing, from the other patients. The County of Orange would bill him for his stay in the lock-up. As a matter of fact his total bill, including that portion covering his time in the cardiac intensive care ward, came to over two thousand dollars. Fat had gone to the county hospital in the first place because he didn't have the money to be taken to a private hospital. So now he had learned something else about being crazy: not only does it get you locked up, but it costs you a lot of money. They can bill you for being crazy and if you don't pay or can't pay they can sue you, and if a court judgment is issued against you and you fail to comply, they can lock you up again, as being in contempt of court.

When you consider that Fat's original suicide attempt had emanated out of deep despair, the magic of his present situation, the glamor, somehow had departed. Beside him on the plastic and chrome couch the huge old lady continued to throw up her medication in the plastic basin provided by the hospital for such matters. The psych tech had taken hold of Fat by the arm to lead him to the ward where he would be confined during the two weeks ahead. They called it the North Ward. Unprotestingly, Fat accompanied the psych tech out of the receiving ward, across the hall and into the North Ward, where once again the door got locked behind him.

Fuck, Fat said to himself.

*

The psych tech escorted Fat to his room—which had two beds in it instead of six cots—and then took Fat to a small room to get a questionaire filled out. "This'll only take a few minutes," the psych tech said.

In the small room stood a girl, a Mexican girl, heavy-set, with rough, dark skin and huge eyes, dark and peaceful eyes, eyes like pools of fire; Fat stopped dead in his tracks as he saw the girl's flaming, peaceful huge eyes. The girl held a magazine open on top of a TV set; she displayed a crude drawing printed

51

on the page: a picture of the Peaceful Kingdom. The magazine, Fat realized, was the *Watchtower*. The girl, smiling at him, was a Jehovah's Witness.

The girl said in a gentle and moderated voice, to Fat and not to the psych tech, "Our Lord God has prepared for us a place to live where there will be no pain and no fear and see? The animals lie happily together, the lion and the lamb, as we shall be, all of us, friends who love one another, without suffering or death, forever and ever with our Lord Jehovah who loves us and will never abandon us, whatever we do."

"Debbie, please leave the lounge," the psych tech said.

Still smiling at Fat, the girl pointed to a cow and a lamb in the crude drawing. "All beasts, all men, all living creatures great and small will bask in the warmth of Jehovah's love, when the Kingdom arrives. You think it will be a long time, but Christ Jesus is with us today." Then, closing up the magazine, the girl still smiling but now silent, left the room.

"Sorry about that," the psych tech said to Fat.

"Gosh," Fat said, amazed.

"Did she upset you? I'm sorry about that. She's not supposed to have that literature; somebody must have smuggled it in to her."

Fat said, "I'll be okay." He realized it; it dazed him.

"Let's get this information down," the psych tech said, seating himself with his clipboard and pen. "The date of your birth."

You fool, Fat thought. You fucking fool. God is here in your goddam mental hospital and you don't know it; you see it but you don't know it. You have been invaded and you don't even know it.

He felt joy.

He remembered entry 9 from his exegesis. **He lived a long time ago but he is still alive.** He is still alive, Fat thought. After all that's happened. After the pills, after the slashed wrist, after the car exhaust. After being locked up. He is still alive.

*

After a few days, the patient he liked best in the ward was

52

Doug, a large, young, deteriorated hebephrenic who never put on street clothing but simply wore a hospital gown open at the back. The women in the ward washed, cut and brushed Doug's hair because he lacked the skills to do those things himself. Doug did not take his situation seriously, except when they all got wakened up for breakfast. Every day Doug greeted Fat with terror.

"The TV lounge has devils in it," Doug always said, every morning. "I'm afraid to go in there. Can you feel it? I feel it even walking past it."

When they all made out their lunch-orders Doug wrote:

SWILL

"I'm ordering swill," he told Fat.

Fat said, "I'm ordering dirt."

In the central office, which had glass walls and a locked door, the staff watched the patients and made notations. In Fat's case it got noted down that when the patients played cards (which took up half their time, since no therapy existed) Fat never joined in. The other patients played poker and blackjack, while Fat sat off by himself reading.

"Why don't you play cards?" Penny, a psych tech, asked him.

"Poker and blackjack are not card games but money games," Fat said, lowering his book. "Since we're not allowed to have any money on us, there's no point in playing."

"I think you should play cards," Penny said.

Fat knew that he had been ordered to play cards, so he and Debbie played kid's card games like "Fish." They played "Fish" for hours. The staff watched from their glass office and noted down what they saw.

One of the women had managed to retain possession of her Bible. For the thirty-five patients it was the only Bible. Debbie was not allowed to look at it. However, at one turn in the corridor—they were locked out of their rooms during the day, so that they could not lie down and sleep—the staff couldn't see what was happening. Fat sometimes turned their copy of the Bible, their communal copy, over to Debbie for a fast look at

53

one of the psalms. The staff knew what they were doing and detested them for it, but by the time a tech got out of the office and down the corridor, Debbie had strolled on.

Mental inmates always move at one speed and one speed only. But some always move slowly and some always run. Debbie, being wide and solid, sailed along slowly, as did Doug. Fat, who always walked with Doug, matched his pace to his. Together they circled around and around the corridor, conversing. Conversations in mental hospitals resemble conversations in bus stations, because in a Greyhound Bus Station everyone is waiting, and in a mental hospital—especially a county lock-up mental hospital—everyone is waiting. They wait to get out.

Not much goes on in a mental ward, contrary to what mythic novels relate. Patients do not really overpower the staff, and the staff does not really murder the patients. Mostly people read or watch TV or just sit smoking or try to lie down on a couch and sleep, or drink coffee or play cards or walk, and three times a day trays of food are served. The passage of time is designated by the arrival of the food carts. At night visitors show up and they always smile. Patients in a mental hospital can never figure out why people from the outside smile. To me, it remains a mystery to this day.

Medication, which is always referred to as "meds," gets doled out at irregular intervals, from tiny paper cups. Everyone is given Thorazine plus something else. They do not tell you what you are getting and they watch to make sure you swallow the pills. Sometimes the meds nurses fuck up and bring the same tray of medication around twice. The patients always point out that they just took their meds ten minutes ago and the nurses give them the meds again anyhow. The mistake is never discovered until the end of the day, and the staff refuses to talk about it to the patients, all of whom now have twice as much Thorazine in their systems as they are supposed to have.

I have never met a mental patient, even the paranoid ones, who believed that double-dosing was a tactic to oversedate the ward deliberately. It is patently obvious that the nurses are dumb. The nurses have enough trouble figuring out which patient is which, and finding each patient's little paper cup.

This is because a ward population constantly changes; new people arrive; old people get discharged. The real danger in a mental ward is that someone spaced out on PCP* will be admitted by mistake. The policy of many mental hospitals is to refuse PCP users and force the armed police to process them. The armed police constantly try to force the PCP users onto the unarmed mental hospital patients and staffs. Nobody wants to deal with a PCP user, for good reasons. The newspapers constantly relate how a PCP freak, locked up in a ward somewhere, bit off another person's nose or tore out his own eyes.

Fat was spared this. He did not even know such horrors existed. This came about through the wise planning of OCMC, which made sure that no PCP-head wound up in the North Ward. In point of fact, Fat owed his life to OCMC (as well as two thousand dollars), although his mind remained too fried for him to appreciate this.

When Beth read the itemized bill from OCMC, she could not believe the number of things they had done for her husband to keep him alive; the list ran to five pages. It even included oxygen. Fat did not know it, but the nurses at the intensive cardiac care ward believed that he would die. They monitored him constantly. Every now and then, in the intensive cardiac care ward, an emergency warning siren sounded. It meant someone had lost vital signs. Fat, lying in his bed attached as he was to the video screen, felt as if he had been placed next to a switching yard for railroad trains; life support mechanisms constantly sounded their various noises.

It is characteristic of the mentally ill to hate those who help them and love those who connive against them. Fat still loved Beth and he detested OCMC. This showed he belonged in the North Ward; I have no doubt of it. Beth knew when she took Christopher and left for parts unknown that Fat would try suicide; he'd tried it in Canada. In fact, Beth planned to move back in as soon as Fat offed himself. She told him so later. Also, she told him that it had infuriated her that he'd failed to kill himself. When he asked her why that had infuriated her, Beth said:

* Also known as Angel Dust.

55

"You have once again shown your inability to do anything."

The distinction between sanity and insanity is narrower than the razor's edge, sharper than a hound's tooth, more agile than a mule deer. It is more elusive than the merest phantom. Perhaps it does not even exist; perhaps it *is* a phantom.

Ironically, Fat hadn't been tossed into the lock-up because he was crazy (although he was); the reason, technically, consisted of the "danger to yourself" law. Fat constituted a menace to his own well-being, a charge that could be brought against many people. At the time he lived in the North Ward a number of pyschological tests were administered to him. He passed them, but on the other hand he had the good sense not to talk about God. Though he passed all the tests, Fat had faked them out. To while away the time he drew over and over again pictures of the German knights who Alexander Nevsky had lured onto the ice, lured to their deaths. Fat identified with the heavily-armored Teutonic knights with their slot-eyed masks and ox-horns projecting out on each side; he drew each knight carrying a huge shield and a naked sword; on the shield Fat wrote: *"In hoc signo vinces,"* which he got from a pack of cigarettes. It means, "In this sign you shall conquer." The sign took the form of an iron cross. His love of God had turned to anger, an obscure anger. He had visions of Christopher racing across a grassy field, his little blue coat flapping behind him, Christopher running and running. No doubt this was Horselover Fat himself running, the child in him, anyhow. Running from something as obscure as his anger.

In addition he several times wrote:

Dico per spiritum sanctum. Haec veritas est. Mihi crede et mecum in aeternitate vivebis. Entry 28.

This meant, "I speak by means of the Holy Spirit. This is the truth. Believe me and you will live with me in eternity."

One day on a list of printed instructions posted on the wall of the corridor he wrote:

Ex Deo nascimur, in Jesu mortimur, per spiritum sanctum reviviscimus.

Doug asked him what it meant.

" 'From God we are born,' " Fat translated, " 'in Jesus we die, by the Holy Spirit we live again.' "

"You're going to be here ninety days," Doug said.

One time Fat found a posted notice that fascinated him. The notice stipulated what could not be done, in order of descending importance. Near the top of the list all parties concerned were told:

NO ONE IS TO REMOVE ASHTRAYS FROM THE WARD.

And later down the list it stated:

FRONTAL LOBOTOMIES ARE NOT TO BE PER-FORMED WITHOUT THE WRITTEN CONSENT OF THE PATIENT.

"That should read 'prefrontal,'" Doug said, and wrote in the "pre."

"How do you know that?" Fat said.

"There's two ways of knowing," Doug said. "Either knowledge arises through the sense organs and is called empirical knowledge, or it arises within your head and it's called *a priori*." Doug wrote on the notice:

IF I BRING BACK THE ASHTRAYS, CAN I HAVE MY PREFRONTAL?

"You'll be here ninety days," Fat said.

Outside the building rain poured down. It had been raining since Fat arrived in the North Ward. If he stood on top of the washing machine in the laundry room, he could see out through a barred window to the parking lot. People parked their cars and then ran through the rain. Fat felt glad he was indoors in the ward.

Dr. Stone, who had charge of the ward, interviewed him one day.

"Did you ever try suicide before?" Dr. Stone asked him.

"No," Fat said, which of course wasn't true. At that moment he no longer remembered Canada. It was his impression that his life had begun two weeks ago when Beth walked out.

57

"I think," Dr. Stone said, "that when you tried to kill yourself you got in touch with reality for the first time."

"Maybe so," Fat said.

"What I am going to give you," Dr. Stone said, opening a black suitcase on his small cluttered desk, "we term the Bach remedies." He pronounced it *batch*. "These organic remedies are distilled from certain flowers which grow in Wales. Dr. Bach wandered through the fields and pastures of Wales experiencing every negative mental state that exists. With each state that he experienced he gently held one flower after another. The proper flower trembled in the cup of Dr. Bach's hand and he then developed unique methods of acquiring an essence in elixir form of each flower and combinations of flowers which I have prepared in a rum base." He put three bottles together on the desk, found a larger, empty bottle, and poured the contents of the three into it. "Take six drops a day," Dr. Stone said. "There is no way the Bach remedies can hurt you. They are not toxic chemicals. They will remove your sense of helplessness and fear and inability to act. My diagnosis is that those are the three areas you have blocks: fear, helplessness and an inability to act. What you should have done instead of trying to kill yourself would have been, take your son away from your wife—it's the law in California that a minor child must remain with his father until there is a court order to the contrary. And then you should have lightly struck your wife with a rolled-up newspaper or a phonebook."

"Thank you," Fat said, accepting the bottle. He could see that Dr. Stone was totally crazy, but in a good way. Dr. Stone was the first person at the North Ward, outside the patients, who had talked to him as if he were human.

"You have much anger in you," Dr. Stone said. "I am lending you a copy of the *Tao Te Ching*. Have you ever read Lao Tzu?"

"No," Fat admitted.

"Let me read you this part here," Dr. Stone said. He read aloud.

> "Its upper part is not dazzling;
> Its lower part is not obscure.

58

Dimly visible, it cannot be named
And returns to that which is without substance.
This is called the shape that has no shape,
The image that is without substance.
This is called indistinct and shadowy.
Go up to it and you will not see its head;
Follow behind it and you will not see its rear."

Hearing this, Fat remembered entries 1 and 2 from his journal. He quoted them, from memory, to Dr. Stone.

1. One Mind there is; but under it two principles contend.

2. The Mind lets in the light, then the dark; in interaction; so time is generated. At the end Mind awards victory to the light; time ceases and the Mind is complete.

"But," Dr. Stone said, "if Mind awards victory to the light, and the dark disappears, then reality will disappear, since reality is a compound of Yang and Yin equally."

"Yang is Form I of Parmenides," Fat said. "Yin is Form II. Parmenides argued that Form II does not in fact exist. Only Form I exists. Parmenides believed in a monistic world. People *imagine* that both forms exist, but they are wrong. Aristotle relates that Parmenides equates Form I with 'that which is' and Form II with 'that which is not.' Thus people are deluded."

Eying him, Dr. Stone said, "What's your source?"

"Edward Hussey," Fat said.

"He's at Oxford," Dr. Stone said. "I attended Oxford. In my opinion Hussey has no peer."

"You're right," Fat said.

"What else can you tell me?" Dr. Stone said.

Fat said, "Time does not exist. This is the great secret known to Apollonius of Tyana, Paul of Tarsus, Simon Magus, Paracelsus, Boehme and Bruno. The universe is contracting into a unitary entity which is completing itself. Decay and disorder are seen by us in reverse, as increasing. Entry 18 of my exegesis reads: **'Real time ceased in 70 C.E. with the fall of the Temple of Jerusalem. It began again in 1974. The intervening period was a perfect spurious interpolation aping the Creation of the Mind.'**"

"Interpolated by whom?" Dr. Stone asked.

"The Black Iron Prison, which is an expression of the Empire. What has been—" Fat had started to say, "What has been revealed to me." He rechose his words. "What has been most important in my discoveries is this: 'The Empire never ended.'"

Leaning against his desk, Dr. Stone folded his arms, rocked forward and back and studied Fat, waiting to hear more.

"That's all I know," Fat said, becoming belatedly cautious.

"I'm very interested in what you're saying," Dr. Stone said.

Fat realized that one of two possibilities existed and only two; either Dr. Stone was totally insane—not just insane but totally so—or else in an artful, professional fashion he had gotten Fat to talk; he had drawn Fat out and now knew that Fat was totally insane. Which meant that Fat could look forward to a court appearance and ninety days.

This is a mournful discovery.

1) Those who agree with you are insane.
2) Those who do not agree with you are in power.

Those were the twin realizations which now percolated through Fat's head. He decided to go for broke, to tell Dr. Stone the most fantastic entry in his exegesis.

"Entry number twenty-four," Fat said. "'In dormant seed form, as living information, the plasmate slumbered in the buried library of codices at Chenoboskion until—'"

"What is 'Chenoboskion'?" Dr. Stone interrupted.

"Nag Hammadi."

"Oh, the Gnostic library." Dr. Stone nodded. "Found and read in 1945 but never published. 'Living information'?" His eyes fixed themselves in intent scrutiny of Fat. "'Living information,'" he echoed. And then he said, "The Logos."

Fat trembled.

"Yes," Dr. Stone said. "The Logos would be living information, capable of replicating."

"Replicating not through information," Fat said, "in information, but *as* information. This is what Jesus meant when he spoke elliptically of the 'mustard seed' which, he said, 'would grow into a tree large enough for birds to roost in.'"

"There is no mustard tree," Dr. Stone agreed. "So Jesus could not have meant that literally. That fits with the so-called 'secrecy' theme of Mark; that he didn't want outsiders to know the truth. And you know?"

"**Jesus foresaw not only his own death but that of all—**" Fat hesitated. "**Homoplasmates.** That's a human being to which the plasmate had crossbonded. Interspecies symbiosis. **As living information the plasmate travels up the optic nerve of a human to the pineal body. It uses the human brain as a female host—**"

Dr. Stone grunted and squeezed himself violently.

"**—in which to replicate itself into its active form,**" Fat said. "**The Hermetic alchemists knew of it in theory from ancient texts but could not duplicate it, since they could not locate the dormant buried plasmate.**"

"But you're saying the plasmate—the Logos—was dug up at Nag Hammadi!"

"Yes, when the codices were read."

"You're sure it wasn't in dormant seed form at Qumran? In Cave Five?"

"Well," Fat said, uncertainly.

"Where did the plasmate originally come from?"

After a pause Fat said, "From another star system."

"You wish to identify that star system?"

"Sirius," Fat said.

"Then you believe that the Dogon People of the western Sudan are the source of Christianity."

"They use the fish sign," Fat said. "For Nommo, the benign twin."

"Who would be Form I or Yang."

"Right," Fat said.

"And Yurugu is Form II. But you believe that Form II doesn't exist."

"Nommo had to slay her," Fat said.

"That's what the Japanese myth stipulates, in a sense," Dr. Stone said. "Their cosmogonical myth. The female twin dies giving birth to fire; then she descends under the ground. The male twin goes after her to restore her but finds her

61

decomposing and giving birth to monsters. She pursues him and he seals her up under the ground."

Amazed, Fat said, "She's decomposing and yet she's still giving birth?"

"Only to monsters," Dr. Stone said.

*

About this time two new propositions entered Fat's mind, due to this particular conversation.

1) Some of those in power are insane.
2) And they are right.

By "right" read "in touch with reality." Fat had reverted back to his most dismal insight, that the universe and the Mind behind it which governed it are both totally irrational. He wondered if he should mention this to Dr. Stone, who seemed to understand Fat better than anyone else during all Fat's life.

"Dr. Stone," he said, "there's something I want to ask you. I want your professional opinion."

"Name it."

"Could the universe possibly be irrational?"

"You mean not guided by a mind. I suggest you turn to Xenophanes."

"Sure," Fat said. "Xenophanes of Colophon. 'One god there is, in no way like mortal creatures either in bodily form or in the thought of his mind. The whole of him sees, the whole of him thinks, the whole of him hears. He stays always motionless in the same place; it is not right—' "

" 'Fitting,' " Dr. Stone corrected. " 'It is not fitting that he should move about now this way, now that.' And the important part, *Fragment 25*. 'But, effortlessly, he wields all things by the thought of his mind.' "

"But he could be irrational," Fat said.

"How would we know?"

"The whole universe would be irrational."

Dr. Stone said, "Compared with what?"

That, Fat hadn't thought of. But as soon as he thought of it

62

he realized that it did not tear down his fear; it increased it. If the whole universe were irrational, because it was directed by an irrational—that is to say, insane—mind, whole species could come into existence, live and perish and never guess, precisely for the reason that Stone had just given.

"The Logos isn't rational," Fat decided out loud. "What I call the plasmate. Buried as information in the codices at Nag Hammadi. Which is back with us now, creating new homoplasmates. The Romans, the Empire, killed all the original ones."

"But you say real time ceased in 70 A.D. when the Romans destroyed the Temple. Therefore these are still Roman times; the Romans are still here. This is roughly—" Dr. Stone calculated. "About 100 A.D."

Fat realized, then, that this explained his double exposure, the superimposition he had seen of ancient Rome and California 1974. Dr. Stone had solved it for him.

The psychiatrist in charge of treating him for his lunacy had ratified it. Now Fat would never depart from faith in his encounter with God. Dr. Stone had nailed it down.

5

Fat spent thirteen days at North Ward, drinking coffee and reading and walking around with Doug, but he never got to talk to Dr. Stone again because Stone had too many responsibilities, inasmuch as he had charge of the whole ward and everyone in it, staff and patients alike.

Well, he did have one brief dipshit hurried interchange at the time of his discharge from the ward.

"I think you're ready to leave," Stone said cheerfully.

Fat said, "But let me ask you. I'm not talking about no mind at all directing the universe. I'm talking about a mind like Xenophanes conceived of, but the mind is insane."

"The Gnostics believed that the creator deity was insane," Stone said. "Blind. I want to show you something. It hasn't been published yet; I have it in a typescript from Orval Wintermute who is currently working with Bethge in translating the Nag Hammadi codices. This quote comes from *On the Origin of the World*. Read it."

Fat read it to himself, holding the precious typescript.

"He said, 'I am god and no other one exists except me.' But when he said these things, he sinned against all of the immortal (imperishable) ones, and they protected him. Moreover, when Pistis saw the impiety of the chief ruler, she was angry. Without being seen, she said, 'You err, Samael,' i.e. 'the blind god.' 'An enlightened, immortal man exists before you. This will appear within your molded bodies. He will trample upon you like potter's clay, (which) is trampled. And you will go with those who are yours down to your mother, the abyss.'"

64

At once, Fat understood what he had read. Samael was the creator deity and he imagined that he was the only god, as stated in Genesis. However, he was blind, which is to say, occluded. "Occluded" was Fat's salient term. It embraced all other terms: insane, mad, irrational, whacked out, fucked up, fried, psychotic. In his blindness (state of irrationality; i.e. cut off from reality), he did not realize that—

What did the typescript say? Feverishly, he searched over it, at which Dr. Stone thereupon patted him on the arm and told him he could keep the typescript; Stone had Xeroxed it several times over.

An enlightened, immortal man existed before the creator deity, and that enlightened, immortal man would appear within the human race which Samael was going to create. And that enlightened, immortal man who had existed *before* the creator deity would trample upon the fucked-up blind deluded creator like potter's clay.

Hence Fat's encounter with God—the true God—had come through the little pot Oh Ho which Stephanie had thrown for him on her kickwheel.

"Then I'm right about Nag Hammadi," he said to Dr. Stone.

"You would know," Dr. Stone said, and then he said something that no one had ever said to Fat before. "You're the authority," Dr. Stone said.

Fat realized that Stone had restored his—Fat's—spiritual life. Stone had saved him; he was a master psychiatrist. Everything which Stone had said and done *vis-à-vis* Fat had a therapeutic basis, a therapeutic thrust. Whether the content of Stone's information was correct was not important; his purpose from the beginning had been to restore Fat's faith in himself, which had vanished when Beth left—which had vanished, actually, when he had failed to save Gloria's life years ago.

Dr. Stone wasn't insane; Stone was a healer. He held down the right job. Probably he healed many people and in many ways. He adapted his therapy to the individual, not the individual to the therapy.

I'll be goddamned, Fat thought.

65

In that simple sentence, "You're the authority," Stone had given Fat back his soul.

The soul which Gloria, with her hideous malignant psychological death-game, had taken away.

They—note the "they"—paid Dr. Stone to figure out what had destroyed the patient entering the ward. In each case a bullet had been fired at him, somewhere, at some time, in his life. The bullet entered him and the pain began to spread out. Insidiously, the pain filled him up until he split in half, right down the middle. The task of the staff, and even of the other patients, was to put the person back together but this could not be done so long as the bullet remained. All that lesser therapists did was note the person split into two pieces and begin the job of patching him back into a unity; but they failed to find and remove the bullet. The fatal bullet fired at the person was the basis of Freud's original attack on the psychologically injured person; Freud had understood: he called it a trauma. Later on, everyone got tired of searching for the fatal bullet; it took too long. Too much had to be learned about the patient. Dr. Stone had a paranormal talent, like his paranormal Bach remedies which were a palpable hoax, a pretext to listen to the patient. Rum with a flower dipped in it—nothing more, but a sharp mind hearing what the patient said.

Dr. Leon Stone turned out to be one of the most important people in Horselover Fat's life. To get to Stone, Fat had had to nearly kill himself physically, matching his mental death. Is this what they mean about God's mysterious ways? How else could Fat have linked up with Leon Stone? Only some dismal act of the order of a suicide attempt, a truly lethal attempt, would have achieved it; Fat had to die, or nearly die, to be cured. Or nearly cured.

I wonder where Leon Stone practices now. I wonder what his recovery rate is. I wonder how he got his paranormal abilities. I wonder a lot of things. The worst event in Fat's life—Beth leaving him, taking Christopher, and Fat trying to kill himself—had brought on limitless benign consequences. If you judge the merits of a sequence by their final outcome, Fat had just gone through the best period of his life; he emerged from North Ward as strong as he would ever get. After all, no man is infinitely strong; for every creature that runs, flies, hops or crawls there is a terminal nemesis which he will not circumvent, which will finally do him in. But Dr. Stone had added the missing element to Fat, the element taken away from him, half-deliberately, by Gloria Knudson, who wished to take as many people with her as she could: self-confidence. "You are the authority," Stone had said, and that sufficed.

I've always told people that for each person there is a sentence—a series of words—which has the power to destroy him. When Fat told me about Leon Stone I realized (this came years after the first realization) that another sentence exists, another series of words, which will heal the person. If you're lucky you will get the second; but you can be certain of getting the first: that is the way it works. On their own, without training, individuals know how to deal out the lethal sentence, but training is required to deal out the second. Stephanie had come close when she made the little ceramic pot Oh Ho and presented it to Fat as her gift of love, a love she lacked the verbal skills to articulate.

How, when Stone gave Fat the typescript material from the Nag Hammadi codex, had he known the significance of *pot* and *potter* to Fat? To know that, Stone would have to be telepathic. Well, I have no theory. Fat, of course, has. He believes that like Stephanie, Dr. Stone was a micro-form of God. That's why I say Fat is nearly healed, not healed.

Yet by regarding benign people as micro-forms of God, Fat at least remained in touch with a good god, not a blind, cruel or evil one. That point should be considered. Fat had a high regard for God. If the Logos was rational, and the Logos equaled God, then God had to be rational. This is why the Fourth Gospel's statement about the identity of the Logos is so important: "*Kai theos en ho logos*" which is to say "and the word was God." In the New Testament, Jesus says that no one has seen God but him; that is, Jesus Christ, the Logos of the Fourth Gospel. If that be correct, what Fat experienced was the Logos. But the Logos *is* God; so to experience Christ is to experience God. Perhaps a more important statement shows up in a book of the New Testament which most people don't

67

read; they read the gospels and the letters of Paul, but who reads *One John?*

> "My dear people, we are already the children of God but what we are to be in the future has not yet been revealed; all we know is, that we shall be like him because we shall see him as he really is."
>
> (*1 John 3:1/2.*)

It can be argued that this is the most important statement in the New Testament; certainly it is the most important not-generally-known statement. *We shall be like him.* That means that man is isomorphic with God. *We shall see him as he really is.* There will occur a theophany, at least to some. Fat could base the credentials for his whoe encounter on this passage. He could claim that his encounter with God consisted of a fulfillment of the promise of *I John 3:1/2*—as Bible scholars indicate it, a sort of code which they can read off in an instant, as cryptic as it looks. Oddly, to a certain extent this passage dovetails with the Nag Hammadi typescript that Dr. Stone handed to Fat the day Fat got discharged from North Ward. Man and the true God are identical—as the Logos and the true God are—but a lunatic blind creator and his screwed-up world separate man from God. That the blind creator sincerely imagines that he is the true God only reveals the extent of his occlusion. This is Gnosticism. In Gnosticism, man belongs with God *against* the world and the creator of the world (both of which are crazy, whether they realize it or not). The answer to Fat's question, "Is the universe irrational, and is it irrational because an irrational mind governs it?" receives this answer, via Dr. Stone: "Yes it is, the universe is irrational; the mind governing it is irrational; but above them lies another God, the true God, and he is *not* irrational; in addition that true God has outwitted the powers of this world, ventured here to help us, and we know him as the Logos," which, according to Fat, is living information.

Perhaps Fat had discerned a vast mystery, in calling the Logos living information. But perhaps not. Proving things of this sort is difficult. Who do you ask? Fat, fortunately, asked

Leon Stone. He might have asked one of the staff, in which case he would still be in North Ward drinking coffee, reading, walking around with Doug.

Above everything else, outranking every other aspect, object, quality of his encounter. Fat had witnessed a benign power *which had invaded this world*. No other term fitted it: the benign power, whatever it was, had *invaded* this world, like a champion ready to do battle. That terrified him but it also excited his joy because he understood what it meant. Help had come.

The universe might be irrational, but something rational had broken into it, like a thief in the night breaks into a sleeping household, unexpectedly in terms of place, in terms of time. Fat had seen it—not because there was anything special about him—but because it had wanted him to see it.

Normally it remained camouflaged. Normally when it appeared no one could distinguish it from ground—set to ground, as Fat correctly expressed it. He had a name for it.

Zebra. Because it blended. The name for this is mimesis. Another name is mimicry. Certain insects do this; they mimic other things: sometimes other insects—poisonous ones—or twigs and the like. Certain biologists and naturalists have speculated that higher forms of mimicry might exist, since lower forms—which is to say, forms which fool those intended to be fooled but not us—have been found all over the world.

What if a high form of sentient mimicry existed—such a high form that no human (or few humans) had detected it? What if it could only be detected if it *wanted* to be detected? Which is to say, not truly detected at all, since under these circumstances it had advanced out of its camouflaged state to disclose itself. "Disclose" might in this case equal "theophany." The astonished human being would say, I saw God; whereas in fact he saw only a highly evolved ultra-terrestrial life form, a UTI, or an extra-terrestrial life form (an ETI) which had come here at some time in the past . . . and perhaps, as Fat conjectured, had slumbered for nearly two thousand years in dormant seed form as living information in the codices at Nag Hammadi, which explained why reports of its existence had broken off abruptly around 70 A.D.

Entry 33 in Fat's journal (i.e. his exegesis):
This loneliness, this anguish of the bereaved Mind, is felt by
every constituent of the universe. All its constituents are alive.
Thus the ancient Greek thinkers were hylozoists.

A "hylozoist" believes that the universe is alive; it's about
the same idea as pan-psychism, that everything is animated.
Pan-psychism or hylozoism falls into two belief-classes:

1) Each object is independently alive.
2) Everything is one unitary entity; the universe is one
thing, alive, with one mind.

Fat had found a kind of middle ground. The universe
consists of one vast irrational entity *into which* has broken a
high-order life form which camouflages itself by a sophisticated
mimicry; thereby as long as it cares to it remains—by
us—undetected. It mimics objects and causal processes (this is
what Fat claims); not just objects but what the objects do.
From this, you can gather that Fat conceives of Zebra as very
large.

After a year of analyzing his encounter with Zebra, or God,
or the Logos, whatever, Fat came first to the conclusion that it
had invaded our universe; and a year later he realized that it
was consuming—that is, devouring—our universe. Zebra
accomplished this by a process much like transubstantiation.
This is the miracle of communion in which the two species, the
wine and bread, invisibly become the blood and body of
Christ.

Instead of seeing this in church, Fat had seen it out in the
world; and not in micro-form but in macro-form, which is to
say, on a scale so vast that he could not estimate its limits. The
entire universe, possibly, is in the invisible process of turning
into the Lord. And with this process comes not just sentience
but—sanity. For Fat this would be a blessed relief. He had put
up with insanity for too long, both in himself and outside
himself. Nothing could have pleased him more.

If Fat was psychotic, you must admit that it is a strange sort
of psychosis to believe that you have encountered an inbreaking
of the rational into the irrational. How do you treat it? Send the

70

afflicted person back to square one? In that case, he is now cut off from the rational. This makes no sense, in terms of therapy; it is an oxymoron, a verbal contradiction.

But an even more basic semantic problem lies exposed, here. Suppose I say to Fat, or Kevin says to Fat, "You did not experience God. You merely experienced something with the qualities and aspects and nature and powers and wisdom and goodness of God." This is like the joke about the German proclivity toward double abstractions; a German authority on English literature declares, "*Hamlet* was not written by Shakespeare; it was merely written by a man named Shakespeare." In English the distinction is verbal and without meaning, although German as a language will express the difference (which accounts for some of the strange features of the German mind).

"I saw God," Fat states, and Kevin and I and Sherri state, "No, you just saw something *like* God, exactly like God." And having spoke, we do not stay to hear the answer, like jesting Pilate, upon his asking, "What is truth?"

Zebra broke through into our universe and fired beam after beam of information-rich colored light at Fat's brain, right through his skull, blinding him and fucking him up and dazing and dazzling him, but imparting to him knowledge beyond the telling. For openers, it saved Christopher's life.

More accurately speaking, it didn't break through to fire the information; it had at some past date broken through. What it did was step forward out of its state of camouflage; it disclosed itself as set to ground and fired information at a rate our calculations will not calibrate; it fired whole libraries at him in nanoseconds. And it continued to do this for eight hours of real elapsed time. Many nanoseconds exist in eight hours of RET. At flash-cut speed you can load the right hemisphere of the human brain with a titanic quantity of graphic data.

Paul of Tarsus had a similar experience. A long time ago. Much of it he refused to discuss. According to his own statement, much of the information fired at his head—right between the eyes, on his trip to Damascus—died with him unsaid. Chaos reigns in the universe, but St. Paul knew who he had talked to. He mentioned that. Zebra, too, identified itself,

71

to Fat. It termed itself "St. Sophia," a designation unfamiliar to Fat. "St. Sophia" is an unusual hypostasis of Christ.

Men and the world are mutually toxic to each other. But God—the true God—has penetrated both, penetrated man and penetrated the world, and sobers the landscape. But that God, the God from outside, encounters fierce opposition. Frauds—the deceptions of madness—abound and mask themselves as their mirror opposite: pose as sanity. The masks, however, wear thin and the madness reveals itself. It is an ugly thing.

The remedy is here but so is the malady. As Fat repeats obsessively, **The Empire never ended.** In a startling response to the crisis, the true God mimics the universe, the very region he has invaded: he takes on the likeness of sticks and trees and beer cans in gutters—he presumes to be trash discarded, debris no longer noticed. Lurking, the true God literally ambushes reality and us as well. God, in very truth, attacks and injures us, in his role as antidote. As Fat can testify to, it is a scary experience to be bushwhacked by the Living God. Hence we say, the true God is in the habit of concealing himself. Twenty-five hundred years have passed since Heraclitus wrote, "Latent form is the master of obvious form," and, "The nature of things is in the habit of concealing itself."

So the rational, like a seed, lies concealed within the irrational bulk. What purpose does the irrational bulk serve? Ask yourself what Gloria gained by dying; not in terms of her death *vis-à-vis* herself but in terms of those who loved her. She paid back their love with—well, with what? Malice? Not proven. Hate? Not proven. With the irrational? Yes; proven. In terms of the effect on her friends—such as Fat—no lucid purpose was served but purpose there was: purpose without purpose, if you can conceive of that. Her motive was no motive. We're talking about nihilism. Under everything else, even under death itself and the will towards death, lies something else and that something else is nothing. The bedrock basic stratum of reality is irreality; the universe is irrational because it is built not on mere shifting sand—but on that which is not.

No help to Fat to know this: the *why* of Gloria's taking him with her—or doing her best to—when she went "Bitch," he could have said if he could have grabbed her. "Just tell me why; why the fucking why?" To which the universe would hollowly respond, "My ways cannot be known, oh man." Which is to say, "My ways do not make sense, nor do the ways of those who dwell in me."

The bad news coming down the pipe for Fat was mercifully still unknown to him, at this point, at the time of his discharge from North Ward. He could not return to Beth, so who could he return to, when he hit the outside world? In his mind, during his stay at North Ward, Sherri, who was in remission from her cancer, had faithfully visited him. Therefore Fat had engrammed onto her, believing that if he had one true friend in all the world it was Sherri Solvig. His plan had unfolded like a bright star: he would live with Sherri, helping to keep up her morale during her remission, and if she lost her remission, he would care for her as she had cared for him during his time in the hospital.

In no sense had Dr. Stone cured Fat, when the motor driving Fat got later exposed. Fat homed in on death more rapidly and more expertly this time than he had ever done before. He had become a professional at seeking out pain; he had learned the rules of the game and now knew how to play. What Fat in his lunacy—acquired from a lunatic universe; branded so by Fat's own analysis—sought was to be dragged down along with someone who wanted to die. Had he gone through his address book he could not have yielded up a better source than Sherri, "Smart move, Fat," I would have told him if I had known what he was planning for his future, during his stay at North Ward. "You've really scored this time." I knew Sherri; I knew she spent all her time trying to figure out a way to lose her remission. I knew that because she expressed fury and hatred, constantly, at the doctors who had saved her. But I did not know what Fat had planned. Fat kept it a secret, even from Sherri. I will help her, Fat said to himself in the depths of his fried mind. I will help Sherri stay healthy but if and when she gets sick again, there I will be at her side, ready to do anything for her.

His error, when deconstructed, amounted to this: Sherri did not merely plan to get sick again; she like Gloria planned to take as many people with her as possible—in direct proportion to their love toward her. Fat loved her and, worse, felt gratitude towards her. Out of this clay, Sherri could throw a pot with the warped kickwheel she used as a brain that would smash what Leon Stone had done, smash what Stephanie had done, smash what God had done. Sherri had more power in her weakened body than all these other entities combined, including the living God.

Fat had decided to bind himself to the Antichrist. And out of the highest possible motives: out of love, gratitude and the desire to help her.

Exactly what the powers of hell feed on: the best instincts in man.

*

Sherri Solvig, being poor, lived in a tiny rundown room with no kitchen; she had to wash her dishes in the bathroom sink. The ceiling showed a vast water stain, from a toilet upstairs which had overflowed. Having visited her there a couple of times Fat knew the place and considered it depressing. He had the impression that if Sherri moved out and into a nice appartment, a modern one, and with a kitchen, her spirits would pick up.

Needless to say, the realization had never penetrated to Fat's mind that Sherri sought out this kind of abode. Her dingy surroundings came as a result of her affliction, not as a cause; she could recreate these conditions wherever she went—which Fat eventually discovered.

At this point in time, however, Fat had geared up his mental and physical assembly line to turn out an endless series of good acts toward the person who, before all other persons, had visited him in the cardiac intensive care ward and later at North Ward. Sherri had official documents declaring her a Christian. Twice a week she took communion and one day she would enter a religious order. Also, she called her priest by his first name. You cannot get any closer to piety than that.

A couple of times Fat had told Sherri about his encounter with God. This hadn't impressed her, since Sherri Solvig believed that one encounters God only through channels. She

74

herself has access to these channels, which is to say her priest Larry.

Once Fat had read to Sherri from the *Britannica* about the "secrecy theme" in Mark and Matthew, the idea that Christ veiled his teachings in parable form so that the multitude—that is, the many outsiders—would not understand him and so would not be saved. Christ, according to this view or theme, intended salvation only for his little flock. The *Britannica* discussed this up front.

"That's bullshit," Sherri said.

Fat said, "You mean this *Britannica* is wrong or the Bible is wrong? The *Britannica* is just—"

"The Bible doesn't say that," Sherri said, who read the Bible all the time, or at least had a copy of it always with her.

It took Fat hours to find the citation in Luke; finally he had it, to set before Sherri:

"His disciples asked him what this parable might mean, and he said, "The mysteries of the kingdom of God are revealed to you, for the rest there are only parables, so that they might see but not perceive, listen but not understand.'" *(Luke 8:9/10.)*

"I'll ask Larry if that's one of the corrupt parts of the Bible," Sherry said.

Pissed off, Fat said irritably, "Sherri, why don't you cut out all the sections of the Bible you agree with and paste them together? And not have to deal with the rest."

"Don't be snippy," Sherri said, who was hanging up clothes in her tiny closet.

Nonetheless, Fat imagined that basically he and Sherri shared a common bond. They both agreed that God existed; Christ had died to save man; people who didn't believe this didn't know what was going on. He had confided to her that he had seen God, news which Sherri received placidly (at that moment she had been ironing).

"It's called a theophany," Fat said. "Or an epiphany."

"An epiphany," Sherri said, pacing her voice to the rate of her slow ironing, "is a feast celebrated on January sixth,

75

marking the baptism of Christ. I always go. Why don't you go? It's a lovely service. You know, I heard this joke—" She droned on. Hearing this, Fat was mystified. He decided to change the subject; now Sherri had switched to an account of an instance when Larry—who was Father Minter to Fat—had poured the sacramental wine down the front of a kneeling female communicant's low-cut dress.

"Do you think John the Baptist was an Essene?" he asked Sherri.

Never at any time did Sherri Solvig admit she didn't know the answer to a theological question; the closest she came surfaced in the form of responding, "I'll ask Larry." To Fat she now said calmly. "John the Baptist was Elijah who returns before Christ comes. They asked Christ about that and he said John the Baptist was Elijah who had been promised."

"But was he an Essene."

Pausing momentarily in her ironing, Sherri said, "Didn't the Essenes live in the Dead Sea?"

"Well, at the Qumran Wadi."

"Didn't your friend Bishop Pike die in the Dead Sea?"

Fat had known Jim Pike, a fact he always proudly narrated to people given a pretext. "Yes," he said. "Jim and his wife had driven out onto the Dead Sea Desert in a Ford Cortina. They had two bottles of Coca-Cola with them; that's all."

"You told me," Sherri said, resuming her ironing.

"What I could never figure out," Fat said, "is why they didn't drink the water in the car radiator. That's what you do when your car breaks down in the desert and you're stranded." For years Fat had brooded about Jim Pike's death. He imagined that it was somehow tied in with the murders of the Kennedys and Dr. King, but he had no evidence whatsoever for it.

"Maybe they had anti-freeze in their radiator," Sherri said.

"In the Dead Sea Desert?"

Sherri said, "My car has been giving me trouble. the man at the Exxon station on Seventeenth says that the motor mounts are loose. Is that serious?"

Not wanting to talk about Sherri's beat-up old car but wanting instead to rattle on about Jim Pike, Fat said, "I don't know." He tried to think how to get the topic back to his friend's perplexing death but could not.

"That damn car," Sherri said.

"You didn't pay anything for it; that guy gave it to you."

" 'Didn't pay anything'? He made me feel like he owned me for giving me that damn car."

"Remind me never to give you a car," Fat said.

All the clues lay before him that day. If you did something for Sherri she felt she should feel gratitude—which she did not—and this she interpreted as a burden, a despised obligation. However, Fat had a ready rationalization for this, which he had already begun to employ. He did not do things for Sherri to get anything back; *ergo*, he did not expect gratitude. *Ergo*, if he did not get it that was okay.

What he failed to notice was that not only was there no gratitude (which he could psychologically handle) but downright malice showed itself instead, Fat had noted this but had written it off as nothing more than irritability, a form of impatience. He could not believe that someone would return malice for assistance. Therefore he discounted the testimony of his senses.

Once, when I lectured at the University of California at Fullerton, a student asked me for a short, simple definition of reality. I thought it over and answered, "Reality is that which when you stop believing in it, it doesn't go away."

Fat did not believe that Sherri returned malice for assistance given her. But that failure to believe changed nothing. Therefore her response lay within the framework of what we call "reality." Fat, whether he liked it or not, would in some way have to deal with it, or else stop seeing Sherri socially.

One of the reasons Beth left Fat stemmed from his visits to Sherri at her rundown room in Santa Ana. Fat had deluded himself into believing that he visited her out of charity. Actually he had become horny, due to the fact that Beth had lost interest in him sexually and he was not, as they say, getting any. In many ways Sherri struck him as pretty; in fact Sherri was pretty; we all agreed. During her chemotherapy she wore a wig. David had been fooled by the wig and often complimented her on her hair, which amused her. We regarded this as macabre, on both their parts.

77

In his study of the form that masochism takes in modern man, Theodor Reik puts forth an interesting view. Masochism is more widespread than we realize because it takes an attenuated form. The basic dynamism is as follows: a human being sees something bad which is coming as inevitable. There is no way he can halt the process; he is helpless. This sense of helplessness generates a need to gain some control over the impending pain—any kind of control will do. This makes sense; the subjective feeling of helplessness is more painful than the impending misery. So the person seizes control over the situation in the only way open to him: he connives to bring on the impending misery; he hastens it. This activity on his part promotes the false impression that he enjoys pain. Not so. It is simply that he cannot any longer endure the helplessness or the supposed helplessness. But in the process of gaining control over the inevitable misery he becomes, automatically, anhedonic (which means being unable or unwilling to enjoy pleasure). Anhedonia sets in stealthily. Over the years it takes control of him. For example, he learns to defer gratification; this is a step in the dismal process of anhedonia. In learning to defer gratification he experiences a sense of self-mastery; he has become stoic, disciplined; he does not give way to impulse. He has *control.* Control over himself in terms of his impulses and control over the external situation. He is a controlled and controlling person. Pretty soon he has branched out and is controlling other people, as part of the situation. He becomes a manipulator. Of course, he is not consciously aware of this; all he intends to do is lessen his own sense of impotence. But in his task of lessening this sense, he insidiously overpowers the freedom of others. Yet, he derives no pleasure from this, no positive psychological gain; all his gains are essentially negative.

Sherri Solvig had had cancer, lymphatic cancer, but due to valiant efforts by her doctors she had gone into remission. However, encoded in the memory-tapes of her brain was the datum that patients with lymphoma who go into remission usually eventually lose their remission. They aren't cured; the ailment has somehow mysteriously passed from a palpable state into a sort of metaphysical state, a limbo. It is there but it is not there. So despite her current good health, Sherri (her mind told her) contained a ticking clock, and when the clock chimed she would die. Nothing could be done about it, except the frantic promotion of a second remission. But even if a second remission were obtained, that remission, too, by the same logic, the same inexorable process, would end.

Time had Sherri in its absolute power. Time contained one outcome for her: terminal cancer. This is how her mind had factored the situation out; it had come to this conclusion, and no matter how good she felt or what she had going for her in her life, this fact remained a constant. A cancer patient in remission, then, represents a stepped-up case of the status of all humans; eventually you are going to die.

In the back of her mind, Sherri thought about death ceaselessly. Everything else, all people, objects and processes had become reduced to the status of shadows. Worse yet, when she contemplated other people she contemplated the injustice of the universe. They did not have cancer. This meant that, psychologically speaking, they were immortal. This was unfair. Everyone had conspired to rob her of her youth, her happiness and eventually her life; in place of those, everyone else had piled infinite pain on her, and probably they secretly enjoyed it. "Enjoying themselves" and "enjoying it" amounted to the same evil thing. Sherri, therefore, had motivation for wishing that the whole world would go to hell in a handbasket.

Of course, she did not say this aloud. But she lived it. Due to her cancer she had become totally anhedonic. How can one deny the sense in this? Logically, Sherri should have squeezed every moment of pleasure out of life during her remission, but the mind does not function logically, as Fat had figured out. Sherri spent her time anticipating the loss of her remission.

In this respect she did not postpone gratification; she enjoyed her returning lymphoma now.

Fat couldn't make this complex mental process out. He only saw a young woman who had suffered a lot and who had been dealt a bum hand. He reasoned that he could improve her life. That was a good thing to do. He would love her, love himself and God would love the both of them. Fat saw love, and Sherri

79

saw impending pain and death over which she had no control. There can be no meeting of such two different worlds.

In summary (as Fat would say), the modern-day masochist does not enjoy pain; he simply can't stand being helpless. "Enjoying pain" is a semantic contradiction, as certain philosophers and psychologists have pointed out. "Pain" is defined as something that you experience as unpleasant. "Unpleasant" is defined as something you don't want. Try to define it otherwise and see where it gets you. "Enjoying pain" means "enjoying what you find unpleasant." Reik had the handle on the situation; he decoded the true dynamism of modern attenuated masochism . . . and saw it spread out among almost all of us, in one form or another and to some degree. It has become an ubiquity.

One could not correctly accuse Sherri of enjoying cancer. Or even wanting to have cancer. But she believed that cancer lay in the deck of cards in front of her, buried somewhere in the pack; she turned one card over each day, and each day cancer failed to show up. But if that card is in the pack and you are turning the cards over one by one eventually you will turn the cancer card over, and there it ends.

So, through no real fault of her own, Sherri was primed to fuck Fat over as he had never been fucked over before. The difference between Gloria Knudson and Sherri was obvious; Gloria wanted to die for strictly imaginary reasons. Sherri would literally die whether she wanted to or not. Gloria had the option to cease playing her malignant death-game any time she psychologically wished, *but Sherri did not*. It was as if Gloria, upon smashing herself to bits on the pavement below the Oakland Synanon Building, had been reborn twice the size with twice the mental strength. Meanwhile, Beth's leaving with Christopher had whittled Horselover Fat down to half his normal size. The odds did not favor a sanguine outcome.

The actual motivation in Fat's head for feeling attracted to Sherri was the locking-in onto death which had begun with Gloria. But, imagining that Dr. Stone had cured him, Fat now sailed out into the world with renewed hope—sailed unerringly into madness and death; he had learned nothing. True, the bullet had been pulled from his body and the wound healed.

80

But he was primed for another, *eager* for another. He couldn't wait to move in with Sherri and save her.

If you'll remember, helping people was one of the two basic things Fat has been told long ago to give up; helping people and taking dope. He had stopped taking dope, but all his energy and enthusiasm were now totally channeled into saving people.

Better he had kept on with the dope.

6

The machinery of divorce chewed Fat up into a single man, freeing him to go forth and abolish himself. He could hardly wait.

Meanwhile he had entered therapy through the Orange County Mental Health people. They had assigned him a therapist named Maurice. Maurice was not your standard therapist. During the Sixties he had run guns and dope into California, using the port of Long Beach; he had belonged to SNCC and CORE and had fought as an Israeli commando against the Syrians; Maurice stood six-foot-two inches high and his muscles bulged under his shirt, nearly popping the buttons. Like Horselover Fat he had a black, curly beard. Generally, he stood facing Fat across the room, not sitting; he yelled at Fat, punctuating his admonitions with, "And I mean it." Fat never doubted that Maurice meant what he said; it wasn't an issue.

The game plan on Maurice's part had to do with bullying Fat into enjoying life instead of saving people. Fat had no concept of enjoyment; he understood only meaning. Initially, Maurice had him draw up a written list of ten things he most wanted.

The term "wanted," as in "wanted to do," puzzled Fat.

"What I want to do," he said, "is help Sherri. So she doesn't get sick again."

Maurice roared, "You think you *ought* to help her. You think it makes you a good person. Nothing will ever make you a good person. You have no value to anyone."

Feebly, Fat protested that that wasn't so.

"You're worthless," Maurice said.

"And you're full of shit," Fat said, to which Maurice grinned. Maurice had begun to get what he wanted.

82

"Listen to me," Maurice said, "and I mean it. Go smoke dope and ball some broad that's got big tits, not one who's dying. You know Sherri's dying; right? She's going to die and then what're you going to do? Go back to Beth? Beth tried to kill you."

"She did?" Fat said, amazed.

"Sure she did. She set you up to die. She knew you'd try to ice yourself if she took your son and split."

"Well," Fat said, partly pleased; this meant he wasn't paranoid, anyhow. Underneath he knew that Beth had engineered his suicide attempt.

"When Sherri dies," Maurice said, "you're going to die. You want to die? I can arrange it right now." He examined his big wristwatch which showed everything including the position of the stars. "Let's see; it's two-thirty. What about six this evening?"

Fat couldn't tell if Maurice were serious. but he believed that Maurice possessed the capability, as the term goes.

"Listen," Maurice said, "and I mean this. There are easier ways to die than you've glommed onto. You're doing it the hard way. What you've set up is, Sherri dies and then you have another pretext to die. You don't need a pretext—your wife and son leaving you, Sherri croaking. That'll be the big pay-off when Sherri croaks. In your grief and love for her—"

"But who says Sherri is going to die?" Fat interrupted. He believed that through his magical powers he could save her; this in fact underlay all his strategy.

Maurice ignored the question. "Why do you want to die?" he said, instead.

"I don't," Fat said, who honestly believed that he didn't.

"If Sherri didn't have cancer would you want to shack up with her?" Maurice waited and got no answer, mainly because Fat had to admit to himself that, no, he wouldn't. "Why do you want to die?" Maurice repeated.

"Well," Fat said, at a loss.

"Are you a bad person?"

"No," Fat said.

"Is someone telling you to die? A voice? Someone flashing you 'die' messages?"

"No."

"Did your mother want you to die?"

"Well, ever since Gloria—"

"Fuck Gloria. Who's Gloria? You never even slept with her. You didn't even know her. You were already preparing to die. Don't give me that shit." Maurice, as usual had begun to yell. "If you want to help people, go up to L.A. and give them a hand at the Catholic Workers' Soup Kitchen, or turn as much of your money over to CARE as you possibly can. Let professionals help people. You're lying to yourself; you're lying that Gloria meant something to you, that what's-her-name—Sherri—isn't going to die—of course she's going to die! That's why you're shacking up with her, so you can be there when she dies. She wants to pull you down with her and you want her to; it's a collusion between the two of you. Everybody who comes in this door wants to die. That's what mental illness is all about. You didn't know that? I'm telling you. I'd like to hold your head under water until you fought to live. If you didn't fight, then fuck it. I wish they'd let me do it. Your friend who has cancer—she got it on purpose. Cancer represents a deliberate failure of the immune system of the body; the person turns it off. It's because of loss, the loss of a loved one. See how death spreads out? Everyone has cancer cells floating around in their bodies, but their immune system takes care of it."

"She did have a friend who died," Fat admitted. "He had a *grand mal* seizure. And her mother died of cancer."

"So Sherri felt guilty because her friend died and her mother died. You feel guilty because Gloria died. Take responsibility for your own life for a change. It's your job to protect yourself."

Fat said, "It's my job to help Sherri."

"Let's see your list. You better have that list."

Handing over his list of the ten things he most wanted to do, Fat asked himself silently if Maurice had all his marbles. Surely Sherri didn't want to die; she had put up a stubborn and brave fight; she had endured not only the cancer but the chemotherapy.

"You want to walk on the beach at Santa Barbara," Maurice said, examining the list. "That's number one."

"Anything wrong with that?" Fat said, defensively.

84

"No. Well? Why don't you do it?"

"Look at number two," Fat said. "I have to have a pretty girl with me."

Maurice said, "Take Sherri."

"She—" He hesitated. He had, as a matter of fact, asked Sherri to go to the beach with him, up to Santa Barbara to spend a weekend at one of the luxurious beach hotels. She had answered that her church work kept her too busy.

"She won't go," Maurice furnished for him. "She's too busy. Doing what?"

"Church."

They looked at each other.

"Her life won't differ much when her cancer returns," Maurice said finally. "Does she talk about her cancer?"

"Yes."

"To clerks in stores? Everyone she meets?"

"Yes."

"Okay, her life will differ; she'll get more sympathy. She'll be better off."

With difficulty, Fat said, "One time she told me—" He could barely say it. "That getting cancer was the best thing that ever happened to her. Because then—"

"The Federal Government funded her."

"Yes." He nodded.

"So she'll never have to work again. I presume she's still drawing SSI even though she's in remission."

"Yeah," Fat said glumly.

"They're going to catch up with her. They'll check with her doctor. Then she'll have to get a job."

Fat said, with bitterness, "She'll never get a job."

"You hate this girl," Maurice said. "And worse, you don't respect her. She's a girl bum. She's a rip-off artist. She's ripping you off, emotionally and financially. You're supporting her, right? And she also gets the SSI. She's got a racket, the cancer racket. And you're the mark." Maurice regarded him sternly. "Do you believe in God?" he asked suddenly.

You can infer from this question that Fat had cooled his Godtalk during his therapeutic sessions with Maurice. He did not intend to wind up in North Ward again.

"In a sense," Fat said. But he couldn't let it lie there; he had to amplify. "I have my own concept of God," he said. "Based on my own—" He hesitated, envisioning the trap built from his words; the trap bristled with barbed wire. "Thoughts," he finished.

"Is this a sensitive topic with you?" Maurice said.

Fat could not see what was coming, if anything. For example, he did not have access to his North Ward files and he did not know if Maurice had read them—or what they contained.

"No," he said.

"Do you believe man is created in God's image?" Maurice said.

"Yes," Fat said.

Maurice, raising his voice, shouted, "Then isn't it an offense against God to ice yourself? Did you ever think of that?"

"I thought of that," Fat said. "I thought of that a lot."

"Well? And what did you decide? Let me tell you what it says in *Genesis*, in case you've forgotten. 'Then God said, "Let us make man in our image and likeness to rule the fish in the sea, the birds of heaven, the cattle, all—"'"

"Okay," Fat broke in, "but that's the creator deity, not the true God."

"What?" Maurice said.

Fat said, "That's Yaldaboath. Sometimes called Samael, the blind god. He's deranged."

"What the hell are you talking about?" Maurice said.

"Yaldaboath is a monster spawned by Sophia who fell from the Pleroma," Fat said. "He imagines he's the only god but he's wrong. There's something the matter with him; he can't see. He creates our world but because he's blind he botches the job. The real God sees down from far above and in his pity sets to work to save us. Fragments of light from the Pleroma are—"

Staring at him, Maurice said, "Who made up this stuff? You?"

"Basically," Fat said, "my doctrine is Valentinian, second century C.E."

"What's 'C.E.'?"

"Common Era. The designation replaces A.D. Valentinus's

86

Gnosticism is the more subtle branch as opposed to the Iranian, which of course was strongly influenced by Zoroastrianism dualism. Valentinus perceived the ontological salvific value of the gnosis, since it reversed the original, primal condition of ignorance, which represents the state of the fall, the impairment of the Godhead which resulted in the botched creation of the phenomenal or material world. The true God, who is totally transcendent, did not create the world. However, seeing what Yaldaboath had done—"

"Who's this 'Yaldaboath'? Yahweh created the world! It says so in the Bible!"

Fat said, "The creator deity imagined that he was the only god; that's why he was jealous and said, 'You shall have no other gods before me,' to which—"

Maurice shouted, "Haven't you read the Bible?"

After a pause, Fat tried another turn. He was dealing with a religious idiot. "Look," he said, as reasonably as possible. "A number of opinions exist as to the creation of the world. For instance, if you regard the world as artifact—which it may not be; it may be an organism, which is how the ancient Greeks regarded it—you still can't reason back to a creator; for instance, there may have been a number of creators at several times. The Buddhist idealists point this out. But even if—"

"You've never read the Bible," Maurice said with incredulity. "You know what I want you to do? And I mean this. I want you to go home and study the Bible. I want you to read *Genesis* over twice; you hear me? Two times. Carefully. And I want you to write an outline of the main ideas and events in it, in descending order of importance. And when you show up here next week I want to see that list." He obviously was genuinely angry.

Bringing up the topic of God had been a poor idea, but of course Maurice hadn't known that in advance. All he intended to do was appeal to Fat's ethics. Being Jewish, Maurice assumed that religion and ethics couldn't be separated, since they are combined in the Hebrew monotheism. Ethics devolve directly from Yahweh to Moses; everybody knows that. Everybody but Horselover Fat, whose problem, at that moment, was that he knew too much.

Breathing heavily, Maurice began going through his appoint-

87

ment book. He hadn't iced Syrian assassins by regarding the cosmos as a sentient entelechy with psyche and soma, a macrocosmic mirror to man the microcosm.

"Let me just say one thing," Fat said.

Irritably, Maurice nodded.

"The creator deity," Fat said, "may be insane and therefore the universe is insane. What we experience as chaos is actually irrationality. There is a difference." He was silent, then.

"The universe is what you make of it," Maurice said. "It's what you do with it that counts. It's your responsibility to do something life-promoting with it, not life-destructive."

"That's the existential position," Fat said. "Based on the concept that We are what we do, rather than, We are what we think. It finds its first expression in Goethe's *Faust*, Part One, where Faust says, '*Im Anfang war das Wort*.' He's quoting the opening of the Fourth Gospel; 'In the beginning was the Word.' Faust says, '*Nein, Im Anfang war die Tat*.' 'In the beginning was the deed.' From this, all existentialism comes."

Maurice stared at him as if he were a bug.

*

Driving back to the modern two-bedroom, two-bathroom apartment in downtown Santa Ana, a full-security apartment with deadbolt lock in a building with electric gate, underground parking, closed-circuit TV scanning of the main entrance, where he lived with Sherri, Fat realized that he had fallen from the status of authority back to the humble status of crank. Maurice, in attempting to help him, had accidentally erased Fat's bastion of security.

However, on the good side, he now lived in this fortress-like, or jail-like, full security new building, set dead in the center of the Mexican barrio. You needed a magnetic computer card to get the gate to the underground garage to open. This shored up Fat's marginal morale. Since their apartment was up on the top floor he could literally look down on Santa Ana and all the poorer people who got ripped off by drunks and junkies every hour of the night. In addition, of much more importance, he had Sherri with him. She cooked wonderful meals, although he had to do the dishes and the shopping. Sherri did neither. She sewed and ironed a lot, drove off on errands, talked on the telephone to her old girlfriends from high school and kept Fat informed about church matters.

I can't give the name of Sherri's church because it really exists (well, so, too, does Santa Ana), so I will call it what Sherri called it: Jesus' sweatshop. Half the day she manned the phones and the front desk; she had charge of the help programs, which meant that she disbursed food, money for shelter, advice on how to deal with Welfare and weeded the junkies out from the real people.

Sherri detested junkies, and for good reason. They continually showed up with a new scam every day. What annoyed her the most was not so much their ripping off the church to score smack, but their boasting about it later. However, since junkies have no loyalty to one another, junkies generally showed up to tell her which other junkies were doing the ripping off and the boasting. Sherri put their names down on her shit list. Customarily, she arrived home from the church, raving like a madwoman about conditions there, most especially what the creeps and junkies had said and done that day, and how Larry, the priest, did nothing about it.

After a week of living together. Fat knew a great deal more about Sherri than he had known from seeing her socially over the three years of their friendship. Sherri resented every creature on earth, in order of proximity to her; that is, the more she had to do with someone or something the more she resented him, or her or it. The great erotic love in her life took the form of the priest, Larry. During the bad days when she was literally dying from the cancer, Sherri had told Larry that her great desire was to sleep with him, to which Larry had said (this fascinated Fat, who did not regard it as an appropriate answer) that he, Larry, never mixed his social life with his business life (Larry was married, with three children and a grandchild). Sherri still loved him and still wanted to go to bed with him, but she sensed defeat.

On the positive side, one time while living at her sister's—or conversely, dying at her sister's, to hear Sherri tell it—she had gone into seizures and Father Larry had showed up to take her

89

to the hospital. As he picked her up in his arms she had kissed him and he had french-kissed her. Sherri mentioned this several times to Fat. Wistfully, she longed for those days.

"I love you," she informed Fat one night, "but it's really Larry that I really love because he saved me when I was sick." Fat soon developed the opinion that religion was a sideline at Sherri's church. Answering the phone and mailing out stuff took the center ring. A number of nebulous people—who might as well be named Larry, Moe and Curly, as far as Fat was concerned—haunted the church, holding down salaries inevitably larger than Sherri's and requiring less work. Sherri wished death to all of them. She often spoke with relish about their misfortunes, as for instance when their cars wouldn't start or they got speeding tickets or Father Larry expressed dissatisfaction toward them.

"Eddy's going to get the royal boot," Sherri would say, upon coming home. "The little fucker."

One particular indigent chronically provoked annoyance in Sherri, a man named Jack Barbina who, Sherri said, rummaged through garbage cans to find little gifts for her. Jack Barbina showed up when Sherri was alone in the church office, handed her a soiled box of dates and a perplexing note stressing his desire to court her. Sherri pegged him as a maniac the first day she saw him; she lived in fear that he would murder her.

"I'm going to call you the next time he comes in," she told Fat. "I'm not going to be there alone with him. There isn't enough money in the Bishop's Discretionary Fund to pay me for putting up with Jack Barbina, especially on what they do pay me, which is about half what Eddy makes, the little fairy." To Sherri, the world was divided up among slackers, maniacs, junkies, homosexuals and back-stabbing friends. She also had little use for Mexicans and blacks. Fat used to wonder at her total lack of Christian charity, in the emotional sense. How could—why would—Sherri want to work in a church and fix her sights on religious orders when she resented, feared and detested every living human being, and, most of all, complained about her lot in life?

Sherri even resented her own sister, who had sheltered, fed and cared for her all the time she was sick. The reason: Mae

90

drove a Mercedes-Benz and had a rich husband. But most of all Sherri resented the career of her best friend Eleanor, who had become a nun.

"Here I am throwing up in Santa Ana," Sherri frequently said, "and Eleanor's walking around in a habit in Las Vegas."

"You're not throwing up now," Fat pointed out. "You're in remission."

"But she doesn't know that. What kind of place is Las Vegas for a religious order? She's probably peddling her ass in—"

"You're talking about a nun," Fat said, who had met Eleanor; he had liked her.

"I'd be a nun by now if I hadn't got sick," Sherri said.

*

To escape from Sherri's nattering drivel, Fat shut himself up in the bedroom he used as a study and began working once more on his great exegesis. He had done almost 300,000 words, mostly holographically, but from the inferior bulk he had begun to extract what he termed his **Tractate: Cryptica Scriptura** (see Appendix p. 229), which simply means "hidden discourse." Fat found the Latin more impressive as a title.

At this point in the *Meisterwerk* he had begun patiently to fabricate his cosmogony, which is the technical term for, "How the cosmos came into existence." Few individuals compose cosmogonies; usually entire cultures, civilizations, people or tribes are required: a cosmogony is a group production, evolving down through the ages. Fat well knew this, and prided himself on having invented his own. He called it:

TWO SOURCE COSMOGONY

In his journal or exegesis it came as entry 47 and was by far the longest single entry.

The One was and was-not, combined, and desired to separate the was-not from the was. So it generated a diploid sac which contained, like an eggshell, a pair of twins, each an androgyny,

91

spinning in opposite directions (the Yin and Yang of Taoism, with the One as the Tao). The plan of the One was that both twins would emerge into being (wasness) simultaneously; however, motivated by a desire to be (which the One had implanted in both twins), the counter-clockwise twin broke through the sac and separated prematurely; i.e. before full term. This was the dark or Yin twin. Therefore it was defective. At full term the wiser twin emerged. Each twin formed a unitary entelechy, a single living organism made of *psyche* and *soma*, still rotating in opposite directions to each other. The full term twin, called Form I by Parmenides, advanced correctly through its growth stages, but the prematurely born twin, called Form II, languished.

The next step in the One's plan was that the Two would become the Many, through their dialectic interaction. From them as hyperuniverses they projected a hologram-like interface, which is the pluriform universe we creatures inhabit. The two sources were to intermingle equally in maintaining our universe, but Form II continued to languish toward illness, madness and disorder. These aspects she projected into our universe.

It was the One's purpose for our hologramatic universe to serve as a teaching instrument by which a variety of new lives advanced until ultimately they would be isomorphic with the One. However, the decaying condition of hyperuniverse II introduced malfactors which damaged our hologramatic universe. This is the origin of entropy, undeserved suffering, chaos and death, as well as the Empire, the Black Iron Prison; in essence, the aborting of the proper health and growth of the life forms within the hologramatic universe. Also the teaching function was grossly impaired, since only the signal from the hyperuniverse I was information-rich; that from II had become noise.

The psyche of hyperuniverse I sent a micro-form of itself into hyperuniverse II to attempt to heal it. The micro-form was apparent in our hologramatic universe as Jesus Christ. However, hyperuniverse II, being deranged, at once tormented, humiliated, rejected and finally killed the micro-form of the healing *psyche* of her healthy twin. After that, hyperuniverse II continued to decay into blind, mechanical, purposeless causal processes. It then became the task of Christ (more properly the Holy Spirit) to either rescue the life forms in the hologramatic universe, or abolish all influences on it emanating from II. Approaching its task with caution, it prepared to kill the deranged twin, since she cannot be healed; i.e. she will not allow herself to be healed because she does not understand that she is sick. This illness and madness pervades us and makes us idiots living in private, unreal worlds. The original plan of the One can only be realized now by the division of hyperuniverse I into two healthy hyperuniverses, which will transform the hologramatic universe into the successful teaching machine it was designed to be. We will experience this as the "Kingdom of God."

Within time, hyperuniverse II remains alive: "The Empire never ended." But in eternity, where the hyperuniverses exist, she has been killed—of necessity—by the healthy twin of hyperuniverse I, who is our champion. The One grieves for this death, since the One loved both twins; therefore the information of the Mind consists of a tragic tale of the death of a woman, the undertones of which generate anguish into all the creatures of the hologramatic universe without their knowing why. This grief will depart when the healthy twin undergoes mitosis and the "Kingdom of God" arrives. The machinery for this tranformation—the procession within time from the Age of Iron to the Age of Gold—is at work now; in eternity it is already accomplished.

Not long thereafter, Sherri got fed up with Fat working night and day on his exegesis; also she got mad because he asked her to contribute some of her SSI money to pay the rent, since because of a court judgment he had to pay out a lot of spousal and child support to Beth and Christopher. Having found another apartment for which the Santa Ana housing authority would pick up the tab, Sherri wound up living by herself rent-free, without the obligation to fix Fat's dinner; also she could go out with other men, something Fat had objected to while he and Sherri were living together. To this possessiveness, Sherri had said hotly one night, when she came home from walking hand-in-hand with a male friend to find Fat furious:

"I don't have to put up with this crap."

Fat promised not to object to Sherri going out with other men any more, nor would he continue to ask her to contribute toward the rent and food costs, even though at the moment he had only nine dollars in his bank account. This did no good; Sherri was pissed.

"I'm moving out," she informed him.

After she moved out, Fat had to raise funds to purchase all manner of furniture, dishes, TV set, flatware, towels—everything, because he had brought little or nothing with him from his marriage; he had expected to depend on Sherri's chattels. Needless to say, he found life very lonely without her; living by himself in the two-bedroom, two-bathroom apartment which they had shared depressed the hell out of him. His friends worried about him and tried to cheer him up. In February Beth had left him and now in early September Sherri had left him. He was again dying by inches. All he did was sit at his typewriter or with notepad and pen, working on his exegesis; nothing else remained in his life. Beth had moved up to Sacramento, seven hundred miles away, so he did not get to see Christopher. He thought about suicide, but not very much, he knew that Maurice would not approve of such thoughts. Maurice would require of him another list.

What really bothered Fat was the intuition that Sherri would soon lose her remission. From going to class at Santa Ana College and working at the church she became rundown and tired; every time he saw her, which was as often as possible, he noticed how tired and thin she looked. In November she complained of the flu; she had pains in her chest and coughed continuously.

"This fucking flu," Sherri said.

Finally he got her to go to her doctor for an X-ray and blood tests. He knew she had lost her remission by then; she could barely drag herself around.

The day she found out that she had cancer again, Fat was with her; since her appointment with the doctor was at eight in the morning, Fat stayed up the night before, just sitting. He drove her to the doctor, along with Edna, a lifelong friend of Sherri's; he and Edna sat together in the waiting room while Sherri conferred with Dr. Applebaum.

"It's just the flu," Edna said.

Fat said nothing. He knew what it was. Three days before, he and Sherri had walked to the grocery store; she could hardly put one foot before the other. No doubt existed in Fat's mind; as he sat with Edna in the crowded waiting room terror filled him and he wanted to cry. Incredibly, today was his birthday.

When Sherri emerged from Dr. Applebaum's office, she had a Kleenex pressed to her eyes; Fat and Edna ran over to her; he caught Sherri as she fell saying, "It's back, the cancer's back." She had it in the lymph nodes in her neck and she had a malignant tumor in her right lung which was suffocating her. Chemotherapy and radiation would be started in twenty-four hours.

Edna said, stricken, "I was sure it was just flu. I wanted her to go to Melodyland and testify that Jesus had cured her."

To that remark, Fat said nothing.

The argument can be made that at this point Fat no longer had any moral obligation to Sherri. For the most meager reason she had moved out on him, leaving him alone, grieving and desperate, with nothing to do but scribble away at his exegesis. Fat's friends had all pointed this out. Even Edna pointed this out, when Sherri wasn't present in the same room. But Fat still loved her. He now asked her to move back in with him so that he could take care of her, inasmuch as she had become too weak to fix herself meals, and once she began the chemotherapy she would become a lot sicker.

"No thanks," Sherri said, tonelessly.

Fat walked down to her church one day and talked with Father Larry; he begged Larry to put pressure on the State of California Medicare people to provide someone to come in and fix meals for Sherri and to help clean up her apartment, since she would not let him, Fat, do it. Father Larry said he would, but nothing came of it. Again Fat went over to talk to the priest about what could be done to help Sherri, and while he was talking, Fat suddenly began to cry.

To this, Father Larry said enigmatically, "I've cried all the tears I am going to cry for that girl."

Fat could not tell if that meant that Larry had burned out his circuits from grief or that he had calculatedly, as a self-protective device, curtailed his grief. Fat does not know to this day. His own grief had reached critical mass. Now Sherri had been hospitalized; Fat visited her and saw lying in the bed a small sad shape, half the size he was accustomed to, a shape coughing in pain, with wretchcd hopelessness in its eyes. Fat could not drive home after that, so Kevin drove him home. Kevin, who usually maintained his stance of cynicism, could not speak from grief; the two of them drove along and then Kevin slapped him on the shulder, which is the only avenue open to men to show love for each other.

"What am I going to do?" Fat said, meaning, What am I going to do when she dies?

He really loved Sherri, despite her treatment of him—if indeed, as his friends maintained, she had treated him shabbily. He himself—he neither knew nor cared about that. All he knew was that she lay in the hospital bed with metastasized tumors throughout her. Every day he visited her in the hospital, along with everyone else who knew her.

At night he did the only act left open to him: work on his exegesis. He had reached an important entry.

Entry 48. ON OUR NATURE. It is proper to say: we appear to be memory coils (DNA carriers capable of experience) in a computer-like thinking system which, although we have correctly recorded and stored thousands of years of experiential information, and each of us possesses somewhat different deposits from all the other life forms, there is a malfunction—a failure—of memory retrieval. There lies the trouble in our particular subcircuit. "Salvation" through *gnosis*—more properly anamnesis (the loss of amnesia)—although it has individual significance for each of us—a quantum leap in perception, identity, cognition, understanding, world- and self-experience, including immortality—it has greater and further importance for the system as a whole, inasmuch as these memories are data needed by it and valuable to it, to its overall functioning.

Therefore it is in the process of self-repair, which includes: rebuilding our subcircuit via linear and orthogonal time changes, as well as continual signaling to us to stimulate blocked memory banks within us to fire and hence retrieve what is there.

The external information or *gnosis*, then, consists of disinhibiting instructions, with the core content actually intrinsic to us—that is, already there (first observed by Plato; *viz*: that learning is a form of remembering).

The ancients possessed techniques (sacraments and rituals) used largely in the Greco-Roman mystery religions, including early Christianity, to induce firing and retrieval, mainly with a sense of restorative value to the individuals; the Gnostics, however, correctly saw the ontological value to what they called the Godhead Itself, the total entity.

The Godhead is impaired; some primordial crisis occurred in it which we do not understand.

Fat reworked journal entry 29 and added it to his **ON OUR NATURE** entry:

29. We did not fall because of a moral error; we fell because of an intellectual error: that of taking the phenomenal world as real. Therefore we are morally innocent. It is the Empire in its various disguised polyforms which tells us we have sinned. "The Empire never ended."

By now Fat's mind was going totally. All he did was work on his exegesis or his *tractate* or just listen to his stereo or visit Sherri in the hospital. He began to install entries in the *tractate* without logical order or reason.

30. The phenomenal world does not exist; it is a hypostasis of the information processed by the Mind.

27. If the centuries of spurious time are excised, the true date is not 1978 C.E. but 103 C.E. Therefore the New Testament says that the Kingdom of the Spirit will come before "some now living die." We are living, therefore, in apostolic times.

20. The Hermetic alchemists knew of the secret race of three-eyed invaders but despite their efforts could not contact them. therefore their efforts to support Frederick V, Elector Palatine, King of Bohemia, failed. "The Empire never ended."

21. The Rose Cross Brotherhood wrote, *"Ex Deo nascimur, in Jesu mortimur, per spiritum sanctum reviviscimus,"* which is to say, "From God we are born, in Jesus we die, by the Holy Spirit we live again." This signifies that they had rediscovered the lost formula for immortality which the Empire had destroyed. "The Empire never ended."

10. Apollonius of Tyana, writing as Hermes Trismegistos, said, "That which is above is that which is below." By this he meant to tell us that our universe is a hologram, but he lacked the term.

12. The Immortal One was known to the Greeks as Dionysos; to the Jews as Elijah; to the Christians as Jesus. He moves on when each human host dies, and thus is never killed or caught. Hence Jesus on the cross said, *"Eli, Eli, lama sabachthani,"* to which some of those present correctly said, "The man is calling on Elijah." Elijah had left him and he died alone.

At this moment as he made this entry. Horselover Fat was dying alone. Elijah, or whatever divine presence it was that had fired tons of information into his skull in 1974, had indeed left him. The dreadful question that Fat asked himself over and over again did not get put down in his journal or *tractate;* the question could be put this way:

> If the divine presence knew about Christopher's birth defect and did something to correct it, why doesn't it do something about Sherri's cancer? How could it let her lie there dying?

Fat could not figure this out. The girl had gone an entire year wrongly diagnosed; why hadn't Zebra fired that information to Fat or to Sherri's doctor or to Sherri—to *someone?*
Fired it in time to save her!
One day when Fat visited Sherri in the hospital, a grinning fool stood there by her bed, a simp who Fat had met; this thing used to shamble in while Fat and Sherri lived together and

would put his arms around Sherri, kiss her and tell her he loved her—never mind Fat. This childhood friend of Sherri's, when Fat entered the hospital room, was saying to Sherri:

"What'll we do when I'm king of the world and you're queen of the world?"

To which Sherri, in agony, murmured, "I just want to get rid of these lumps in my throat."

Fat had never come so close to coldcocking anybody into tomorrow as at that moment. Kevin, who had accompanied him, had to physically hold Fat back.

On the drive back to Fat's lonely apartment, where he and Sherri had lived together for such a short time, Fat said to Kevin, "I'm going crazy. I can't take it."

"That's a normal reaction," Kevin said, showing nothing of his cynical pose, these days.

"Tell me," Fat said, "why God doesn't help her." He kept Kevin up on the progress of his exegesis; his encounter with God in 1974 was known to Kevin, so Fat could talk openly.

Kevin said, "It's the mysterious ways of the Great Punta."

"What the fuck is that?" Fat said.

"I don't believe in God," Kevin said. "I believe in the Great Punta. And the ways of the Great Punta are mysterious. No one knows why he does what he does, or doesn't do."

"Are you kidding me?"

"No," Kevin said.

"Where did the Great Punta come from?"

"Only the Great Punta knows."

"Is he benign?"

"Some say he is; some say he isn't."

"He could help Sherri if he wanted to."

Kevin said, "Only the Great Punta knows that."

They started laughing.

Obsessed with death, and going crazy from grief and worry about Sherri, Fat wrote entry 15 in his tractate.

15. The Sibyl of Cumae protected the Roman Republic and gave timely warnings. In the first century C.E. she foresaw the murders of the two Kennedy brothers, Dr. King and Bishop Pike. She saw the two common denominators in the four murdered

99

men: first, they stood in defense of the liberties of the Republic; and second, each man was a religious leader. For this they were killed. The Republic had once again become an empire with a caesar. "The Empire never ended."

16. The Sibyl said in March 1974, "The conspirators have been seen and they will be brought to justice." She saw them with the third or *ajna* eye, the Eye of Shiva which gives inward discernment, but which when turned outward blasts with desiccating heat. In August 1974 the justice promised by the Sibyl came to pass.

Fat decided to put down on the *tractate* all the prophetic statements fired into his head by Zebra.

7. The Head Apollo is about to return. St. Sophia is going to be born again; she was not acceptable before. The Buddha is in the park. Siddhartha sleeps (but is going to awaken). The time you have waited for has come.

Knowing this, by direct route from the divine, made Fat a latter-day prophet. But, since he had gone crazy, he also entered absurdities into his *tractate*.

50. The primordial source of all our religions lies with the ancestors of the Dogon tribe, who got their cosmogony and cosmology directly from the three-eyed invaders who visited long ago. The three-eyed invaders are mute and deaf and telepathic, could not breathe our atmosphere, had the elongated misshapen skull of Ikhnaton and emanated from a planet in the star-system Sirius. Although they had no hands, but had, instead, pincer claws such as a crab has, they were great builders. They covertly influence our history toward a fruitful end.

By now Fat had finally lost touch with reality.

7

You can understand why Fat no longer knew the difference between fantasy and divine revelation—assuming there is a difference, which has never been established. He imagined that Zebra came from a planet in the star-system Sirius, had overthrown the Nixon tyranny in August 1974, and would eventually set up a just and peaceful kingdom on Earth where there would be no sickness, no pain, no loneliness, and the animals would dance with joy.

Fat found a hymn by Ikhnaton and copied parts of it out of the reference book and into his *tractate*.

"... When the fledgling in the egg chirps in the egg,
Thou givest him breath therein to preserve him alive.
When thou hast brought him together
To the point of bursting the egg,
He cometh forth from the egg,
To chirp with all his might.
He goeth about upon his two feet
When he hath come from therefrom.

How manifold are thy works!
They are hidden from before us,
O sole god, whose powers no other possesseth.
Thou didst create the earth according to thy heart
While thou wast alone:
Men, all cattle large and small,
All that go about upon their feet;
All that are on high,
That fly with their wings.

101

Thou art in my heart,
There is no other that knoweth thee
Save thy son Ikhnaton.
Thou hast made him wise
In thy designs and in thy might.
The world is in thy hands . . ."

Entry 52 shows that Fat at this point in his life reached out for any wild hope which would shore up his confidence that some good existed somewhere.

52. Our world is still secretly ruled by the hidden race descended from Ikhnaton, and his knowledge is the information of the Macro-Mind itself.

"All cattle rest upon their pasturage,
The trees and the plants flourish,
The birds flutter in their marshes,
Their wings uplifted in adoration to thee.
All the sheep dance upon their feet,
All winged things fly,
They live when thou hast shone upon them."

From Ikhnaton this knowledge passed to Moses, and from Moses to Elijah, the Immortal Man, who became Christ. But underneath all the names there is only one Immortal Man; *and we are that man.*

Fat still believed in God and Christ—and a lot else—but he wished he knew why Zebra, his term for the Almighty Divine One, had not given early warning about Sherri's condition and did not now heal her, and this mystery assailed Fat's brain and turned him into a maddened thing.

Fat, who had sought death, could not comprehend why Sherri was being allowed to die, and die horribly.

I myself am willing to step forth and offer some possibilities. A little boy menaced by a birth defect isn't in the same category with a grown woman who desires to die, who is playing a

102

malignant game, as malignant as her physical analog, the lymphoma destroying her body. After all, the Almighty Divine One had not stepped forward to interfere with Fat's own suicide attempt; the Divine Presence had allowed Fat to down the forty-nine tabs of high-grade pure digitalis; nor had the Divine authority prevented Beth from abandoning him and taking his son away from him, the very son for whom the medical information was put forth in theophanic disclosure.

This mention of three-eyed invaders with claws instead of hands, mute, deaf and telepathic creatures from another star, interested me. Regarding this topic, Fat showed a natural sly reticence; he knew enough not to shoot his mouth off about it. In March 1974 at the time he had encountered God (more properly Zebra), he had experienced vivid dreams about the three-eyed people—he had told me that. They manifested themselves as cyborg entities: wrapped up in glass bubbles staggering under masses of technological gear. An odd aspect cropped up that puzzled both Fat and me; sometimes in these vision-like dreams, Soviet technicians could be seen, hurrying to repair malfunctions of the sophisticated technological communications apparatus enclosing the three-eyed people.

"Maybe the Russians beamed microwave psychogenic or psychotronic or whatever-they-call-it signals at you," I said, having read an article on alleged Soviet boosting of telepathic messages by means of microwaves.

"I doubt if the Soviet Union is interested in Christopher's hernia," Fat said sourly.

But the memory plagued him that in these visions or dreams or hypnagogic states he had heard Russian words spoken and had seen page upon page, hundreds of pages, of what appeared to be Russian technical manuals, describing—he knew this because of the diagrams—engineering principles and constructs.

"You overheard a two-way transmission," I suggested. "Between the Russians and an extra-terrestrial entity."

"Just my luck," Fat said.

At the time of these experiences Fat's blood pressure had gone up to stroke level; his doctor had briefly hospitalized him. The doctor warned him not to take uppers.

"I'm not taking uppers," Fat had protested, truthfully.

The doctor had run every test possible, during Fat's stay in the hospital, to find a physical cause for the elevated blood pressure, but no cause had been found. Gradually his hypertension had diminished. The doctor was suspicious; he continued to believe that Fat had abreacted in his lifestyle to the days when he did uppers. But both Fat and I knew better. His blood pressure had registered 280 over 178, which is a lethal level. Normally, Fat ran about 135 over 90, which is normal. The cause of the temporary elevation remains a mystery to this day. That, and the deaths of Fat's pets.

I tell you these things for what they are worth. They are true things; they happened.

In Fat's opinion his apartment had been saturated with high levels of radiation of some kind. In fact he had seen it: blue light dancing like St. Elmo's Fire.

And, what was more, the aurora that sizzled around the apartment behaved as if it were sentient and alive. When it entered objects it interfered with their causal processes. And when it reached Fat's head it transferred—not just information to him, which it did—but also a personality. A personality which wasn't Fat's. A person with different memories, customs, tastes and habits.

For the first and only time in his life, Fat stopped drinking wine and bought beer, foreign beer. And he called his dog "he" and his cat "she," although he knew—or had previously known—that the dog was a she and the cat a he. This had annoyed Beth.

Fat wore different clothes and carefully trimmed down his beard. When he looked in the bathroom mirror while trimming it he saw an unfamiliar person, although it was his regular self not changed. Also the climate seemed wrong; the air was too dry and too hot: not the right altitude and not the right humidity. Fat had the subjective impression that a moment ago he'd been living in a high, cool, moist region of the world and not in Orange County, California.

Plus the fact that this inner ratiocination took the form of *koine* Greek, which he did not understand as a language, nor as a phenomenon going on in his head.

And he had a lot of trouble driving his car; he couldn't figure out where the controls were; they all seemed to be in the wrong places.

Perhaps most remarkable of all, Fat experienced a particularly vivid dream—if "dream" it was—about a Soviet woman who would be contacting him by mail. In the dream he was shown a photograph of her; she had blonde hair, and, he was told, "Her name is Sadassa Ulna." An urgent message fired into Fat's head that he *must* respond to her letter when it came.

Two days later, a registered air mail letter arrived from the Soviet Union, which shocked Fat into a state of terror. The letter had been sent by a man, who Fat had never heard of (Fat wasn't used to getting letters from the Soviet Union anyhow) who wanted:

1) A photograph of Fat.
2) A specimen of Fat's handwriting, in particular his signature.

To Beth, Fat said, "Today is Monday. On Wednesday, another letter will come. This will be from the woman."

On Wednesday, Fat received a plethora of letters: seven in all. Without opening them he fished among them and pointed out one, which had no return name or address on it. "That's it," he said to Beth, who, by now, was also freaked. "Open it and look at it, but don't let me see her name and address or I'll answer it."

Beth opened it. Instead of a letter *per se* she found a Xerox sheet on which two book reviews from the left-wing New York newspaper *The Daily World* had been juxtaposed. The reviewer described the author of the books as a Soviet national living in the United States. From the reviews it was obvious that the author was a Party member.

"My God," Beth, turning the Xerox sheet over. "The author's name and address is written on the back."

"A woman?" Fat said.

"Yes," Beth said.

I never found out from Fat and Beth what they did with the two letters. From hints Fat dropped I deduced that he finally answered the first one, having decided that it was innocent; but

105

what he did with the Xerox one, which really wasn't a letter in the strict sense of the term, I do not to this day know, nor do I want to know. Maybe he burned it. Maybe he turned it over to the police or the FBI or the CIA; in any case I doubt if he answered it.

For one thing, he refused to look at the back of the Xerox sheet where the woman's name and address appeared; he had the conviction that if he saw this information he would answer her whether he wanted to or not. Maybe so. Who can say? First eight hours of graphic information is fired at you from sources unknown, taking the form of lurid phosphene activity in eighty colors arranged like modern abstract paintings; then you dream about three-eyed people in glass bubbles and electronic gear; then your apartment fills up with St. Elmo's Fire plasmatic energy which appears to be alive and to think; your animals die; you are overcome by a different personality who thinks in Greek; you dream about Russians; and finally you get a couple of Soviet letters within a three-day period—which you were told were coming. But the total impression isn't bad because some of the information saves your son's life. Oh yes; one more thing: Fat found himself seeing ancient Rome superimposed over California 1974. Well, I'll say this: Fat's encounter may not have been with God, but it certainly was with *something*.

No wonder Fat started scratching out page after page of his exegesis. I'd have done the same. He wasn't just theory-mongering for the sake of it; he was trying to figure out what the fuck had happened to him.

If Fat had simply been crazy he certainly found a unique form, an original way of doing it. Being in therapy at the time (Fat was always in therapy) he asked that a Rorschach Test be given to him to determine if he had become a schizophrenic. The test, upon his taking it, showed only a mild neurosis. So much for that theory.

*

In my novel *A Scanner Darkly*, published in 1977, I ripped off Fat's account of his eight hours of lurid phosphene activity.

106

"He had, a few years ago, been experimenting with disinhibiting substances affecting neural tissue, and one night, having administered to himself an IV injection considered safe and mildly euphoric, had experienced a disastrous drop in the GABA fluid of his brain. Subjectively, he had then witnessed lurid phosphene activity projected on the far wall of his bedroom, a frantically progressing montage of what, at the time, he imagined to be modern-day abstract paintings.

For about six hours, entranced, S.A. Powers had watched thousands of Picasso paintings replace one another at flash-cut speed, and then he had been treated to Paul Klees, more than the painter had painted during his entire lifetime. S.A. Powers, now viewing Modigliani paintings replacing themselves at furious velocity, had conjectured (one needs a theory for everything) that the Rosicrucians were telepathically beaming pictures at him, probably boosted by microrelay systems of an advanced order; but then, when Kandinsky paintings began to harass him, he recalled that the main art museum at Leningrad specialized in just such nonobjective moderns, and he decided that the Soviets were attempting telepathically to contact him.

In the morning he remembered that a drastic drop in the GABA fluid of the brain normally produced such phosphene activity; nobody was trying to contact him telepathically, with or without microwave boosting . . ."*

The GABA fluid of the brain blocks neural circuits from firing; it holds them in a dormant or latent state until a disinhibiting stimulus—the correct one—is presented to the organism, in this case Horselover Fat. In other words, these are neural circuits designed to fire on cue at a specific time under specific circumstances. Had Fat been presented with a disinhibiting stimulus prior to the lurid phosphene activity— the indication of a drastic drop in the level of GABA fluid in

* *A Scanner Darkly*, Doubleday, 1977, pgs. 15/16.

107

his brain, and hence the firing of previously blocked circuits, meta-circuits, so to speak?

All these events took place in March 1974. The month before that, Fat had had an impacted wisdom tooth removed. For this the oral surgeon administered a hit of IV sodium pentathol. Later that afternoon, back at home and in great pain, Fat had gotten Beth to phone for some oral pain medication. Being as miserable as he was, Fat himself had answered the door when the pharmacy delivery person knocked. When he opened the door, he found himself facing a lovely darkhaired young woman who held out a small white bag containing the Darvon N. But Fat, despite his enormous pain, cared nothing about the pills, because his attention had fastened on the gleaming gold necklace about the girl's neck; he couldn't take his eyes off it. Dazed from pain—and from the sodium pentathol—and exhausted by the ordeal he had gone through, he nonetheless managed to ask the girl what the symbol shaped in gold at the center of the necklace represented. It was a fish, in profile.

Touching the golden fish with one slender finger, the girl said, "This is a sign used by the early Christians."

Instantly, Fat experienced a flashback. He remembered—just for a half-second. Remembered ancient Rome and himself: as an early Christian; the entire ancient world and his furtive frightened life as a secret Christian hunted by the Roman authorities burst over his mind . . . and then he was back in California 1974 accepting the little white bag of pain pills.

A month later as he lay in bed unable to sleep, in the semi-gloom, listening to the radio, he started to see floating colors. Then the radio shrilled hideous, ugly sentences at him. And, after two days of this, the vague colors began to rush toward him as if he were himself moving forward, faster and faster; and, as I depicted in my novel *A Scanner Darkly*, the vague colors abruptly froze into sharp focus in the form of modern abstract paintings, literally tens of millions of them in rapid succession.

Meta-circuits in Fat's brain had been disinhibited by the fish sign and the words spoken by the girl.

It's as simple as that.

A few days later, Fat woke up and saw ancient Rome superimposed on California 1974 and thought in *koine* Greek, the *lingua franca* of the Near East part of the Roman world, which was the part he saw. He did not know that the *koine* was their *lingua franca*; he supposed that Latin was. And in addition, as I've already told you, he did not recognize the language of his thoughts even as a language.

Horselover Fat is living in two different times and two different places; i.e. in two space-time continua; that is what took place in March 1974 because of the ancient fish-sign presented to him the month before: his two space-time continua ceased to be separate and merged. And his two identities—personalities—also merged. Later, he heard a voice think inside his head:

"There's someone else living in me and he's not in this century."

The other personality had figured it out. The other personality was thinking. And Fat—especially just before he fell asleep at night—could pick up the thoughts of this other personality, as recently as a month ago; which is to say, four-and a half years after the compartmentalization of the two persons broke down.

*

Fat himself expressed it very well to me in early 1975 when he first began to confide in me. He called the personality in him living in another century and at another place "Thomas."

"Thomas," Fat told me, "is smarter than I am, and he knows more than I do. Of the two of us Thomas is the master personality." He considered that good; woe unto someone who has an evil or stupid other-personality in his head!

I said, "You mean once you were Thomas. You're a reincarnation of him and you remembered him and his—"

"No, he's living now. Living in ancient Rome *now*. And he is not me. Reincarnation has nothing to do with it."

"*But your body*," I said.

Fat stared at me, nodding. "Right. It means my body is either in two space-time continua simultaneously, *or else my body is nowhere at all*."

Entry 14 from the *tractate*: **The universe is information and we are stationary in it, not three-dimensional and not in space or time.** The information fed to us we hypostatize into the phenomenal world

Entry 30, which is a restatement for emphasis: **The phenomenal world does not exist; it is a hypostasis of the information processed by the Mind.**

Fat had scared the shit out of me. He had extrapolated entries 14 and 30 from his experience, inferred them from discovering that someone else existed in his head and that someone else was living in a different place at a different time—two thousand years ago and eight thousand miles away.

We are not individuals. We are stations in a single Mind. We are supposed to remain separate from one another at all times. However, Fat had received by accident a signal (the golden fish sign) intended for Thomas. It was Thomas who dealt in fish signs, not Fat. If the girl hadn't explained the meaning of the sign, the breakdown of compartmentalization would not have occurred. But she did and it did. Space and time were revealed to Fat—and to Thomas!—as mere mechanisms of separation. Fat found himself viewing a double exposure of two realities superimposed, and Thomas probably found himself doing the same. Thomas probably wondered what the hell foreign language was happening in *his* head. Then he realized it wasn't even his head:

"There's someone else living in me and he's not in this century." That was Thomas thinking that, not Fat. But it applied to Fat equally.

But Thomas had the edge over Fat, because, as Fat said, Thomas was smarter; he was the master personality. He took over Fat, switched him off wine and onto beer, trimmed his beard, had trouble with the car . . . but more important. Thomas remembered—if that is the word—other selves, one in Minoan Crete, which is from 3000 B.C.E. to 1100 B.C.E., a long, long time ago. Thomas even remembered a self before that: one which had come to this planet from the stars.

Thomas was the ultimate non-fool of Post Neolithic times. As an early Christian, of the apostolic age; he had not seen

110

Jesus but he knew people who had—my God, I'm losing control, here, trying to write this down. Thomas had figured out how to reconstitute himself after his physical death. *All* the early Christians knew how. It worked through anamnesis, the loss of amnesia which—well, the system was supposed to work this way: when Thomas found himself dying, he would engram himself on the Christian fish sign, eat some strange pink—the same pink color as in the light which Fat had seen—some strange pink food and drink from a sacred pitcher kept in a cool cupboard, and then die, and when he was reborn, he would grow up and be a later person, not himself, *until* he was shown the fish sign.

He had anticipated this happening about forty years after his death. Wrong. It took almost two thousand years.

In this way, through this mechanism, time was abolished. Or, put another way, the tyranny of death was abolished. The promise of eternal life which Christ held out to his little flock was no hoax. Christ had taught them how to do it; it had to do with the immortal plasmate which Fat talked about, the living information slumbering at Nag Hammadi century after century. The Romans had found and murdered all the homoplasmates—all the early Christians crossbonded to the plasmate; they died, the plasmate escaped to Nag Hammadi and slumbered as information on the codices.

Until, in 1945, the library was discovered and dug up—and read. So Thomas had to wait—not forty years—but two thousand; because the golden fish sign wasn't enough. Immortality, the abolition of time and space, comes only through the Logos or plasmate; only it is immortal.

We are talking about Christ. He is an extra-terrestrial life form which came to this planet thousands of years ago, and, as living information, passed into the brains of human beings already living here, the native population. We are talking about interspecies symbiosis.

Before being Christ he was Elijah. The Jews know all about Elijah and his immortality—and his ability to extend immortality to others by "dividing up his spirit." The Qumran people knew this. They sought to receive part of Elijah's spirit.

"You see, my son, here time changes into space."

111

First you change it into space and then you walk through it, but as Parsifal realized, he was not moving at all; he stood still and the landscape changed; it underwent a metamorphosis. For a while he must have experienced a double exposure, a superimposition, as Fat did. This is the dream-time, which exists now, not in the past, the place where the heroes and gods dwell and their deeds take place.

The single most striking realization that Fat had come to was his concept of the universe as irrational and governed by an irrational mind, the creator deity. If the universe were taken to be rational, not irrational, then something breaking into it might seem irrational, since it would not belong. But Fat, having reversed everything, saw the rational breaking into the irrational. The immortal plasmate had invaded our world and the plasmate was totally rational, whereas our world is not. This structure forms the basis of Fat's world-view. It is the bottom line.

For two thousand years the single rational element in our world had slumbered. In 1945 it woke up, came out of its dormant seed state and began to grow. It grew within himself, and presumably within other humans, and it grew outside, in the macro-world. He could not estimate its vastness, as I have said. When something begins to devour the world, a serious matter is taking place. If the devouring entity is evil or insane, the situation is not merely serious; it is grim. But Fat viewed the process the other way around. He viewed it exactly as Plato had viewed it in his own cosmology: the rational mind (*noös*) persuades the irrational (chance, blind determinism, *ananke*), into cosmos.

This process had been interrupted by the Empire.

"The Empire never ended." Until now; until August 1974 when the Empire suffered a crippling, perhaps terminal, blow, at the hands—so to speak—of the immortal plasmate, now restored to active form and using humans as its physical agents.

Horselover Fat was one of those agents. He was, so to speak, the hands of the plasmate, reaching out to injure the Empire.

Out of this, Fat deduced that he had a mission, that the plasmate's invasion of him represented its intention to employ him for its benign purposes.

112

*

I have had dreams of another place myself, a lake up north and the cottages and small rural houses around its south shore. In my dream I arrive there from Southern California, where I live; this is a vacation spot, but it is very old-fashioned. All the houses are wooden, made of the brown shingles so popular in California before World War Two. The roads are dusty. The cars are older, too. What is strange is that no such lake exists in the northern part of California. In real life I have driven all the way north to the Oregon border and into Oregon itself. Seven hundred miles of dry country exists only.

Where does this lake—and the houses and roads around it—actually exist? Countless times I dream about it. Since in the dreams I am aware that I am on vacation, that my real home is in southern California, I sometimes drive back down here to Orange County in these inter-connected dreams. But when I arrive back down here I live in a house, whereas in actuality I live in an apartment. In the dreams, I am married. In real life, I live alone. Stranger still, my wife is a woman I have never actually seen.

In one dream, the two of us are outside in the back yard watering and tending our rose garden. I can see the house next door; it's a mansion, and we share a common cement retaining wall with it. Wild roses have been planted up the side of the wall, to make it attractive. As I carry my rake past the green plastic garbage cans which we have stuffed with the clippings of trimmed plants, I glance at my wife—she is watering with the hose—and I gaze up at the retaining wall with its wild rose bushes, and I feel good; I think, It wouldn't be possible to live happily in southern California if we didn't have this nice house with its beautiful back garden. I'd prefer to own the mansion next door, but anyhow I get to see it, and I can walk over into its more spacious garden. My wife wears blue jeans; she is slender and pretty.

As I wake up I think, I should drive north to the lake; as beautiful as it is down here, with my wife and the back garden and the wild roses, the lake is nicer. But then I realize that this is

113

January and there will be snow on the highway when I get north of the Bay Area; this is not a good time to drive back to the cabin on the lake. I should wait until summer; I am really, after all, a rather timid driver. My car's a good one, though; a nearly new red Capri. And then as I wake up more I realize that I am living in an apartment in southern California alone. I have no wife. There is no such house, with the back garden and the high retaining wall with wild rose bushes. Stranger still, not only do I not have a cabin on the lake up north but no such lake in California exists. The map I hold mentally during my dream is a counterfeit map; it does not depict California. Then what state does it depict? Washington? There is a large body of water at the north of Washington; I have flown over it going to and returning from Canada, and once I visited Seattle.

Who is this wife? Not only am I single; I have never been married to nor seen this woman. Yet in the dreams I felt deep, comfortable and familiar love towards her, the kind of love which grows only with the passage of many years. But how do I even know that, since I have never had anyone to feel such love for?

Getting up from bed—I've been napping in the early evening—I walk into the living room of my apartment and am struck dumb by the synthetic nature of my life. Stereo (that's synthetic); television set (that's certainly synthetic); books, a second-hand experience, at least compared with driving up the narrow, dusty road which follows the lake, passing under the branches of trees, finally reaching my cabin and the place I park. What cabin? What lake? I can even remember being taken there originally, years ago, by my mother. Now, sometimes, I go by air. There's a direct flight between southern California and the lake . . . except for a few miles after the airfield. What airfield? But, most of all, how can I endure the ersatz life I lead here in this plastic apartment, alone, specifically without her, the slender wife in blue jeans?

If it wasn't for Horselover Fat and his encounter with God or Zebra or the Logos, and this other person living in Fat's head but in another century and place, I would dismiss my dreams as nothing. I can remember articles dealing with the people who have settled near the lake; they belong to a mild

114

religious group, somewhat like the Quakers (I was raised as a Quaker); except, it is stated, they held the strong belief that children should not be put in wooden cradles. This was their special heretical thrust. Also—and I can actually see the pages of the written article about them—it is said of them that "every now and then one or two wizards are born," which has some bearing on their aversion to wooden cradles; if you put an infant or baby who is a wizard—a future wizard—into a wooden cradle, evidently he will gradually lose his powers.

Dreams of another life? But where? Gradually the envisioned map of California, which is spurious, fades out, and, with it, the lake, the houses, the roads, the people, the cars, the airport, the clan of mild religious believers with their peculiar aversion to wooden cradles; but for this to fade out, a host of inter-connected dreams spanning years of real elapsed time must fade, too.

The only connection between this dream landscape and my actual world consists of my red Capri.

Why does that one element hold true in both worlds?

It has been said of dreams that they are a "controlled psychosis," or, put another way, a psychosis is a dream breaking through during waking hours. What does this mean in terms of my lake dream which includes a woman I never knew for whom I feel a real and comfortable love? Are there two persons in my brain, as there are in Fat's? Partitioned off, but, in my case no disinhibiting symbol accidentally triggered the "other" one into bursting through the partition into my personality and my world?

Are we all like Horselover Fat, but don't know it?

How many worlds do we exist in simultaneously?

Groggy from my nap I turn on the TV and try to watch a program called "Dick Clark's Good Ol' Days Part II." Morons and simps appear on the screen, drool like pinheads and waterheads; zitfaced kids scream in ecstatic approval of total banality. I turn the TV set off. My cat wants to be fed. What cat? In the dreams, my wife and I own no pets; we own a lovely house with a large, well-tended yard in which we spend our weekends. We have a two-car garage . . . suddenly I realize with a distinct jolt that this is an expensive house; in my inter-

115

related dreams I am well-to-do. I live an upper-middleclass life. It's not me. I'd never live like that; or if I did I'd be acutely uncomfortable. Wealth and property make me uneasy; I grew up in Berkeley and have the typical Berkeley left wing socialist conscience, with its suspicion of the cushy life.

The person in the dream also owns lake-front property. But the goddam Capri is the same. Earlier this year I went out and bought a brand new Capri Ghia, which normally I can't afford; it is the kind of car the person in the dream would own. There is a logic to the dream, then. As that person I would have the same car.

An hour after I have woken up from the dream I can still see in my mind's eye—whatever that may be; the third or *ajna* eye?—the garden hose which my wife in her blue jeans is dragging across the cement driveway. Little details, and no plot. I wish I owned the mansion next to our house. I do? In real life, I wouldn't own a mansion on a bet. These are rich people; I detest them. Who am I? How many people am I? Where am I? This plastic little apartment in southern California is not my home, but now I am awake, I guess, and here I live, with my TV (hello, Dick Clark), and my stereo (hello, Olivia Newton-John) and my books (hello nine million stuffy titles). In comparison to my life in the inter-connected dreams, this life is lonely and phony and worthless; unfit for an intelligent and educated person. *Where are the roses? Where is the lake? Where is the slim, smiling, attractive woman coiling and tugging the green garden hose?* The person that I am now, compared with the person in the dream, has been baffled and defeated and only supposes he enjoys a full life. In the dreams, I see what a full life really consists of, and it is not what I really have.

Then a strange thought comes to me. I am not close to my father, who is still alive, in his eighties, living up in northern California, in Menlo Park. Only twice did I ever visit his house, and that was twenty years ago. His house was like that which I owned in the dream. His aspirations—and accomplishments— dovetail with those of the person in the dream. Do I become my father during my sleep? The man in the dream—myself— was about my own actual age, *or younger.* Yes; I infer from the

116

woman, my wife: much younger. I have gone back in time in my dreams, not back to my own youth but back to my father's youth! In my dreams, I hold my father's view of the good life, of what things should be like; the strength of his view is so strong that it lingers an hour after I wake up. Of course I felt dislike for my cat upon awakening; my father hates cats.

My father, in the decade before I was born, used to drive up north to Lake Tahoe. He and my mother probably had a cabin there. I don't know; I've never been there.

Phylogenic memory, memory of the species. Not my own memory, ontogenic memory. "Phylogeny is recapitulated in ontogeny," as it is put. The individual contains the history of his entire race, back to its origins. Back to ancient Rome, to Minos at Crete, back to the stars. All I got down to, all I abreacted to, in sleep, was one generation. This is gene pool memory, the memory of the DNA. That explains Horselover Fat's crucial experience, in which the symbol of the Christian fish disinhibited a personality from two thousand years in the past . . . because the symbol originated two thousand years in the past. Had he been shown an even older symbol he would have abreacted farther; after all, the conditions were perfect for it: he was coming off sodium penthathol, the "truth drug."

Fat has another theory. He thinks that the date is really 103 C.E. (or A.D. as I put it; damn Fat and his hip modernisms). We're actually in apostolic times, but a layer of *maya* or what the Greeks called "*dokos*" obscures the landscape. This is a key concept with Fat: *dokos*, the layer of delusion or the merely seeming. The situation has to do with time, with whether time is real.

I'll quote Heraclitus on my own, without getting Fat's permission: "Time is a child at play, playing draughts; a child's is the kingdom." Christ! What does this mean? Edward Hussey about this passage: "Here, as probably in Anaximander, 'Time' is a name for God, with an etymological suggestion of his eternity. The infinitely old divinity is a child playing a board game as he moves the cosmic pieces in combat according to rule." Jesus Christ, what are we dealing with, here? Where are we and when are we and who are we? How many people in how

117

many places at how many times? Pieces on a board, moved by the "infinitely old divinity" who is a "child"!

Back to the cognac bottle. Cognac calms me down. Sometimes, especially after I've spent an evening talking to Fat, I get freaked and need something to calm me. I have the dreadful sense that he is into something real and awfully frightening. Personally, I don't want to break any new theological or philosophical ground. But I had to meet Horselover Fat; I had to get to know him and share his harebrained ideas based on his peculiar encounter with God knows what. With ultimate reality, maybe. Whatever it was, it was alive and it thought. And in no way did it resemble us, despite the quote from *1 John 3:1/2*.

Xenophanes was right.

"One god there is, *in no way like mortal creatures* either in bodily form or in the thought of his mind."

*

Isn't it an oxymoron to say, I am not myself? Isn't this a verbal contradiction, a statement semantically meaningless? Fat turned out to be Thomas; and I, upon studying the information in my dream, conclude that I am my own father, married to my mother, when she was young—before my own birth. I think the cryptic mention that, "Now and then one or two wizards are born" is supposed to tell me something. A sufficiently advanced technology would seem to us to be a form of magic; Arthur C. Clarke has pointed that out. A wizard deals with magic; *ergo*, a "wizard" is someone in possession of a highly sophisticated technology, one which baffles us. Someone is playing a board game with time, someone we can't see. It is not God. That is an archaic name given to this entity by societies in the past, and by people now who're locked into anachronistic thinking. We need a new term, but what we are dealing with is not new.

Horselover Fat is able to travel through time, travel back thousands of years. The three-eyed people probably live in the far future; they are our descendents, highly-evolved. And it is probably their technology which permitted Fat to do his time-

118

traveling. In point of fact, Fat's master personality may not lie in the past but ahead of us—but it expressed itself outside of him in the form of Zebra. I am saying that the St. Elmo's Fire which Fat recognized as alive and sentient probably abreacted back to this time-period and is one of our own children.

8

I did not think I should tell Fat that I thought his encounter with God was in fact an encounter with himself from the far future. Himself so evolved, so changed, that he had become no longer a human being. Fat had remembered back to the stars, and had encountered a being ready to return to the stars, and several selves along the way, several points along the line. All of them are the same person.

Entry 13 in the *tractate:* **Pascal said, "All history is one immortal man who continually learns." This is the Immortal One whom we worship without knowing his name. "He lived a long time ago but he is still alive," and, "The Head Apollo is about to return." The name changes.**

On some level Fat guessed the truth; he had encountered his past selves and his future selves—two future selves; an early-on one, the three-eyed people, and then Zebra, who is discorporate.

Time somehow got abolished for him, and the recapitulation of selves along the linear time-axis caused the multitude of selves to laminate together into a common entity.

Out of the lamination of selves, Zebra, which is supra- or trans-temporal, came into existence: pure energy, pure living information. Immortal, benign, intelligent and helpful. The essence of the *rational* human being. In the center of an irrational universe governed by an irrational Mind stands rational man, Horselover Fat being just one example. The in-breaking deity that Fat encountered in 1974 was himself. However, Fat seemed happy to believe that he had met God.

After some thought I decided not to tell him my views. After all, I might be wrong.

It all had to do with time. "Time can be overcome," Mircea Eliade wrote. That's what it's all about. The great mystery of Eleusis, of the Orphics, of the early Christians, of Sarapis, of the Greco-Roman mystery religions, of Hermes Trismegistos, of the Renaissance Hermetic alchemists, of the Rose Cross Brotherhood, of Apollonius of Tyana, of Simon Magus, of Asklepios, of Paracelsus, of Bruno, consists of the abolition of time. The techniques are there. Dante discusses them in the *Comedy*. It has to do with the loss of amnesia; when forgetfulness is lost, true memory spreads out backward and forward, into the past and into the future, and also, oddly, into alternate universes; it is orthogonal as well as linear.

This is why Elijah could be said correctly to be immortal; he had entered the Upper Realm (as Fat calls it) and is no longer subject to time. Time equals what the ancients called "astral determinism." The purpose of the mysteries was to free the initiate from astral determinism, which roughly equals fate. About this, Fat wrote in his *tractate:*

Entry 48. Two realms there are, upper and lower. The upper, derived from hyperuniverse I or Yang, Form I of Parmenides, is sentient and volitional. The lower realm, or Yin, Form II of Parmenides, is mechanical, driven by blind, efficient cause, deterministic and without intelligence, since it emanates from a dead source. In ancient times it was termed "astral determinism." We are trapped, by and large, in the lower realm, but are through the sacraments, by means of the plasmate, extricated. Until astral determinism is broken, we are not even aware of it, so occluded are we. "The Empire never ended."

Siddhartha, the Buddha, remembered all his past lives; this is why he was given the title of buddha which means "the Enlightened One." From him the knowledge of achieving this passed to Greece and shows up in the teachings of Pythagoras, who kept much of this occult, mystical *gnosis* secret; his pupil Empedocles, however, broke off from the Pythagorean Brotherhood and went public. Empedocles told his friends privately that he was Apollo. He, too, like the Buddha and Pythagoras, could remember his past lives. What they did not talk about was their ability to "remember" future lives.

The three-eyed people who Fat saw represented himself at an enlightened stage of his evolving development through his various lifetimes. In Buddhism it's called the "super-human divine eye" (*dibba-cakkhu*), the power to see the passing away and rebirth of beings. Gautama the Buddha (Siddhartha) attained it during his middle watch (ten P.M. to two A.M.). In his first watch (six P.M. to ten P.M.) he gained the knowledge of all—repeat: *all*—his former existences (*pubbeni-vasanussati-nana*). I did not tell Fat this, but technically he had become a Buddha. It did not seem to me like a good idea to let him know. After all, if you are a Buddha you should be able to figure it out for yourself.

It strikes me as an interesting paradox that a Buddha—an enlightened one—would be unable to figure out, even after four-and-a-half years, that he had become enlightened. Fat had become totally bogged down in his enormous exegesis, trying futilely to determine what had happened to him. He resembled more a hit-and-run accident victim than a Buddha.

"Holy fuck!" as Kevin would have put it, about the encounter with Zebra. "What was THAT?"

No wimpy hype passed muster before Kevin's eyes. He considered himself the hawk and the hype the rabbit. He had little use for the exegesis, but remained Fat's good friend. Kevin operated on the principle, Condemn the deed not the doer.

These days, Kevin felt fine. After all, his negative opinion of Sherri had proven correct. This brought him and Fat closer together. Kevin knew her for what she was, her cancer notwithstanding. In the final analysis, the fact that she was dying mattered to him not in the least. He had mulled it over and concluded that the cancer was a scam.

Fat's obsessive idea these days, as he worried more and more about Sherri, was that the Savior would soon be reborn—or had been already. Somewhere in the world he walked or soon would walk the ground once more.

What did Fat intend to do when Sherri died? Maurice had

122

shouted that at him in the form of a question. Would he die, too?

Not at all. Fat, pondering and writing and doing research and receiving dribs and drabs of messages from Zebra during hypnagogic states and in dreams, and attempting to salvage something from the wreck of his life, had decided to go in search of the Savior. He would find him wherever he was.

This was the mission, the divine purpose, which Zebra had placed on him in March 1974: the mild yoke, the burden light. Fat, a holy man now, would become a modern-day magus. All he lacked was a clue—some hint as to where to seek. Zebra would tell him, eventually; the clue would come from God. This was the whole purpose of Zebra's theophany: to send Fat on his way.

Our friend David, upon being told of this, asked, "Will it be Christ?" Thus showing his Catholicism.

"It is a fifth Savior," Fat said enigmatically. After all, Zebra had referred to the coming of the Savior in several—and in a sense conflicting—ways: as St. Sophia, who was Christ; as the Head Apollo; as the Buddha or Siddhartha.

Being eclectic in terms of his theology, Fat listed a number of saviors: the Buddha, Zoroaster, Jesus and Abu Al-Qasim Muhammad Ibn Abd Allah Abd Al-Muttalib Ibn Hashim (i.e. Muhammad). Sometimes he also listed Mani. Therefore, the next Savior would be number five, by the abridged list, or number six by the longer list. At certain times, Fat also included Asklepios, which, when added to the longer list, would make the next Savior number seven. In any case, this forthcoming savior would be the last; he would sit as king and judge over all nations and people. The sifting bridge of Zoroastrianism had been set up, by means of which good souls (those of light) became separated from bad souls (those of darkness). Ma'at had put her feather in the balance to be weighed against the heart of each man in judgment, as Osiris the Judge sat. It was a busy time.

Fat intended to be present, perhaps to hand the *Book of Life* to the Supreme Judge, the Ancient of Days mentioned in the *Book of Daniel*.

We all pointed out to Fat that hopefully the *Book of Life*—in

123

which the names of all who were saved had been inscribed—would prove too heavy for one man to lift; a winch and power crane would be necessary. Fat wasn't amused.

"Wait'll the Supreme Judge sees my dead cat," Kevin said.

"You and your goddam dead cat," I said. "We're tired of hearing about your dead cat."

After listening to Fat disclose his sly plans to seek out the Savior—no matter how far he had to travel to find him—I realized the obvious: Fat actually was in search of the dead girl Gloria, for whose death he considered himself responsible. He had totally blended his religious life and goals with his emotional life and goals. For him "savior" stood for "lost friend." He hoped to be reunited with her, but this side of the grave. If he couldn't go to her, on the other side, he would instead find her here. So although he was no longer suicidal he was still nuts. But this seemed to me to be an improvement; *thanatos* was losing out to *eros*. As Kevin put it, "Maybe Fat'll get laid by some fox somewhere along the way."

By the time Fat took off on his sacred quest he would be searching for two dead girls: Gloria and Sherri. This updated version of the Grail saga made me wonder if equally erotic underpinnings had motived the Grail knights at Montsavat, the castle where Parsifal wound up. Wagner says in his text that only those who the Grail itself calls find their way there. The blood of Christ on the cross had been caught in the same cup from which he had drunk at the Last Supper; so literally it had wound up containing his blood. In essence the blood, not the Grail, summoned the knights; the blood never died. Like Zebra, the contents of the Grail were a plasma or, as Fat termed it, plasmate. Probably Fat had it down somewhere in his exegesis that Zebra equaled plasmate equaled the sacred blood of the crucified Christ.

The spilled blood of the girl broken and drying on the pavement outside the Oakland Synanon Building called to Fat, who, like Parsifal, was a complete fool. That's what the word "parsifal" is supposed to mean in Arabic; it's supposed to have been derived from *"Falparsi,"* an Arabic word meaning "pure fool." This of course isn't the actual case, although in the opera *Parsifal*, Kundry addresses Parsifal this way. The name

"Parsifal" is in fact derived from "Perceval," which is just a name. However, one point of interest remains: via Persia the Grail is identified with the pre-Christian *"lapis exilix,"* which is a magical stone. This stone shows up in later Hermetic alchemy as the agent by which human metamorphosis is achieved. On the basis of Fat's concept of interspecies symbiosis, the human being crossbonded with Zebra or the Logos or plasmate to become a homoplasmate, I can see a certain continuity in all this. Fat believed himself to have crossbonded with Zebra; therefore he had already become that which the Hermetic alchemists sought. It would be natural, then, for him to seek out the Grail; he would be finding his friend, himself and his home.

Kevin held the role of the evil magician Klingsor by his continual lampooning of Fat's idealistic aspirations. Fat, according to Kevin, was horny. In Fat, *thanatos*—death—fought it out with *eros*—which Kevin identified not with life but with getting laid. This probably isn't far off; I mean Kevin's basic description of the dialectical struggle surging back and forth inside Fat's mind. Part of Fat desired to die and part desired life. *Thanatos* can assume any form it wishes; it can kill *eros*, the life drive, and then simulate it. Once thanatos does this to you, you are in big trouble; you suppose you are driven by *eros* but it is *thanatos* wearing a mask. I hoped Fat hadn't gotten into this place; I hoped his desire to seek out and find the Savior stemmed from *eros*.

The true Savior, or the true God for that matter, carries life with him; he *is* life. Any "savior" or "god" who brings death is nothing but *thanatos* wearing a savior mask. This is why Jesus identified himself as the true Savior—even when he didn't want to so identify himself—by his healing miracles. The people knew what healing miracles pointed to. There is a wonderful passage at the very end of the Old Testament where this matter is clarified. God says, "But for you who fear my name, the sun of righteousness shall rise with healing in his wings, and you shall break loose like calves released from the stall."

In a sense Fat hoped that the Savior would heal what had become sick, restore what had been broken. On some level, he actually believed that the dead girl Gloria could be restored to

125

life. This is why Sherri's unrelieved agony, her growing cancer, baffled him and defeated his spiritual hopes and beliefs. According to his system as put forth in his exegesis, based on his encounter with God, Sherri should have been made well.

Fat was in search of a very great deal. Although technically he could understand why Sherri had cancer, spiritually he could not. In fact, Fat could not really make out why Christ, the Son of God, had been crucified. Pain and suffering made no sense to Fat; he could not fit it into the grand design. Therefore, he reasoned, the existence of such dreadful afflictions pointed to irrationality in the universe, an affront to reason.

Beyond doubt, Fat was serious about his proposed quest. He had squirreled away almost twenty thousand dollars in his savings account.

"Don't make fun of him," I said to Kevin one day. "This is important to him."

His eyes gleaming with customary cynical mockery, Kevin said, "Ripping off a piece of ass is important to me, too."

"Come off it," I said. "You're not funny."

Kevin merely continued to grin.

A week later, Sherri died.

Now, as I had foreseen, Fat had two deaths on his conscience. He had been unable to save either girl. When you are Atlas you must carry a heavy load and if you drop it a lot of people suffer, an entire world of people, an entire world of suffering. This now lay over Fat spiritually rather than physically, this load. Tied to him the two corpses cried for rescue—cried even though they had died. The cries of the dead are terrible indeed; you should try not to hear them.

What I feared was a return by Fat to suicide and if that failed, then another stretch in the rubber lock-up.

To my surprise when I dropped by Fat's apartment I found him composed.

"I'm going," he told me.

"On your quest?"

"You got it," Fat said.

"Where?"

"I don't know. I'll just start going and Zebra will guide me."

I had no motivation to try to talk him out of it; what did his alternatives consist of? Sitting by himself in the apartment he and Sherri had lived in together? Listening to Kevin mock the sorrows of the world? Worst of all, he could spend his time listening to David prattle about how "God brings good out of evil." If anything were to put Fat in the rubber lock-up it would be finding himself caught in a cross-fire between Kevin and David: the stupid and pious and credulous versus the cynically cruel. And what could I add? Sherri's death had torn me down, too, had deconstructed me into basic parts, like a toy disassembled back to what had arrived in the gaily-colored kit. I felt like saying, "Take me along, Fat. Show me the way home."

While Fat and I sat there together grieving, the phone rang. It was Beth, wanting to be sure Fat knew that he had fallen behind a week in his child support payment.

As he hung up the phone, Fat said to me, "My ex-wives are descended from rats."

"You've got to get out of here," I said.

"Then you agree I should go."

"Yes," I said.

"I've got enough money to go anywhere in the world. I've thought of China. I've thought, Where is the least likely place He would be born? A Communist country like China. Or France."

"Why France?" I asked.

"I've always wanted to see France."

"Then go to France," I said.

" 'What will you do,' " Fat murmured.

"Pardon?"

"I was thinking about that American Express Travelers' Checks TV ad. 'What will you do. What *will* you do.' That's how I feel right now. They're right."

I said, "I like the one where the middle-aged man says, 'I had six hundred dollars in that wallet. It's the worst thing that ever happened to me in my life.' If that's the worst thing that ever happened to him—"

"Yeah," Fat said, nodding. "He's led a sheltered life."

I knew what vision had conjured itself up in Fat's mind: the vision of the dying girls. Either broken on impact or burst open

127

from within. I shivered and felt, myself, like weeping.

"She suffocated," Fat said, finally, in a low voice. "She just fucking suffocated; she couldn't breathe any longer."

"I'm sorry," I said.

"You know what the doctor said to me to cheer me up?" Fat said. " 'There are worse diseases than cancer.' "

"Did he show you slides?"

We both laughed. When you are nearly crazy with grief, you laugh at what you can.

"Let's walk down to Sombrero Street," I said; that was a good restaurant and bar where we all liked to go. "I'll buy you a drink."

We walked down to Main St. and seated ourselves in the bar at Sombrero Street.

"Where's that little brown-haired lady you used to come in here with?" the waitress asked Fat as she served us our drinks.

"In Cleveland," Fat said. We both started to laugh again. The waitress remembered Sherri. It was too awful to take seriously.

"I knew this woman," I said to Fat as we drank, "and I was talking about a dead cat of mine and I said, 'Well, he's at rest in perpetuity' and she immediately said, completely seriously, 'My cat is buried in Glendale.' We all chimed in and compared the weather in Glendale compared to the weather in perpetuity." Both Fat and I were laughing so hard now that other people stared at us. "We have to knock this off," I said, calming down.

"Isn't it colder in perpetuity?" Fat said.

"Yes, but there's less smog."

Fat said, "Maybe that's where I'll find him."

"Who?" I said.

"Him. The fifth savior."

"Do you remember the time at your apartment," I said, "when Sherri was starting chemotherapy and her hair was falling out—"

"Yeah, the cat's water dish."

"She was standing by the cat's water dish and her hair kept falling into the water dish and the poor cat was puzzled."

" 'What the hell is this?' " Fat said, quoting what the cat would have said could it talk. " 'Here in my water dish?' " He

128

grinned, but no joy could be seen in his grin. Neither of us could be funny any longer, even between us. "We need Kevin to cheer us up," Fat said. "On second thought," he murmured, "maybe we don't."

"We just have to keep on truckin'," I said.

"Phil," Fat said, "if I don't find him, I'm going to die."

"I know," I said. It was true. The Savior stood between Horselover Fat and annihilation.

"I am programmed to self-destruct," Fat said. "The button has been pressed."

"The sensations that you feel—" I began.

"They're rational," Fat said. "In terms of the situation. It's true. This is not insanity. I have to find him, wherever he is, or die."

"Well, then I'll die, too," I said. "If you do."

"That's right," Fat said. He nodded. "You got it. You can't exist without me and I can't exist without you. We're in this together. Fuck. What kind of life is this? Why do these things happen?"

"You said it yourself. The universe—"

"I'll find him," Fat said. He drank his drink and set the empty glass down and stood up. "Let's go back to my apartment. I want you to hear the new Linda Ronstadt record, *Living In the USA*. It's real good."

As we left the bar, I said, "Kevin says Ronstadt's washed up."

Pausing at the door out, Fat said, "Kevin is washed up. He's going to whip that goddam dead cat out from under his coat on Judgment Day and they're going to laugh at him like he laughs at us. That's what he deserves: a Great Judge exactly like himself."

"That's not a bad theological idea," I said. "You find yourself facing yourself. You think you'll find him?"

"The Savior? Yeah, I'll find him. If I run out of money I'll come home and work some more and go look again. He has to be somewhere. Zebra said so. And Thomas inside my head—he knew it; he remembered Jesus just having been there a little while ago, and he knew he'd be back. They were all joyful, completely joyful, making preparations to welcome him back.

129

The bridegroom back. It was so goddam festive, Phil; totally joyful and exciting, and everyone running around. They were running out of the Black Iron Prison and just laughing and laughing; they had fucking blown it up, Phil; the whole prison. Blew it up and got out of there . . . running and laughing and totally, totally happy. And I was one of them."

"You will be again," I said.

"I will be," Fat said, "when I find him. But until then I won't be; I can't be; there's no way." He halted on the sidewalk, hands in his pockets. "I miss him, Phil; I fucking miss him. I want to be with him; I want to feel his arm around me. Nobody else can do that. I saw him—sort of—and I want to see him again. That love, that warmth—that delight on his part that it's me, seeing me, being glad it's me: *recognizing* me. He *recognized* me!"

"I know," I said, awkwardly.

"Nobody knows what it's like," Fat said, "to have seen him and then not to see him. Almost five years now, five years of—" He gestured. "Of what? And what before that?"

"You'll find him," I said.

"I have to," Fat said, "or I am going to die. And you, too, Phil. And we know it."

*

The leader of the Grail knights, Amfortas, has a wound which will not heal. Klingsor has wounded him with the spear which pierced Christ's side. Later, when Klingsor hurls the spear at Parsifal, the pure fool catches the spear—which has stopped in midair—and holds it up, making the sign of the Cross with it, at which Klingsor and his entire castle vanish. They were never there in the first place; they were a delusion, what the Greeks call *dokos;* what the Indians call the *veil of máya*.

There is nothing Parsifal cannot do. At the end of the opera, Parsifal touches the spear to Amfortas's wound, the wound heals. Amfortas, who only wanted to die, is healed. Very mysterious words are repeated, which I never understood, although I can read German:

"Gesegnet sei dein Leiden,
Das Mitleids höchste Kraft,
Und reinsten Wissens Macht
Denn zagen Toren gab!"

This is one of the keys to the story of Parsifal, the pure fool who abolishes the delusion of the magician Klingsor and his castle, and heals Amfortas's wound. But what does it mean?

"May your suffering be blessed,
Which gave the timid fool
Pity's highest power
And purest knowledge's might!"

I don't know what this means. However, I know that in our case, the pure fool, Horselover Fat, himself had the wound which would not heal, and the pain that goes with it. All right; the wound is caused by the spear which pierced the Savior's side, and only that same spear can heal it. In the opera, after Amfortas is healed, the shrine is at last opened (it has been closed for a long time) and the Grail is revealed, at which point heavenly voices say:

"Erlösung dem Erlöser!"

Which is very strange, because it means:

"The Redeemer redeemed!"

In other words, Christ has saved himself. There's a technical term for this: *Salvator salvandus*. The "saved savior."

"The fact that in the discharge of his task the eternal messenger must himself assume the lot of incarnation and cosmic exile, and the further fact that, at least in the Iranian variety of the myth, he is in a sense identical with those he calls—the once lost parts of the divine self—give rise to the moving idea of the 'saved savior' (*salvator salvandus*)."

131

My source is reputable: *The Encyclopedia of Philosophy*, Macmillan Publishing Company, New York, 1967; in the article on "Gnosticism." I am trying to see how this applies to Fat. What is this "pity's highest power"? In what way does pity have the power to heal a wound? And can Fat feel pity for himself and so heal his own wound? *Would this, then, make Horselover Fat the Savior himself, the savior saved*? That seems to be the idea which Wagner expresses. The savior idea is Gnostic in origin. How did it get into *Parsifal*?

Maybe Fat was searching for himself when he set out in search of the Savior. To heal the wound made by first the death of Gloria and then the death of Sherri. But what in our modern world is the analog for Klingsor's huge stone castle?

That which Fat calls the Empire? The Black Iron Prison?

Is the Empire "which never ended" an illusion?

The words which Parsifal speaks which cause the huge stone castle—and Klingsor himself—to disappear are:

"*Mit diesem Zeichen bann' Ich deinen Zauber.*"
"With this sign I abolish your magic."

The sign, of course, is the sign of the Cross. Fat's Savior is Fat himself, as I already figured out; Zebra is all the selves along the linear time-axis, laminated into one supra- or trans-temporal self which cannot die, and which has come back to save Fat. But I don't dare tell Fat that he is searching for himself. He is not ready to entertain such a notion, because like the rest of us he seeks an external savior.

"Pity's highest power" is just bullshit. Pity has no power. Fat felt vast pity for Gloria and vast pity for Sherri and it didn't do a damn bit of good in either case. Something was lacking. Everyone knows this, everyone who has gazed down helplessly at a sick or dying human or a sick or dying animal, felt terrible pity, overpowering pity, and realized that this pity, however great it might be, is totally useless.

Something else healed the wound.

For me and David and Kevin this was a serious matter, this wound in Fat which would not heal, but which had to be healed and would be healed—*if* Fat found the Savior. Did some magic scene lie in the future where Fat would come to his senses, recognize that he was the Savior, and thereby automatically be healed? Don't bet on it. I wouldn't.

Parsifal is one of those corkscrew artifacts of culture in which you get the subjective sense that you've learned something from it, something valuable or even priceless; but on closer inspection you suddenly begin to scratch your head and say, "Wait a minute. This makes no sense." I can see Richard Wagner standing at the gates of heaven. "You have to let me in," he says. "I wrote *Parsifal*. It has to do with the Grail, Christ, suffering, pity and healing. Right?" And they answer, "Well, we read it and it makes no sense." *SLAM*. Wagner is right and so are they. It's another Chinese fingertrap.

Or perhaps I'm missing the point. What we have here is a Zen paradox. That which makes no sense makes the *most* sense. I am being caught in a sin of the highest magnitude: using Aristotelian two-value logic: "A thing is either A or not-A." (The Law of the Excluded Middle.) Everybody knows that Aristotelian two-value logic is fucked. What I am saying is that—

If Kevin were here he'd say, "Deedle-deedle queep," which is what he says to Fat when Fat reads aloud from his exegesis. Kevin has no use for the Profound. He's right. All I am doing is going, "Deedle-deedle queep" over and over again in my attempts to understand how Horselover Fat is going to heal—save—Horselover Fat. Because Fat cannot be saved. Healing Sherri was going to make up for losing Gloria; but Sherri died. The death of Gloria caused Fat to take forty-nine tablets of poison and now we are hoping that upon Sherri's death he will go forth, find the Savior (what Savior?) and be healed—healed of a wound that prior to Sherri's death was virtually terminal for him. Now there is no Horselover Fat; only the wound remains.

Horselover Fat is dead. Dragged down into the grave by two malignant women. Dragged down because he is a fool. That's another nonsense part in *Parsifal*, the idea that being stupid is salvific. Why? In *Parsifal* suffering gave the timid fool "purest knowledge's might." How? Why? Please explain.

Please show me how Gloria's suffering and Sherri's suffering

133

contributed anything good to Fat, to anyone, to anything. It's a lie. It's an evil lie. Suffering is to be abolished. Well, admittedly, Parsifal did that by healing the wound; Amfortas's agony ceased.

What we really need is a doctor, not a spear. Let me give you entry 45 from Fat's *tractate*.

45. In seeing Christ in a vision I correctly said to him, "We need medical attention." In the vision there was an insane creator who destroyed what he created, without purpose; which is to say, irrationally. This is the deranged streak in the Mind; Christ is our only hope, since we cannot now call on Asklepios. Asklepios came before Christ and raised a man from the dead; for this act, Zeus had a Kyklopes slay him with a thunderbolt. Christ also was killed for what he had done: raising a man from the dead. Elijah brought a boy back to life and disappeared soon thereafter in a whirlwind. "The Empire never ended."

46. The physician has come to us a number of times under a number of names. But we are not yet healed. The Empire identified him and ejected him. This time he will kill the Empire by phagocytosis.

In many ways Fat's exegesis makes more sense than *Parsifal.* Fat conceives of the universe as a living organism into which a toxic particle has come. The toxic particle, made of heavy metal, has embedded itself in the universe-organism and is poisoning it. The universe-organism dispatches a phagocyte. The phagocyte is Christ. It surrounds the toxic metal particle—the Black Iron Prison—and begins to destroy it.

41. The Empire is the institution, the codification, of derangement; it is insane and imposes its insanity on us by violence, since its nature is a violent one.

42. To fight the Empire is to be infected by its derangement. This is a paradox; whoever defeats a segment of the Empire becomes the Empire; it proliferates like a virus, imposing its form on its enemies. Thereby it becomes its enemies.

43. Against the Empire is posed the living information, the plasmate or physician, which we know as the Holy Spirit or Christ discorporate. These are the two principles, the dark (the Empire) and the light (the plasmate). In the end, Mind will give victory to the latter. Each of us will die or survive according to which he aligns himself and his efforts. Each of us contains a component of each. Eventually one or the other component will triumph in each human. Zoroaster knew this, because the Wise Mind informed him. He was the first savior.* Four have lived in all. A fifth is about to be born, who will differ from the others: he will rule and he will judge us.

In my opinion, Kevin may go "deedle-deedle queep" whenever Fat reads or quotes from his *tractate*, but Fat is onto something. Fat sees a cosmic phagocytosis in progress, one in which in micro-form we are each involved. A toxic metal particle is lodged in each of us: "That which is above (the macrocosm) is that which is below (the microcosm or man)." We are all wounded and we all need a physician—Elijah for the Jews, Asklepios for the Greeks, Christ for the Christians, Zoroaster for the Gnostics, the followers of Mani, and so forth. We die because we are born sick—born with a heavy metal splinter in us, a wound like Amfortas's wound. And when we are healed we will be immortal; this is how it was supposed to be, but the toxic metal splinter entered the macrocosm and simultaneously entered each of its microcosmic pluriforms: ourselves.

Consider the cat dozing on your lap. He is wounded, but the wound does not yet show. Like Sherri, something is eating him away. Do you want to gamble against this statement? Laminate all the cat's images in linear time into one entity; what you get is pierced, injured and dead. But a miracle occurs. An invisible physician restores the cat.

"So everything lingers but a moment, and hastens on to death. The plant and the insect die at the end of summer,

* Fat has left out Buddha, perhaps he doesn't understand who and what the Buddha is.

135

the brute and the man after a few years: death reaps unweariedly. Yet notwithstanding this, nay, as if this were not so at all, everything is always there and in its place, just as if everything were imperishable . . . This is temporal immortality. In consequence of this, notwithstanding thousands of years of death and decay, nothing has been lost, not an atom of the matter, still less anything of the inner being, that exhibits itself as nature. Therefore every moment we can cheerfully cry, 'In spite of time, death and decay, we are still all together!' " (Schopenhauer.)

Somewhere Schopenhauer says that the cat which you see playing in the yard is the cat which played three hundred years ago. This is what Fat had encountered in Thomas, in the three-eyed people, and most of all in Zebra who had no body. An ancient argument for immortality goes like this: if every creature really dies—as it appears to—then life continually passes out of the universe, passes out of being; and so eventually all life will have passed out of being, since there are no known exceptions to this. *Ergo*, despite what we see, life somehow must *not* turn to death.

Along with Gloria and Sherri, Fat had died, but Fat still lived on, as the Savior he now proposed to seek.

136

9

Wordsworth's "Ode" carries the sub-title: "Intimations of
Immortality from Recollections of Early Childhood." In Fat's
case, the "intimations of immortality" were based on recollections of a future life.

In addition, Fat could not write poetry worth shit, despite
his best efforts. He loved Wordsworth's "Ode," and wished he
could come up with its equal. He never did.

Anyhow, Fat's thoughts had turned to travel. These
thoughts had acquired a specific nature; one day he drove to
Wide-World Travel Bureau (Santa Ana branch) and conferred
with the lady behind the counter, the lady and her computer
terminal.

"Yes, we can put you on a slow boat to China," the lady said
cheerfully.

"How about a fast plane?" Fat said.

"Are you going to China for medical reasons?" the lady
asked.

Fat was surprised at the question.

"A number of people from Western countries are flying to
China for medical services," the lady said. "Even from
Sweden, I'm given to understand. Medical costs in China are
exceptionally low . . . but perhaps you already know that. Do
you know that? Major operations run approximately thirty
dollars in some cases." She rummaged among pamphlets,
smiling cheerfully.

"I guess so," Fat said.

"Then you can deduct it on your income tax," the lady said.
"You see how we help you here at Wide-World Travel?"

The irony of this side-issue struck Fat forcefully—that he, who sought the fifth Savior, could write his quest off on his state and Federal Income Tax. That night when Kevin dropped over he mentioned it to him, expecting Kevin to be wryly amused.

Kevin, however, had other fish to fry. In an enigmatic tone Kevin said, "What about going to the movies tomorrow night?"

"To see what?" Fat had caught the dark current in his friend's voice. It meant Kevin was up to something. But of course, true to his nature, Kevin would not amplify.

"It's a science fiction film," Kevin said, and that was all he would say.

"Okay," Fat said.

The next night, he and I and Kevin drove up Tustin Avenue to a small walk-in theater; since they intended to see a science fiction film I felt that for professional reasons I should go along.

As Kevin parked his little red Honda Civic we caught sight of the theater marquee.

"*Valis*," Fat said, reading the words. "With Mother Goose. What's 'Mother Goose'?"

"A rock group," I said, disappointed; it did not appear to me to be something I'd like. Kevin had odd tastes, both in films and in music; evidently he had managed to combine the two tonight.

"I've seen it," Kevin said cryptically. "Bear with me. You won't be disappointed."

"You've seen it?" Fat said, "and you want to see it again?"

"Bear with me," Kevin repeated.

As we sat in our seats inside the small theater we noticed that the audience seemed to be mostly teenagers.

"Mother Goose is Eric Lampton," Kevin said. "He wrote the screenplay for *Valis* and he stars in it."

"He sings?" I said.

"Nope," Kevin said, and that was all he had to say; he then lapsed into silence.

"Why are we here?" Fat said.

Kevin glanced at him without answering.

138

"Is this like your belch record?" Fat said. One time, when he'd been especially depressed, Kevin had brought over an album which he, Kevin, assured him, Fat, would cheer him up. Fat had to put on his electrostatic Stax headphones and really crank it up. The track turned out to consist of belching.

"Nope," Kevin said.

The lights dimmed; the audience of teenagers fell silent; the titles and credits appeared.

"Does Brent Mini mean anything to you?" Kevin said. "He did the music. Mini works with computer-created random sounds which he calls 'Synchronicity Music.' He's got three LPs out. I've got the second two, but I can't find the first."

"Then this is serious stuff," Fat said.

"Just watch," Kevin said.

Electronic noises sounded.

"God," I said, with aversion. On the screen a vast blob of colors appeared, exploding in all directions; the camera panned in for a tight shot. Low budget sci-fi flick, I said to myself. This is what gives the field a bad reputation.

The drama started abruptly; all at once the credits vanished. An open field, parched, brown, with a few weeds here and there, appeared. Well, I said to myself, here is what we'll see. A jeep with two soldiers in it, bumping across the field. Then something vivid flashes across the sky.

"Looks like a meteor, captain," one soldier says.

"Yes," the other soldier agrees thoughtfully. "But maybe we'd better investigate."

I was wrong.

*

The film *Valis* depicted a small record firm called Meritone Records, located in Burbank, owned by an electronics genius named Nicholas Brady. The time—by the style of the cars and the particular kind of rock being played—suggested the late Sixties or early Seventies, but odd incongruities prevailed. For example, Richard Nixon didn't seem to exist; the President of the United States bore the name Ferris F. Fremount, and he was very popular. During the first part of the film there were

139

abrupt segues to TV news footage of Ferris Fremount's spirited campaign for re-election.

Mother Goose himself—the actual rock star who in real life is rated with Bowie and Zappa and Alice Cooper—took the form of a song writer who had gotten hooked on drugs, decidedly a loser. Only the fact that Brady kept paying him enabled Goose to survive economically. Goose had an attractive and extremely short-haired wife; this woman possessed an unearthly appearance with her nearly bald head and enormous luminous eyes.

In the film Brady schemed constantly on Linda, Goose's wife (in the film, for some reason, Goose used his real name, Eric Lampton; so the tale narrated had to do with the marginal Lamptons). Linda Lampton wasn't natural; that came across early on. I got the impression that Brady was a son-of-a-bitch despite his wizardry with audio electronics. He had a laser system set up which ran the information—which is to say, the various channels of music—into a mixer unlike anything that actually exists; the damn thing rose up like a fortress—Brady actually entered it through a door, and, inside it, got bathed with laser beams which converted into sound using his brain as a transducer.

In one scene Linda Lampton took off her clothes. She had no sex organs.

Damdest thing Fat and I ever saw.

Meanwhile, Brady schemed on her unaware that no way existed by which he could make it with her, anatomically-speaking. This amused Mother Goose—Eric Lampton—who kept shooting up and writing the worst songs conceivable. It became obvious after a while that his brain was fried; he didn't realize it, either. Nicholas Brady began going through mystifying maneuvers suggesting that by means of his fortress mixer he intended to laser Eric Lampton out of existence, to pave the way for laying Linda Lampton who in fact had no sex organs.

Meanwhile, Ferris Fremount kept showing up in dissolves that baffled us. Fremount kept looking more and more like Brady, and Brady seemed to metamorphose into Fremount. Scenes shot by which showed Brady at enormous gala functions, apparently affairs of state; foreign diplomats

140

wandered around with drinks, and a constant low murmuring hung in the background—an electronic noise resembling the sound created by Brady's mixer.

I didn't understand the picture one bit.

"Do you understand this?" I asked Fat, leaning over to whisper.

"Christ, no," Fat said.

Having lured Eric Lampton into the mixer, Brady stuck a strange black cassette into the chamber and punched buttons. The audience saw a tight shot of Lampton's head explode, literally explode; but instead of brains bursting out, electronic miniaturized parts flew in all directions. Then Linda Lampton walked *through* the mixer, right through the wall of it, did something with an object she carried, and Eric Lampton ran backward in time: the electronic components of his head imploded, the skull returned intact—Brady, meanwhile, staggered out of the Meritone Building onto Alameda, his eyes bulging . . . cut to Linda Lampton putting her husband back together, both of them in the fortress-like mixer.

Eric Lampton opens his mouth to speak and out comes the sound of Ferris F. Fremount's voice. Linda draws back in dismay.

Cut to the White House; Ferris Fremount, who no longer looks like Nicholas Brady but like himself, restored.

"I want Brady taken out," he says grimly, "and taken out now." Two men dressed in skin-tight black shiny uniforms, carrying futuristic weapons, nod silently.

Cut to Brady crossing a parking lot rapidly to his car; he is totally fucked up. Pan to black-suited men on roof scope-sights up with cross-hairs: Brady seating himself and trying to start his car.

Dissolve to huge crowds of young girls dressed in red, white and blue cheerleader uniforms. But they're not cheerleaders; they chant, "Kill Brady! Kill Brady!"

Slow motion. The men in black fire their weapons. All at once, Eric Lampton stands outside the door of Meritone Records; close shot of his face; his eyes turn into something weird. The men in black char into ashes; their weapons melt.

"Kill Brady! Kill Brady!" Thousands of girls dressed in

identical red-white-and-blue uniforms. Some strip off their uniforms in sexual frenzy.

They have no reproductive organs.

Dissolve. Time has passed. *Two* Ferris F. Fremounts sit facing each other at a huge walnut table. Between them: a cube of pulsing pink light. It's a hologram.

Beside me, Fat grunts. He sits forward staring. I stare, too. I recognize the pink light; it's the color Fat described to me regarding Zebra.

Scene of Eric Lampton nude in bed with Linda Lampton. They strip off some kind of plastic membrane and reveal sex organs underneath. They make love, then Eric Lampton slides out of bed. Goes into living room, shoots up whatever dope he's strung out on. Sits down, puts his head wearily down. Dejection.

Long shot. The Lamptons' house below; camera is what they call "camera three." A beam of energy fires at the house below. Quick cut to Eric Lampton; he jerks as if pierced. Holds his hands to his head, convulsing in agony. Tight shot of his face; his eyes explode. (The audience with us gasps, including me and Fat.)

Different eyes replace the ones which exploded. Then, very slowly, his forehead slides open in the middle. A third eye becomes visible, but it lacks a pupil; instead it has a lateral lens.

Eric Lampton smiles.

Segue to recording session; some kind of folk rock group. They are playing a song that really turns them on.

"I never heard you write like this before," a board man says to Lampton.

Camera dollies in on speakers; sound level increases. Then cut to Ampex playback system; Nicholas Brady is playing a tape of the folk rock group. Brady signals to technician at the fortress-like mixer. Laser beams fire in all directions; the audio track undergoes a sinister transformation. Brady frowns, rewinds tape, plays it again. We hear words.

"Kill . . . Ferris . . . Fremount . . . kill . . . Ferris . . . Fremount . . ." Over and over again. Brady stops tape, rewinds it, replays it. This time the original song that Lampton wrote, no mention of killing Fremount.

142

Blackout. No sound, no sight. Then, slowly, Ferris F. Fremount's face appears with a grim expression. As if he had heard the tape.

Bending, Fremount clicks on a desk intercom system. "Give me the Secretary of Defense," he says. "Get him here at once; I must talk to him."

"Yes, Mr. President."

Fremount sits back, opens folder; pictures of Eric Lampton, Linda Lampton, Nicholas Brady, plus data. Fremount studies the data—beam of pink light strikes his head from above, for a split second. Fremount winces, looks puzzled, then, stiffly, like a robot, rises to his feet, walks to a shredder marked SHREDDER and drops the folder and its contents in. His expression is bland; he has totally forgotten everything.

"The Secretary of Defense is here, Mr. President."

Puzzled, Fremount says, "I didn't call for him."

"But sir—"

Cut to Air Force Base. Missile being launched. Tight shot of document marked SECRET. We see it opened.

PROJECT VALIS

Voice off camera; " 'VALIS'? What's that, general?"

Deep authoritative voice. "Vast Active Living Intelligence System. You're never to—"

Whole building detonates, into the same pink light as before. Outdoors: missile rising. Suddenly wobbles. Alarm sirens go off. Voices yelling, "Destruct alert! Destruct alert! Abort mission!"

We now see Ferris F. Fremount making campaign speech at fund-raising dinner; well-dressed people listening . Uniformed officer bends down to whisper in the President's ear. Aloud, Fremount says, "Well, did we get VALIS?"

Agitatedly, the officer says, "Something went wrong, Mr. President. The Satellite is still—" Voice drowned out by crowd noises; crowd senses something is wrong: the well-dressed people have metamorphosed to the girl cheerleaders in red-white-and-blue identical uniforms; they stand motionless. Like robots unplugged.

143

Final scene. Vast cheering crowd. Ferris Fremount, back to camera, making Nixon-type V-for-victory signs with both hands. Obviously he has won re-election. Brief shots of black-clad armed men standing at attention, pleased; general joy.

Some kid holds flowers to Mrs. Fremount; she turns to accept them. Ferris Fremount turns, too; zoom in.

Brady's face.

*

On the drive home, back down Tustin Avenue, Kevin said, after a period of mutual silence among the three of us, "You saw the pink light."

"Yes," Fat said.

"And the lateral-lens third eye," Kevin said.

"Mother Goose wrote the screenplay?" I asked.

"Wrote the screenplay, directed it, starred in it."

Fat said, "Did he ever do a film before?"

"No," Kevin said.

"There was information transfer," I said.

"In the film?" Kevin said. "As story line? Or do you mean from the film and audio track to the audience?"

"I'm not sure I understand—" I began.

"There is subliminal material in that film," Kevin said. "The next time I see it I'm taking a battery-powered cassette tape recorder in with me. I think the information is encoded in Mini's Synchronicity Music, his random music."

"It was an alternate U.S.A.," Fat said. "Where instead of Nixon being president Ferris Fremount was. I guess."

"Were Eric and Linda Lampton human or not?" I said. "First they appeared human; then she turned out not to have any—you know, sex organs. And then they stripped those membranes off and they did have sex organs."

"But when his head exploded," Fat said, "it was full of computer parts."

"Did you notice the pot?" Kevin said. "On Nicholas Brady's desk. The little clay pot—like the one you have, the pot that girl—"

"Stephanie," Fat said.

144

"—made for you."

"No," Fat said. "I didn't notice it. There were a lot of details in the film that kept coming at me so fast, at the audience so fast, I mean."

"I didn't notice the pot the first time," Kevin said. "It shows up in different places; not just on Brady's desk but one time in President Fremount's office, way over in the corner, where only your peripheral vision picks it up. It shows up in different parts of the Lamptons' house; for example in the living room. And in that one scene where Eric Lampton is staggering around he knocks against things and—"

"The pitcher," I said.

"Yes," Kevin said. "It also appears as a pitcher. Full of water. Linda Lampton takes it out of the refrigerator."

"No, that was just an ordinary plastic pitcher," Fat said.

"Wrong," Kevin said. "It was the pot again."

"How could it be the pot again if it was a pitcher?" Fat said.

"At the beginning of the film," Kevin said. "On the parched field. Off to one side; it only registers subliminally unless you're deliberately watching for it. The design on the pitcher is the same as the design on the pot. A woman is dipping it into a creek, a very small, mostly dried-up creek."

I said, "It seemed to me that the Christian fish sign appeared on it once. As the design."

"No," Kevin said emphatically.

"No?" I said.

"I thought so, too, the first time," Kevin said. "This time I looked closer. You know what it is? The double helix."

"That's the DNA molecule," I said.

"Right," Kevin said, grinning. "In the form of a repeated design running around the top of the pitcher."

We all remained silent for a time and then I said, "DNA memory. Gene-pool memory."

"Right," Kevin said. He added, "At the creek when she fills the pitcher—"

" 'She'?" Fat said. "Who was she?"

"A woman," Kevin said. "We never see her again. We never even see her face but she has on a long, old-fashioned dress and she's barefoot. Where she's filling the pot or the pitcher, there's a man fishing. It's flash-cut, just for a fraction of an instant. But he's there. That's why you thought you saw the fish sign. Because you picked up the sight of the man fishing. There may even have been fish lying beside him in a heap; I'll have to look really hard at that when I see it again. You saw the man subliminally and your brain—your right hemisphere—connected it with the double helix design on the pitcher."

"The satellite," Fat said. "VALIS. Vast Active Living Intelligence System. It fires information down to them?"

"It does more than that," Kevin said. "Under certain circumstances it controls them. It can override them when it wants to."

"And they're trying to shoot it down?" I said. "With that missile?"

Kevin said. "The early Christians—the real ones—can make you do anything they want you to do. And see—or *not* see—anything. That's what I get out of the picture."

"But they're dead," I said. "The picture was set in the present."

"They're dead," Kevin said, "if you believe time is real. Didn't you see the time dysfunctions?"

"No," both Fat and I said in unison.

"That dry barren field. That was the parking lot Brady ran across to get into his car when the two men in black were stationed and ready to shoot him."

I hadn't realized that. "How do you know?" I said.

"There was a tree," Kevin said. "Both times."

"I saw no tree," Fat said.

"Well, we'll all have to go see the picture again," Kevin said. "I'm going to; ninety percent of the details are designed to go by you the first time—actually only go by your conscious mind; they register in your unconscious. I'd like to study the film frame by frame."

I said, "Then the Christian fish sign is Crick and Watson's double helix. The DNA molecule where genetic memory is stored; Mother Goose wanted to make that point. That's why—"

"Christians," Kevin agreed. "Who aren't human beings but something without sex organs designed to look like human beings, but on closer inspection they *are* human beings; they do have sex organs and they make love."

"Even if their skulls are full of electronic chips instead of brains," I said.

"Maybe they're immortal," Fat said.

"That's why Linda Lampton is able to put her husband back together," I said. "When Brady's mixer blew him up. They can travel backward in time."

Kevin, not smiling, said, "Right. So now can you see why I wanted you to see *Valis*?" he said to Fat.

"Yes," Fat said, somberly, in deep introspection.

"How could Linda Lampton walk through the wall of the mixer?" I said.

"I don't know," Kevin said. "Maybe she wasn't really there or maybe the mixer wasn't there; maybe she was a hologram."

"'A hologram,'" Fat echoed.

Kevin said. "The satellite had control of them from the get-go. It could make them see what it wanted them to see; at the end, where it turns out that Fremount is Brady—no one notices! His own wife doesn't notice. The satellite has occluded them, all of them. The whole fucking United States."

"Christ," I said; that hadn't dawned on me yet, but the realization had been coming.

"Right," Kevin said. "We see Brady, but obviously they don't; they don't realize what's happened. It's a power struggle between Brady and his electronic know-how and equipment, and Fremount and his secret police—the men in black are the secret police. And those broads who looked like cheerleaders—they're something, on Fremount's side, but I don't know what. I'll figure it out next time." His voice rose. "There's information in Mini's music; as we watch the events on the screen the music—Christ, it isn't music; it's certain pitches at specific intervals—unconsciously cues us. The music is what makes the thing into sense."

"Could that huge mixer actually be something that Mini really built?" I asked.

"Maybe so," Kevin said. "Mini has a degree from MIT."

"What else do you know about him?" Fat said.

"Not very much," Kevin said. "He's English. He visited the

147

Soviet Union one time; he said he wanted to see certain experiments they were conducting with microwave information transfer over long distances. Mini developed a system where—"

"I just realized something," I broke in. "On the credits, Robin Jamison who did the still photography. I know him. He took photos of me to go with an interview I did for the *London Daily Telegraph*. He told me he covered the coronation; he's one of the top still photographers in the world. He said he was moving his family to Vancouver; he said it's the most beautiful city in the world."

"It is," Fat said.

"Jamison gave me his card," I said. "So I could write to him for the negatives after the interview was published."

Kevin said, "He would know Linda and Eric Lampton. And maybe Mini, too."

"He told me to contact him," I said. "He was very nice; he sat for a long time and talked to me. He had motor-driven cameras; the noise fascinated my cats. And he let me look through a wide-angle lens; it was beyond belief, the lenses he had."

"Who put up the satellite?" Fat said. "The Russians?"

"It's never made clear," Kevin said. "But the way they talk about it . . . it didn't suggest the Russians. There's that one scene where Fremount is opening a letter with an antique letter-opener; all of a sudden you have that montage—antique letter-opener and then the military talking about the satellite. If you fuse the two together, you get the idea—I got the idea—the satellite is real old."

"That makes sense," I said. "The time dysfunction, the woman in the old-fashioned long dress, barefoot, dipping water from the creek with a clay pitcher. There was a shot of the sky; did you notice that, Kevin?"

"The sky," Kevin murmured. "Yes; it was a long shot. A panorama shot. Sky, the field . . . the field looks old. Like maybe in the Near East. Like in Syria. And you're right; the pitcher reinforces that impression."

I said, "The satellite is never seen."

"Wrong," Kevin said.

"'Wrong'?" I said.

"Five times," Kevin said. "It appears once as a picture on a wall calendar. Once briefly as a child's toy in a store window. Once in the sky, but it's a flash-cut; I missed it the first time. Once in diagram form when President Fremount is going through that packet of data and photos on the Meritone Record Company . . . I forget the fifth time, now." He frowned.

"The object the taxi runs over," I said.

"What?" Kevin said. "Oh yeah; the taxi speeding along West Alameda. I thought it was a beer can. It rattled off loudly into the gutter." He reflected, then nodded. "You're right. It was the satellite again, mashed up by being run over. It *sounded* like a beer can; that's what fooled me. Mini again; his damn music or noises—whatever. You hear the sound of a beer can so automatically you *see* a beer can." His grin became stark. "Hear it so you see it. Not bad." Although he was driving in heavy traffic he shut his eyes a moment. "Yeah, it's mashed up. But it's the satellite; it has those antennae, but they're broken and bent. And—shit! There're words written on it. Like a label. What do the words say? You know, you'd have to take a fucking magnifying glass and go over stills from the flick, single-frame stills. One by one by one by one. And do some superimpositions. We're getting retinal lag; it's done through the lasers Brady uses. The light is so bright that it leaves—" Kevin paused.

"Phosphene activity," I said. "In the retinas of the audience. That's what you mean. That's why lasers play such a role in the film."

*

"Okay," Kevin said, when we had returned to Fat's apartment. Each of us sat with a bottle of Dutch beer, kicking back and ready to figure it all out.

The material in the Mother Goose flick overlapped with Fat's encounter with God. That's the plain truth. I'd say, "That's God's truth," but I don't think—I certainly didn't think then—that God had anything to do with it.

"The Great Punta works in wonderful ways," Kevin said,

149

but not in a kidding tone of voice. "Fuck. Holy fuck." To Fat he said, "I just assumed you were crazy. I mean, you're in and out of the rubber lock-up."

"Cool it," I said.

"So I take in *Valis*," Kevin said, "I go to the movies to get away for a little while from all this nutso garbage that Fat here lays on us; there I am sitting in the goddam theater watching a sci-fi flick with Mother Goose in it, and what do I see. It's like a conspiracy."

"Don't blame me," Fat said.

Kevin said to him, "You're going to have to meet Goose."

"How'm I going to do that?" Fat said.

"Phil will contact Jamison. You can meet Goose—Eric Lampton—through Jamison; Phil's a famous writer—he can arrange it." To me, Kevin said, "You have any books currently optioned to any movie producer?"

"Yes," I said. "*Do Androids Dream of Electric Sheep?** and also *Three Stigmata.*†"

"Fine," Kevin said. "Then Phil can say maybe there's a film in it." Turning to me he said, "Who's that producer friend of yours? The one at MGM?"

"Stan Jaffly," I said.

"Are you still in touch with him?"

"Only on a personal basis. They let their option on *Man in the High Castle*‡ lapse. He writes to me sometimes; he sent me a huge kit of herb seeds one time. He was going to send me a huge bag of peatmoss later on but fortunately he never did."

"Get in touch with him," Kevin said.

"Look," Fat said. "I don't understand. There were—" He gestured. "Things in *Valis* that happened to me in March of 1974. When I—" Again he gestured and fell silent, a perplexed expression on his face. Almost an expression of suffering, I noticed. I wondered why.

Maybe Fat felt that it reduced the stature of his encounter with God—with Zebra—to discover elements of it cropping up

---

* *Do Androids Dream of Electric Sheep?* Doubleday, 1968.
† *The Three Stigmata of Palmer Eldritch*, Doubleday, 1964.
‡ *The Man in the High Castle*, G.P. Putnam's Sons, 1962.

in a sci-fi movie starring a rock figure named Mother Goose. But this was the first hard evidence we had had that anything existed, here; and it had been Kevin, who could disintegrate a scam with a single bound, that had brought it to our attention.

"How many elements did you recognize?" I said, as quietly and calmly as I could, to the dejected-looking Horselover Fat.

After a time, Fat pulled himself erect in his chair and said, "Okay."

"Write them down," Kevin said; he brought out a fountain pen. Kevin always used fountain pens, the last of a vanishing breed of noble men. "Paper?" he said, glancing around.

When paper had been brought, Fat began the list. "The third eye with the lateral lens."

"Okay." Nodding, Kevin wrote that down.

"The pink light."

"Okay."

"The Christian fish sign. Which I didn't see, but which you say was—"

"Double helix," Kevin said.

"Same thing," I said. "Apparently."

"Anything else?" Kevin asked Fat.

"Well, the whole goddam information transfer. From VALIS. From the satellite. You say it not only fires information to them but it overrides them and controls them."

"That," Kevin said, "was the whole point of the film. The satellite took—look; here's what the picture was about. There is this tyrant obviously based on Richard Nixon called Ferris F. Fremount. He rules the U.S.A. through those black secret police, I mean, men in black uniforms carrying scope-sight weapons, and those fucking cheerleader broads. They're called 'Fappers' in the film."

"I didn't get that," I said, "when I saw it."

"It was on a banner," Kevin said. "Marginally. Fappers— 'Friends of the American People.' Ferris Fremount's citizen army. All alike and all patriotic. Anyhow, the satellite fires beams of information and saves Brady's life. You did get that. Finally the satellite arranges for Brady to replace Fremount at the very end when Fremount has won re-election. It's really Brady who's president, not Fremount. And Fremount knows;

151

there was the scene of him with the dossier of pictures of the people at Meritone Records; he knew what was happening but he couldn't stop it. He gave orders for the military to bring down VALIS but the missile wobbled and had to be destroyed. *Everything* was done by VALIS. Where do you think Brady got his electronics knowledge in the first place? From VALIS. So when Brady became president as Ferris Fremount, it was really the satellite which became president. Now, who or what is the satellite? Who or what is VALIS? The clue is the ceramic pot or the ceramic pitcher; same thing. The fish sign—which your brain has to assemble from separate pieces of information. Fish sign, Christians. Old-fashioned dress on the woman. Time dysfunction. There is some connection between VALIS and the early Christians, but I can't make out what. Anyhow, the film alludes to it elliptically. Everything is in pieces, all the information. For example, when Ferris Fremount is reading the dossier on Meritone Records—did you have time to scan any of the data?"

"No," Fat and I said.

" 'He lived a long time ago,' " Kevin said hoarsely, " 'but he is still alive.' "

"It said that?" Fat said.

"Yes!" Kevin said. "It said that."

"Then I'm not the only one who encountered God," Fat said.

"Zebra," Kevin corrected him. "You don't know it was God; you don't know what the fuck it was."

"A satellite?" I said. "A very old information-firing satellite?"

Irritably, Kevin said, "They wanted to make a sci-fi flick; that's how you would handle it in a sci-fi flick if you had such an experience. You ought to know that, Phil. Isn't that so, Phil?"

"Yes," I said.

"So they call it VALIS," Kevin said, "and make it an ancient satellite. That's controlling people to remove an evil tyranny that grips the United States—obviously based on Richard Nixon."

I said, "Are we to assume that the film *Valis* is telling us that

152

Zebra or God or VALIS or three-eyed people from Sirius removed Nixon from office?"

"Yep," Kevin said.

To Fat, I said, "Didn't the three-eyed Sibyl you dreamed about talk about 'conspirators who had been seen and would be taken care of?'"

"In August 1974," Fat said.

Kevin, harshly, said, "That's the month and year Nixon resigned."

*

Later, as Kevin was driving me home, the two of us talked about Fat and about *Valis*, since presumably neither of them could overhear us.

The opinion Kevin copped to was that all along he had taken it for granted that Fat was simply crazy. He had seen the situation this way: guilt and sorrow over Gloria's suicide had destroyed Fat's mind and he had never recovered. Beth was a tremendous bitch, and, married to her out of desperation, Fat had become even more miserable. At last, in 1974, he had totally lost it. Fat had begun a lurid schizophrenic episode to liven up his drab life: he had seen pretty colors and heard comforting words, all generated out of his unconscious which had risen up and literally swamped him, wiping out his ego. In that psychotic state Fat had flailed around, deriving great solace from his "encounter with God," as he had imagined it to be. For Fat, total psychosis was a mercy. No longer in touch with reality in any way, shape or form, Fat could believe that Christ Himself held Fat in his arms, comforting him. But then Kevin had gone to the movies and now he was not so sure; the Mother Goose flick had shaken him up.

I wondered if Fat still intended to fly to China to find what he termed "the fifth Savior." It would seem that he need go no farther than Hollywood, where VALIS had been shot, or, if that was where he would find Eric and Linda Lampton, Burbank, the center of the American recording industry.

The fifth Savior: a rock star.

"When was *Valis* made?" I asked Kevin.

153

"The film? Or the satellite?"

"The film of course."

Kevin said, "1977."

"And Fat's experience took place in 1974."

"Right," Kevin said. "Probably before work began on the screenplay, from what I can piece together from reviews I've read on *Valis*. Goose says he wrote the screenplay in twelve days. He didn't say exactly when, but apparently he wanted to go into production as soon as possible. I'm sure it was after 1974."

"But you really don't know."

Kevin said, "You can find that out from Jamison, the still photographer; he'd know."

"What if it happened at the same time? March 1974?"

"Beats the fuck out of me," Kevin said.

"You don't think it really is an information satellite, do you?" I said. "That fired a beam at Fat?"

"No; that's a sci-fi film device, a sci-fi way of explaining it." Kevin pondered. "I guess. But there were time dysfunctions in the film; Goose was aware that somehow time's involved. That really is the only way you can understand the film . . . the woman filling the pitcher. How'd Fat get that ceramic pot? Some broad gave it to him?"

"Made it, fired it and gave it to him, around 1971 after his wife left him."

"Not Beth."

"No, some earlier wife."

"After Gloria's death."

"Yes. Fat says God was sleeping in the pot and came out in March 1974—the theophany."

"I know a lot of people who think God sleeps in pot," Kevin said.

"Cheap shot."

"Well, so the barefoot woman was back in Roman times. I saw something tonight in *Valis* I didn't see before that I didn't mention; I didn't want Fat to fizzle around the room like a firecracker. In the background while the woman was by the creek, you could see indistinct shapes. Your still-photographer friend Jamison probably did that. Shapes of buildings. Ancient

154

buildings, from, say, around Roman times. It looked like clouds, but—there are clouds and there are clouds. The first time I saw it I saw clouds and the second time—today—I saw buildings. Does the goddam film change everytime you see it? Holy fuck; what a thought! A different film each time. No, that's impossible."

I said, "So is a beam of pink light that transfers medical information to your brain about your son's birth defect."

"What if I told you that there may have been a time dysfunction in 1974, and the ancient Roman world broke through into our world?"

"You mean as the theme in the film."

"No, I mean really."

"In the real world?"

"Yep."

"That would explain 'Thomas'."

Kevin nodded.

"Broke through," I said, "and then separated again."

"Leaving Richard Nixon walking along a beach in California in his suit and tie wondering what happened."

"Then it was purposeful."

"The dysfunction? Sure."

"Then it's not a dysfunction we're talking about; we're talking about someone or something deliberately manipulating time."

"You got it," Kevin said.

I said, "You've sure gone 180 degrees away from the 'Fat is crazy' theory."

"Well, Nixon is still walking along a beach in California wondering what happened. The first U.S. President ever to be forced out of office. The most powerful man in the world. Which made him in effect the most powerful man who ever lived. You know why the President in *Valis* was named Ferris F. Fremount? I figured it out. 'F' is the sixth letter of the English alphabet. So F equals six. So FFF, Ferris F. Fremount's initials, are in numerical terms 666. That's why Goose called him that."

"Oh God," I said.

"Exactly."

"That makes these the Final Days."

"Well, Fat's convinced the Savior is about to return or has already returned. The inner voice he hears that he identifies with Zebra or God—it told him so in several ways. St. Sophia—which is Christ—and the Buddha and Apollo. And it told him something like, 'The time you've waited for—'"

"'Has now come,'" I finished.

"This is heavy shit," Kevin said. "We've got Elijah walking around, another John the Baptist, saying, 'Make straight in the desert a highway for our Lord.' Freeway, maybe." He laughed.

Suddenly I remembered something I had seen in *Valis*; it came into my mind visually: a tight shot of the car which Fremount at the end of the film, Fremount re-elected but actually now Nicholas Brady, had emerged from to address the crowd. "Thunderbird," I said.

"Wine?"

"Car. Ford car. Ford."

"Ah, shit," Kevin said. "You're right. He got out of a Ford Thunderbird and he was Brady. Jerry Ford."

"It could have been a coincidence."

"In *Valis* nothing was a coincidence. And they zoomed in on the car where the metal thing read Ford. How much else is there in VALIS that we didn't pick up on? Pick up on *consciously*. There's no telling what it's doing to our unconscious minds; the goddam film may be—" Kevin grimaced. "Firing all kinds of information at us, visually and auditorily. I've got to make a tape of the sound track of that flick; I've got to get a tape recorder in there the next time I see it. Which'll be in the next couple of days."

"What kind of music are on the Mini LPs?" I asked.

"Sounds resembling the songs of the humpback whale."

I stared at him, not sure he was serious.

"Really," he said. "In fact I did a tape going from whale noises to the Synchronicity Music and back again. There's an eerie continuity; I mean, you can tell the difference, but—"

"How does the Synchronicity Music affect you? What sort of mood does it put you in?"

Kevin said, "A deep theta state, deep sleep. But I personally had visions."

"Of what? Three-eyed people?"

"No," Kevin said. "Of an ancient Celtic sacred ceremony. A ram being roasted and sacrificed to cause winter to go away and spring to return." Glancing at me he said, "Racially, I'm Celtic."

"Did you know about these myths before?"

"No. I was one of the participants in the sacrifice; I cut the ram's throat. I remembered being there."

Kevin, listening to Mini's Synchronicity Music, had gone back in time to his origins.

10

It would not be in China, nor in India or Tasmania for that matter, that Horselover Fat would find the fifth Savior. *Valis* had shown us where to look: a beer can run over by a passing taxi. That was the source of the information and the help.

That in fact was VALIS, Vast Active Living Intelligence System, as Mother Goose had chosen to term it.

We had just saved Fat a lot of money, plus a lot of wasted time and effort, including the bother of obtaining vaccinations and a passport.

A couple of days later the three of us drove up Tustin Avenue and took in the film *Valis* once more. Watching it carefully I realized that on the surface the movie made no sense whatsoever. Unless you ferreted out the subliminal and marginal clues and assembled them all together you arrived at nothing. But these clues got fired at your head whether you consciously considered them and their meaning or not; you had no choice. The audience was in the same relationship to the film *Valis* that Fat had had to what he called Zebra: a transducer and a percipient, totally receptive in nature.

Again we found mostly teenagers comprising the audience. They seemed to enjoy what they saw. I wondered how many of them left the theater pondering the inscrutible mysteries of the film as we did. Maybe none of them. I had a feeling it made no difference.

We could assign Gloria's death as the cause of Fat's supposed encounter with God, but we could not consider it the cause of the film *Valis*. Kevin, upon first seeing the film, had realized this at once. It didn't matter what the explanation was; what

158

had now been established was that Fat's March 1974 experience was real.

Okay; it mattered what the explanation was. But at least one thing had been proved: Fat might be clinically crazy but he was locked into reality—a reality of some kind, although certainly not the normal one.

Ancient Rome—apostolic times and early Christians—breaking through into the modern world. And breaking through with a purpose. To unseat Ferris F. Fremount, who was Richard Nixon.

They had achieved their purpose, and had gone back home. Maybe the Empire *had* ended after all.

Now himself somewhat persuaded, Kevin began to comb through the two apocalyptic books of the Bible for clues. He came across a part of the *Book of Daniel* which he believed depicted Nixon.

> "In the last days of those kingdoms,
> When their sin is at its height,
> A king shall appear, harsh and grim, a master of
>   stratagem.
> His power shall be great, he shall work havoc untold;
> He shall work havoc among great nations and upon a
>   holy people.
> His mind shall be ever active,
> And he shall succeed in his crafty designs;
> He shall conjure up great plans.
> And, when they least expect it, work havoc on many.
> He shall challenge even the Prince of princes
> And be broken, but not by human hands."

Now Kevin had become a Bible scholar, to Fat's amusement; the cynic had become devout, albeit for a particular purpose.

But on a far more fundamental level Fat felt fear at the turn of events. Perhaps he had always felt reassured to think that his March 1974 encounter with God emanated from mere insanity; viewing it that way he did not necessarily have to take it as real. Now he did. We all did. Something which did not yield up an explanation had happened to Fat, an experience which pointed to a melting of the physical world itself, and to the ontological categories which defined it: space and time.

"Shit, Phil," he said to me that night. "What if the world doesn't exist? If it doesn't, then what does?"

"I don't know," I said, and then I said, quoting, "You're the authority."

Fat glared at me. "It's not funny. Some force or entity melted the reality around me as if everything was a hologram! An interference with our hologram!"

"But in your *tractate*," I said, "that's exactly what you stipulate reality is: a two-source hologram."

"But intellectually thinking it is one thing," Fat said, "and finding out it's true is another!"

"There's no use getting sore at me," I said.

David, our Catholic friend, and his teeny-bopper underage girlfriend Jan went to see *Valis*, on our recommendation. David came out of it pleased. He saw the hand of God squeezing the world like an orange.

"Yeah, well we're in the juice," Fat said.

"But that's the way it should be," David said.

"You're willing to dispense with the whole world as a real thing, then," Fat said.

"Whatever God believes in is real," David said.

Kevin, irked, said, "Can he create a person so gullible that he'll believe nothing exists? Because if nothing exists, what is meant by the word 'nothing'? How is one 'nothing' which exists defined in comparison to another 'nothing' which doesn't exist?"

We, as usual, had gotten caught in the crossfire between David and Kevin, but under altered circumstances.

"What exists," David said, "is God and the Will of God."

"I hope I'm in his will," Kevin said. "I hope he left me more than one dollar."

"All creatures are in his will," David said, not batting an eye; he never let Kevin get to him.

Concern had now, by gradual increments, overcome our little group. We were no longer friends comforting and propping up a deranged member; we were collectively in deep trouble. A total reversal had in fact taken place: instead of

160

mollifying Fat we now had to turn to him for advice. Fat was our link with that entity, VALIS or Zebra, which appeared to have power over all of us, if the Mother Goose film were to be believed.

"Not only does it fire information to us but when it wants to it can take control. It can override us."

That expressed it perfectly. At any moment a beam of pink light could strike us, blind us, and when we regained our sight (if we ever did) we could know everything or nothing and be in Brazil four thousand years ago; space and time, for VALIS, meant nothing.

A common worry unified all of us, the fear that we knew or had figured out too much. We knew that apostolic Christians armed with stunningly sophisticated technology had broken through the space-time barrier into our world, and, with the aid of a vast information-processing instrument had basically deflected human history. The species of creature which stumbles onto such knowledge may not show up too well on the longevity tables.

Most ominous of all, we knew—or suspected—that the original apostolic Christians who had known Christ, who had been alive to receive the direct oral teachings before the Romans wiped those teachings out, were immortal. They had acquired immortality through the plasmate which Fat had discussed in his *tractate*. Although the original apostolic Christians had been murdered, the plasmate had gone into hiding at Nag Hammadi and was again loose in our world, and as angry as a motherfucker, if you'll excuse the expression. It thirsted for vengence. And apparently it had begun to score that vengence, against the modern-day manifestation of the Empire, the imperial United States Presidency.

I hoped the plasmate considered us its friends. I hoped it didn't think we were snitches.

"Where do we hide," Kevin said, "when an immortal plasmate which knows everything and is consuming the world by transubstantiation is looking for you?"

"It's a good thing Sherri isn't alive to hear about all this," Fat said, surprising us. "I mean, it would shake her faith."

We all laughed. Faith shaken by the discovery that the entity

161

believed in actually existed—the paradox of piety. Sherri's theology had congealed; there would have been no room in it for the growth, the expansion and evolution, necessary to encompass our revelations. No wonder Fat and she weren't able to live together.

The question was, How did we go about making contact with Eric Lampton and Linda Lampton and the composer of Synchronicity Music, Mini? Obviously through me and my friendship—if that's what it was—with Jamison.

"It's up to you, Phil," Kevin said. "Get off the pot and onto the stick. Call Jamison and tell him—whatever. You're full of it; you'll think of something. Say you've written a hot-property screenplay and you want Lampton to read it."

"Call it *Zebra*," Fat said.

"Okay," I said, "I'll call it Zebra or Horse's Ass or anything you want. You know, of course, that this is going to shoot down my professional probity."

"What probity?" Kevin said, characteristically. "Your probity is like Fat's. It never got off the ground in the first place."

"What you have to do," Fat said, "is show knowledge of the gnosis disclosed to me by Zebra over and above, which is to say beyond, what appears in *Valis*. That will intrigue him. I'll write down a few statements I've received directly from Zebra."

Presently he had a list for me.

18. Real time ceased in 70 C.E. with the fall of the temple at Jerusalem. It began again in 1974 C.E. The intervening period was a perfect spurious interpolation aping the creation of the Mind. "The Empire never ended," but in 1974 a cypher was sent out as a signal that the Age of Iron was over; the cypher consisted of two words: KING FELIX, which refers to the Happy (or Rightful) King.

19. The two-word cypher signal KING FELIX was not intended for human beings but for the descendents of Ikhnaton, the three-eyed race which, in secret, exists with us.

Reading these entries, I said, "I'm supposed to recite this to Robin Jamison?"

162

"Say they're from your screenplay *Zebra*," Kevin said.

"Is this cypher real?" I asked Fat.

A veiled expression appeared on his face. "Maybe."

"This two-word secret message was actually sent out?" David said.

"In 1974," Fat said. "In February. The United States Army cryptographers studied it, but couldn't discern who it was intended for or what it meant."

"How do you know that?" I said.

"Zebra told him," Kevin said.

"No," Fat said, but he did not amplify.

In this industry you always talk to agents, never to principals. One time I had gotten loaded and tried to get hold of Kay Lenz, who I had a crush on from having seen *Breezy*. Her agent cut me off at the pass. The same thing happened when I tried to get through to Victoria Principal, who herself is now an agent; again, I had a crush on her and again I was ripped when I started phoning Universal Studios. But having Robin Jamison's address and phone number in London made a difference.

"Yes, I remember you," Jamison said pleasantly when I put the call through to London. "The science fiction writer with the child bride, as Mr. Purser described her in his article."

I told him about my dynamite screenplay *Zebra* and that I'd seen their sensational film *Valis* and thought that Mother Goose was absolutely perfect for the lead part; even more so than Robert Redford, who we were also considering and who was interested.

"What I can do," Jamison said, "is contact Mr. Lampton and give him your number there in the States. If he's interested he or his agent will get in touch with you or your agent."

I'd fired my best shot; that was it.

After some more talk I hung up, feeling futile. Also I had a minor twinge of guilt over my devious hype, but I knew that the twinge would abate.

Was Eric Lampton the fifth Savior who Fat sought?

Strange, the relationship between the actuality and the ideal. Fat had been prepared to climb the highest mountain in Tibet, to reach a two-hundred-year-old monk who would say, "The

163

meaning of it all, my son, is—" I thought, Here, my son, time turns into space. But I said nothing; Fat's circuits were already overloaded with information. The last thing he needed was more information; what Fat needed was someone to take the information *from* him.

"Is Goose in the States?" Kevin said.

"Yes," I said, "according to Jamison."

"You didn't tell him the cypher," Fat said.

We all gave Fat a withering look.

"The cypher is for Goose," Kevin said. "When he calls."

"'When,'" I echoed.

"If you have to you can have your agent contact Goose's agent," Kevin said. He had become more earnest about this than even Fat himself. After all, it was Kevin who had discovered *Valis* and thereby put us in business.

"A film like that," David said, "is going to bring a lot of cranks out of the woodwork. Mother Goose is probably being rather careful."

"Thanks," Kevin said.

"I don't mean us," David said.

"He's right," I said, reviewing in my mind some of the mail my own writing generates. "Goose will probably prefer to contact my agent." I thought, If he contacts us at all. His agent to my agent. Balanced minds.

"If Goose does phone you," Fat said to me in a calm, low, very tense voice, unusual for him, "you are to give him the two-word cypher, KING FELIX. Work it into the conversation, of course; this isn't spy stuff. Say it's an alternate title for the screenplay."

I said, irritably, "I can handle it."

Chances were, there wouldn't be anything to handle. A week later I received a letter from Mother Goose himself, Eric Lampton. It contained one word. KING. And after the word a question mark and an arrow pointing to the right of KING.

It scared the shit out of me; I trembled. And wrote in the word FELIX. And mailed the letter back to Mother Goose.

He had included a stamped self-addressed envelope.

No doubt existed: we had linked up.

*

The person referred to by the two-word cypher KING FELIX is the fifth Savior who, Zebra—or VALIS—had said, was either already born or would soon be. This was terribly frightening to me, getting the letter from Mother Goose. I wondered how Goose—Eric Lampton and his wife Linda— would feel when they got the letter back with FELIX correctly added. Correctly; yes, that was it. Only one word out of the hundreds of thousands of English words would do; no, not English: Latin. It is a name in English but a word in Latin.

Prosperous, happy, fruitful . . . the Latin word "Felix" occurs in such injunctions as that by God Himself, who in *Genesis 1:21* says to all the creatures of the world, "Be fruitful and increase, fill the waters of the seas; and let the birds increase on land." This is the essence of the meaning of *Felix*, this command from God, this loving command, this manifestation of his desire that we not only live but that we live happily and prosperously.

FELIX. Fruit-bearing, fruitful, fertile, productive. All the nobler sorts of trees, whose fruits are offered to the superior deities. That brings good luck, of good omen, auspicious, favorable, propitious, fortunate, prosperous, felicitous. Lucky, happy, fortunate. Wholesome. Happier, more successful in.

That last meaning interests me. "More successful in." The King who is more successful in . . . in what? Perhaps in overthrowing the tyrannical reign of the king of tears, replacing that sad and bitter king with his own legitimate reign of happiness: the end of the age of the Black Iron Prison and the beginning of the age of the Garden of Palm Trees in the warm sun of Arabia ("Felix" also refers to the fertile portion of Arabia).

Our little group, upon my receiving the missive from Mother Goose, met in plenipotentiary session.

"Fat is in the fire," Kevin said laconically, but his eyes sparkled with excitement and joy, a joy we all shared.

"You're with me," Fat said.

We had all chipped in to buy a bottle of Courvoisier

165

Napoleon cognac; seated around Fat's living room we warmed our glasses by rubbing their stems like fire sticks, feeling pretty smart.

Kevin, hollowly, intoned, to no one in particular, "It would be interesting if some men in skin-tight black uniforms show up and shoot us all, now. Because of Phil's phonecall."

"Them's the breaks," I said, easily fielding Kevin's wit. "Let's push Kevin out into the hall with the end of a broom handle and see if anyone opens fire on him."

"It would prove nothing," David said. "Half of Santa Ana is tired of Kevin."

Three nights later, at two A.M., the phone rang. When I answered it—I was still up, finishing an introduction for a book of stories culled from twenty-five years of my career*—a man's voice with a slight British accent said, "How many are there of you?"

Bewildered, I said, "Who is this?"

"Goose."

Aw Christ, I thought, and again I trembled. "Four," I said, and my voice shook.

"This is a happy occasion," Eric Lampton said.

"Prosperous," I said.

Lampton laughed. "No, the King isn't financially well-off."

"He—" I couldn't go on.

Lampton said, "Vivit. I think. Vivet? He lives, anyhow, you'll be happy to hear. My Latin isn't very good."

"Where?" I said.

"Where are you? I have a 714 area code, here."

"Santa Ana. In Orange County."

"With Ferris," Lampton said. "You're just north of Ferris's mansion-by-the-sea."

"Right," I said.

"Shall we get together?"

"Sure," I said, and in my head a voice said, This is real.

"You can fly up here, the four of you? To Sonoma?"

* *The Golden Man*, edited by Mark Hurst, Berkley Publishing Corporation, NY., 1980.

166

"Oh yes," I said.

"You'll fly to the Oakland Airport; it's better then San Francisco. You saw *Valis*?"

"Several times." My voice still shook. "Mr. Lampton, is a time dysfunction involved?"

Eric Lampton said, "How can there be a dysfunction in something that doesn't exist?" He paused. "You didn't think of that."

"No," I admitted. "Can I tell you that we thought *Valis* is one of the finest films we ever saw?"

"I hope we can release the uncut version sometime. I'll see that you get a peek at it up here. We really didn't want to cut it, but, you know, practical considerations . . . you're a science fiction writer? Do you know Thomas Disch?"

"Yes," I said.

"He is very good."

"Yes," I said, pleased that Lampton knew Disch's writing. It was a good sign.

"In a way *Valis* was shit," Lampton said. "We had to make it that way, to get the distributors to pick it up. For the popcorn drive-in crowd." There was merriment in his voice, a musical twinkling. "They expected me to sing, you know. 'Hey, Mr. Starman! When You Droppin' In?' I think they were a bit disappointed, do you see."

"Well," I said, nonplussed.

"Then we'll see you up here. You have the address, do you? I won't be in Sonoma after this month, so it must be this month or much later in the year; I'm flying back to the UK to do a TV film for the Granada people. And I have concert engagements . . . I do have a recording date in Burbank; I could meet you there in—what do you call it? The 'Southland'?"

"We'll fly up to Sonoma," I said. "Are there others?" I said. "Who've contacted you?"

" 'Happy King' people? Well, we'll talk about that when we get together, your little group and Linda and Mini; did you know that Mini did the music?"

"Yes," I said. "Synchronicity Music."

"He is very good," Lampton said. "Much of what we get through lies in his music. He doesn't do songs, the prick. I wish he did. He'd do lovely songs. My songs aren't bad but I'm not Paul." He paused. "Simon, I mean."

"Can I ask you," I said, "where *he* is?"

"Oh. Well, yes; you can ask. But no one is going to tell you until we've talked. A two-word message doesn't really tell me very much about you, now does it? Although I've checked you out. You were into drugs for a while and then you switched sides. You met Tim Leary—"

"Only on the phone," I corrected. "Talked to him once on the phone; he was in Canada with John Lennon and Paul Williams—not the singer, but the writer."

"You've not been arrested. For possession?"

"Never," I said.

"You acted as a sort of dope guru to teenagers in—where was it?—oh yes; Marin County. Someone took a shot at you."

"That's not quite it," I said.

"You write very strange books. But you are positive you don't have a police record; we don't want you if you do."

"I don't," I said.

Mildly, pleasantly, Lampton said, "You were mixed up with black terrorists for a while."

I said nothing.

"What an adventure your life has been," Lampton said.

"Yes," I agreed. That certainly was true.

"You're not on drugs now?" Lampton laughed. "I'll withdraw that question. We know you're squared up now. All right, Philip; I'll be glad to meet you and your friends personally. Was it you who got—well, let's see. Got told things."

"The information was fired at my friend Horselover Fat."

"But that's you. 'Philip' means 'Horselover' in Greek, lover of horses. 'Fat' is the German translation of 'Dick.' So you've translated your name."

I said nothing.

"Should I call you 'Horselover Fat'? Are you more comfortable that way?"

"Whatever's right," I said woodenly.

"An expression from the Sixties." Lampton laughed. "Okay, Philip. I think we have enough information on you. We

168

talked to your agent, Mr. Galen; he seemed very astute and forthright."

"He's okay," I said.

"He certainly understands where your head is at, as they say over here. Your publisher is Doubleday, is it?"

"Bantam," I said.

"When will your group be coming up?"

I said, "What about this weekend?"

"Very good," Lampton said. "You'll enjoy this, you know. The suffering you've gone through is over. Do you realize that, Philip?" His tone was no longer bantering. "It is over; it really is."

"Fine," I said, my heart hammering.

"Don't be scared, Philip," Lampton said quietly.

"Okay," I said.

"You've gone through a lot. The dead girl . . . well, we can let that go; that is gone. Do you see?"

"Yes," I said. "I see." And I did. I hoped I did; I tried to understand; I wanted to.

"You don't understand. He's here. The information is correct. 'The Buddha is in the park.' Do you understand?"

"No," I said.

"Gautama was born in a great park called Lumbini. It's a story such as that of Christ at Bethlehem. If the information were 'Jesus is in Bethlehem,' you would know what that meant, wouldn't you?"

I nodded, forgetting I was on the phone.

"He has slept almost two thousand years," Lampton said. "A very long time. Under everything that has happened. But—well, I think I've said enough. He is awake now; that's the point. Linda and I will see you Friday night or early Saturday, then?"

"Right," I said. "Fine. Probably Friday night."

"Just remember," Lampton said. " 'The Buddha is in the park.' And try to be happy."

I said, "Is it him come back? Or another one?"

A pause.

"I mean—" I said.

"Yes, I know what you mean. But you see, time isn't real. It's

169

him again but not him; another one. There are many Buddhas, but only one. The key to understanding it is time . . . when you play a record a second time, do the musicians play the music a second time? If you play the record fifty times, do the musicians play the music fifty times?"

"Once," I said.

"Thank you," Lampton said, and the phone clicked. I set down the receiver.

You don't see that every day, I said to myself. What Goose said.

To my surprise I realized that I had stopped shaking.

*

It was as if I had been shaking all my life, from a chronic undercurrent of fear. Shaking, running, getting into trouble, losing the people I loved. Like a cartoon character instead of a person, I realized. A corny animation from the early Thirties. In back of all I had ever done the fear had forced me on. Now the fear had died, soothed away by the news I had heard. The news, I realized suddenly, that I had waited from the beginning to hear; created, in a sense, to be present when the news came, and for no other reason.

I could forget the dead girl. The universe itself, on its macrocosmic scale, could now cease to grieve. The wound had healed.

Because of the late hour I could not notify the others of Lampton's call. Nor could I call Air California and make the plane reservations. However, early in the morning I called David, then Kevin and then Fat. They had me take care of the travel arrangements; late Friday night sounded fine to them.

We met that evening and decided that our little group needed a name. After some bickering we let Fat decide. In view of Eric Lampton's emphasis on the statement about the Buddha we decided to call ourselves the Siddhartha Society.

"Then count me out," David said. "I'm sorry but I can't go along with it unless there's some suggestion of Christianity. I don't mean to sound fanatic, but—"

"You sound fanatic," Kevin told him.

170

We bickered again. At last we came up with a name convoluted enough to satisfy David; to me the subject wasn't all that important. Fat told us of a dream he had had recently, in which he had been a large fish. Instead of an arm he had walked around with sail-like or fan-like fins; with one of these fins he had tried to hold onto an M-16 rifle but the weapon had slid to the ground, whereupon a voice had intoned:

"Fish cannot carry guns."

Since the Greek word for that kind of fan was *rhipidos*—as with the Rhiptoglossa reptiles—we finally settled on the Rhipidon Society, the name referring elliptically to the Christian fish. This pleased Fat, too, since it alluded back to the Dogon people and their fish symbol for the benign deity.

So now we could approach Lampton—both Eric and Linda Lampton—in the form of an official organization. Small though we were. I guess we were frightened, at this point; intimidated is perhaps the better word.

Taking me off to one side, Fat said in a low voice, "Did Eric Lampton really say we don't have to think about her death any more?"

I put my hand on Fat's shoulder. "It's over," I said. "He told me that. The age of oppression ended in August 1974; now the age of sorrow begins to end. Okay?"

"Okay," Fat said, with a faint smile, as if he could not believe what he was hearing, but wanted to believe it.

"You're not crazy, you know," I said to Fat. "Remember that. You can't use that as a cop-out."

"And he's alive? Already? He really is?"

"Lampton says so."

"Then it's true."

I said, "Probably it's true."

"You believe it."

"I think so," I said. "We'll find out."

"Will he be old? Or a child? I guess he's still a child. Phil—" Fat gazed at me, stricken. "What if he isn't human?"

"Well," I said, "we'll deal with that problem when and if it arises." In my own mind I thought, Probably he's here from the future; that's the most likely possibility. He will not be human in some respects, but in others he will be. Our immortal child

171

. . . the life form of maybe millions of years ahead in time. Zebra, I thought. Now *I* will see you. We all will.

King and judge, I thought. As promised. All the way back to Zoroaster.

All the way back, in fact, to Osiris. And from Egypt to the Dogon people; and from there to the stars.

"A hit of cognac," Kevin said, bringing the bottle into the living room. "As a toast."

"Damn, Kevin," David protested. "You can't toast the Savior, not with cognac."

"Ripple?" Kevin said.

We each accepted a glass of the Courvoisier Napoleon cognac, including David.

"To the Rhipidon Society," Fat said. We touched glasses. I said, "And our motto."

"Do we have a motto?" Kevin said.

"'Fish cannot carry guns,'" I said.

We drank to that.

11

It had been years since I'd visited Sonoma, California, which lies in the heart of the wine country, with lovely hills on three sides of it. Most attractive of all is the town's park, set dead-center, with the old stone courthouse, the pond with ducks, the ancient cannons left over from used-up wars.

The many small shops surrounding the square park pandered by and large to weekend tourists, bilking the unwary with many trashy goods, but a few genuine historically-important buildings from the old Mexican reign still stood, painted and with plaques proclaiming their ancient roles. The air smelled good—especially if you emanate from the Southland—and even though it was night we strolled around before finally entering a bar called Gino's to phone the Lamptons.

In a white VW Rabbit both Eric and Linda Lampton picked us up; they met us in Gino's where the four of us sat at a table drinking Separators, a specialty of the place.

"I'm sorry we couldn't pick you up at the airport," Eric Lampton said as he and his wife came over to our table; apparently he recognized me from my publicity pictures.

Eric Lampton is slender, with long blond hair; he wore red bellbottoms and a T-shirt reading: SAVE THE WHALES. Kevin, of course, identified him at once, as did many of the people in the bar; calls, shouts and hellos greeted the Lamptons, who smiled around them at what obviously were their friends. Beside Eric, Linda walked quickly, also slender, with teeth like Emmylou Harris's. Like her husband she is slender, but her hair is dark and quite soft and long. She wore cut-offs, much washed, and a checkered shirt with a bandana knotted around her neck. Both of them had on boots: Eric's were sideboots and Linda's were granny boots.

173

Shortly, we were squeezed into the Rabbit, sailing down residential streets of relatively modern houses with wide lawns.

"We are the Rhipidon Society," Fat said.

Eric Lampton said, "We are the Friends of God."

Amazed, Kevin reacted violently; he stared at Eric Lampton. The rest of us wondered why.

"You know the name, then," Eric said.

"*Gottesfreunde*," Kevin said. "You go back to the fourteenth century!"

"That's right," Linda Lampton said. "The Friends of God formed originally in Basel. Finally we entered Germany and the Netherlands. You know of Meister Eckehart, then."

Kevin said, "He was the first person to conceive of the Godhead in distinction to God. The greatest of the Christian mystics. He taught that a person can attain union with the Godhead—he held a concept that God exists within the human soul!" We had never heard Kevin so excited. "The soul can actually know God as he is! Nobody today teaches that! And, and—" Kevin stammered; we had never heard him stammer before. "Sankara in India, in the ninth century; he taught the same things Eckehart taught. It's a trans-Christian mysticism in which man can reach beyond God, or merges with God, as or with a spark of some kind that isn't created. Brahman; that's why Zebra—"

"VALIS," Eric Lampton said.

"Whatever," Kevin said; turning to me, he said in agitation, "this would explain the revelations about the Buddha and about St. Sophia or Christ. This isn't limited to any one country or culture or religion. Sorry, David."

David nodded amiably, but appeared shaken. He knew this wasn't orthodoxy.

Eric said, "Sankara and Eckehart, the same person; living in two places at two times."

Half to himself, Fat said, " 'He causes things to look different so it would appear time has passed.' "

"Time and space both," Linda said.

"What is VALIS?" I asked.

"Vast Active Living Intelligence System," Eric said.

"That's a description," I said.

174

"That's what we have," Eric said. "What else is there but that? Do you want a name, the way God had man name all the animals? VALIS is the name; call it that and be satisfied."

"Is VALIS man?" I said. "Or God? Or something else."

Both Eric and Linda smiled.

"Does it come from the stars?" I said.

"This place where we are," Eric said, "is one of the stars; our sun is a star."

"Riddles," I said.

Fat said, "Is VALIS the Savior?"

For a moment, both Eric and Linda remained silent and then Linda said, "We are the Friends of God." Beyond that she added nothing more.

Cautiously, David glanced at me, caught my eye, and made a questioning motion: *Are these people on the level?*

"They are a very old group," I answered, "which I thought had died out centuries ago."

Eric said, "We have never died out and we are much older than you realize. Than you have been told. Than even we will tell you if asked."

"You date back before Eckehart, then," Kevin said acutely.

Linda said, "Yes."

"Centuries?" Kevin asked.

No answer.

"Thousands of years?" I said, finally.

" 'High hills are the haunt of the mountain-goat,' " Linda said, " 'and boulders a refuge for the rock-badger.' "

"What does that mean?" I said; Kevin joined in; we spoke in unison.

"I know what it means," David said.

"It can't be," Fat said; apparently he recognized what Linda had quoted, too.

" 'The stork makes her home in their tops,' " Eric said, after a time.

To me, Fat said, "These are Ikhnaton's race. That's *Psalm 104*, based on Ikhnaton's hymn; it entered our Bible—it's *older* than our Bible."

Linda Lampton said, "We are the ugly builders with clawlike hands. Who hide ourselves in shame. Along with Hephaistos

175

we built great walls and the homes of the gods themselves."

"Yes," Kevin said. "Hephaistos was ugly, too. The builder God. You killed Asklepios."

"These are Kyklopes," Fat said faintly.

"The name means 'Round-eye,'" Kevin said.

"But we have three eyes," Eric said. "So an error in the historic record was made."

"Deliberately?" Kevin said.

Linda said, "Yes."

"You are very old," Fat said.

"Yes, we are," Eric said, and Linda nodded. "Very old. But time is not real. Not to us, anyhow."

"My God," Fat said, as if stricken. "These are the original builders."

"We have never stopped," Eric said. "We still build. We built this world, this space-time matrix."

"You are our creators," Fat said.

The Lamptons nodded.

"You really are the friends of God," Kevin said. "You are literally."

"Don't be afraid," Eric said. "You know how Shiva holds up one hand to show that there is nothing to fear."

"But there is," Fat said. "Shiva is the destroyer; his third eye destroys."

"He is also the restorer," Linda said.

Leaning against me, David whispered in my ear, "Are they crazy?"

They are gods, I said to myself; they are Shiva who both destroys and protects. *They judge.*

Perhaps I should have felt fear. But I did not. They had already destroyed—brought down Ferris F. Fremount, as he had been depicted in the film *Valis*.

The period of Shiva the Restorer had begun. The restoration, I thought, of all we have lost. Of two dead girls.

As in the film *Valis*, Linda Lampton could turn time back, if necessary; and restore everything to life.

I had begun to understand the film.

The Rhipidon Society, I realized, fish though it be, is out of its depth.

176

*

An irruption from the collective unconscious, Jung taught, can wipe out the fragile individual ego. In the depths of the collective the archetypes slumber; if aroused, they can heal or they can destroy. This is the danger of the archetypes; the opposite qualities are not yet separated. Bipolarization into paired opposites does not occur until consciousness occurs.

So, with the gods, life and death—protection and destruction —are one. This secret partnership exists outside of time and space.

It can make you very much afraid, and for good reason. After all, your existence is at stake.

The real danger, the ultimate horror, happens when the creating and protecting, the sheltering, comes first—and then the destruction. Because if this is the sequence, everything built up ends in death.

Death hides within every religion.

And at any time it can flash forth—not with healing in its wings but with poison, with that which wounds.

But we had started out wounded. And VALIS had fired healing information at us, medical information. VALIS approached us in the form of the physician, and the age of the injury, the Age of Iron, the toxic iron splinter, had been abolished.

And yet . . . the risk is, potentially, always there.

It is a kind of terrible game. Which can go either way.

Libera me, Domine, I said to myself. *In die illa*. Save me, protect me, God, in this day of wrath. There is a streak of the irrational in the universe, and we, the little hopeful trusting Rhipidon Society, may have been drawn into it, to perish.

As many have perished before.

I remembered something which the great physician of the Renaissance had discovered. Poisons, in measured doses, are remedies; Paracelsus was the first to use metals such as mercury as medication. For this discovery—the measured use of poisonous metals as medications—Paracelsus has entered our

177

history books. There is, however, an unfortunate ending to the great physician's life.

He died of metal poisoning.

So put another way, medications can be poisonous, can kill. And it can happen at any time.

"Time is a child at play, playing draughts; a child's is the kingdom." As Heraclitus wrote twenty-five hundred years ago. In many ways this is a terrible thought. The most terrible of all. A child playing a game . . . with all life, everywhere.

I would have preferred an alternative. I saw now the binding importance of our motto, the motto of our little Society, binding upon all occasions as the essence of Christianity, from which we could never depart:

FISH CANNOT CARRY GUNS!

If we abandoned that, we entered the paradoxes, and, finally, death. Stupid as our motto sounded, we had fabricated in it the insight we needed. There was nothing more to know.

In Fat's quaint little dream about dropping the M-16 rifle, the Divine had spoken to us. *Nihil Obstat.* We had entered love, and found ourselves a land.

But the divine and the terrible are so close to each other. Nommo and Yurugu are partners; both are necessary. Osiris and Seth, too. In the *Book of Job*, Yahweh and Satan form a partnership. For us to live, however, these partners must be split. The behind-the-scenes partnership must end as soon as time and space and all the creatures come into being.

It is not God nor the gods which must prevail; it is wisdom, Holy Wisdom. I hoped that the fifth Savior would be that: splitting the bipolarities and emerging as a unitary thing. Not of three persons or two but *one*. Not Brahma the creator, Vishnu the sustainer and Shiva the destroyer, but what Zoroaster called the Wise Mind.

God can be good and terrible—not in succession—but at the same time. This is why we seek a mediator between us and him; we approach him through the mediating priest and attenuate and enclose him through the sacraments. It is for our own safety: to trap him within confines which render him safe. But

178

now, as Fat had seen, God had escaped the confines and was transubstantiating the world; God had become free.

The gentle sounds of the choir singing "Amen, amen" are not to calm the congregation but to pacify the god.

When you know this you have penetrated to the innermost core of religion. And the worst part is that the god can thrust himself outward and into the congregation until he becomes them. You worship a god and then he pays you back by taking you over. This is called "*enthousiasmos*" in Greek, literally "to be possessed by the god." Of all the Greek gods the one most likely to do this was Dionysos. And, unfortunately, Dionysos was insane.

Put another way—stated backward—if your god takes you over, it is likely that no matter what name he goes by he is actually a form of the mad god Dionysos. He was also the god of intoxication, which may mean, literally, to take in toxins; that is to say, to take a poison. The danger is there.

If you sense this, you try to run. But if you run he has you anyhow, for the demigod Pan was the basis of panic which is the uncontrollable urge to flee, and Pan is a subform of Dionysos. So in trying to flee from Dionysos you are taken over anyhow.

I write this literally with a heavy hand; I am so weary I am dropping as I sit here. What happened at Jonestown was the mass running of panic, inspired by the mad god—panic leading into death, the logical outcome of the mad god's thrust.

For them no way out existed. You must be taken over by the mad god to understand this, that once it happens there is no way out, because the mad god is everywhere.

It is not reasonable for nine hundred people to collude in their own deaths and the deaths of little children, but the mad god is not logical, not as we understand the term.

*

When we reached the Lamptons' house we found it to be a stately old farm mansion, set in the middle of grape vines; after all, this is wine country.

I thought, Dionysos is the god of wine.

179

"The air smells good here," Kevin said as we got out of the VW Rabbit.

"We sometimes get pollution," Eric said. "Even here."

Entering the house, we found it warm and attractive; huge posters of Eric and Linda, framed behind non-reflecting glass, covered all the walls. This gave the old wooden house a modern look, which linked us back to the Southland.

Linda said, smiling, "We make our own wine, here. From our own grapes."

I imagine you do, I said to myself.

A huge complex of stereo equipment rose up along one wall like the fortress in VALIS which was Nicholas Brady's sound-mixer. I could see where the visual idea had originated.

"I'll put on a tape we made," Eric said, going over to the audio fortress and clicking switches to on. "Mini's music but my words. I'm singing but we're not going to release it; it's just an experiment."

As we seated ourselves, music at enormous dBs filled the living room, rebounding off all the walls.

"I want to see you, man.
As quickly as I can.
Let me hold your hand
I've got no hand to hold
And I'm old, old; very old.

Why won't you look at me?
Afraid of what you see?
I'll find you anyhow,
Later or now; later or now."

Jesus, I thought, listening to the lyrics. Well, we came to the right place. No doubt about that. We wanted this and we got this. Kevin could amuse himself by deconstructing the song lyrics, which did not need to be deconstructed. Well, he could turn his attention to Mini's electronic noises, then.

Linda, bending down and putting her lips to my ears, shouted over the music, "Those resonances open the higher chakras."

180

I nodded.

When the song ended, we all said how terrific it was, David included. David had passed into a trance-state; his eyes were glazed over. David did this when he was faced by what he could not endure; the church had taught him how to phase himself out mentally for a time, until the stress situation was over.

"Would you like to meet Mini?" Linda Lampton said.

"Yes!" Kevin said.

"He's probably upstairs sleeping," Eric Lampton said. He started out of the living room. "Linda, you bring some cabernet sauvignon, the 1972, up from the cellar."

"Okay," she said, starting out of the room in the other direction. "Make yourselves comfortable," she said over her shoulder to us. "I'll be right back."

Over at the stereo, Kevin gazed down in rapture.

David walked up to me, his hands stuck deep in his pockets, a complex expression on his face. "They're—"

"They're crazy," I said.

"But in the car you seemed—"

"Crazy," I said.

"Good crazy?" David said; he stood close beside me, as if for protection. "Or—the other thing."

"I don't know," I said, truthfully.

Fat stood with us now; he listened, but did not speak. He looked deeply sobered. Meanwhile, Kevin, by himself, continued to analyze the audio system.

"I think we should—" David began, but at that moment Linda Lampton returned from the wine cellar, carrying a silver tray on which stood six wine glasses and a bottle still corked.

"Would one of you open the wine?" Linda said. "I usually get cork in it; I don't know why." Without Eric she seemed shy with us, and completely unlike the woman she had played in Valis.

Rousing himself, Kevin took the wine bottle from her.

"The opener is somewhere in the kitchen," Linda said.

From above our heads thumping and scraping noises could be heard, as if something awfully heavy were being dragged across the upper-story floor.

Linda said, "Mini—I should tell you this—has multiple

181

myeloma. It's very painful and he's in a wheelchair."

Horrified, Kevin said, "Plasma cell myeloma is always fatal."

"Two years is the life span," Linda said. "His has just been diagnosed. He'll be hospitalized in another week. I'm sorry."

Fat said, "Can't VALIS heal him?"

"That which is to be healed will be healed," Linda Lampton said. "That which is to be destroyed will be destroyed. But time is not real; nothing is destroyed. It is an illusion."

David and I glanced at each other.

Bump-bump. Something awkward and enormous dragged its way down a flight of stairs. Then, as we stood unmoving, a wheel chair entered the living room. In it a crushed little heap smiled at us in humour, love and the warmth of recognition. From both ears ran cords: double hearing aids. Mini, the composer of Synchronicity Music, was partially deaf.

Going up to Mini one by one we shook his faltering hand and identified ourselves, not as a society but as persons.

"Your music is very important," Kevin said.

"Yes it is," Mini said.

We could see his pain and we could see that he would not live long. But in spite of the suffering he held no malice toward the world; he did not resemble Sherri. Glancing at Fat, I could see that he was remembering Sherri, now, as he gazed at the stricken man in the wheelchair. To come this far, I thought, and to find this again—this, which Fat had fled from. Well, as I already said, no matter which direction you take, when you run the god runs with you because he is everywhere, inside you and out.

"Did VALIS make contact with you?" Mini said. "The four of you? Is that why you're here?"

"With me," Fat said. "These others are my friends."

"Tell me what you saw," Mini said.

"Like St. Elmo's Fire," Fat said. "And information—"

"There is always information when VALIS is present," Mini said, nodding and smiling. "He is information. Living information."

"He healed my son," Fat said. "Or anyhow fired the medical information necessary to heal him at me. And VALIS told me

182

that St. Sophia and the Buddha and what he or it called the 'Head Apollo' is about to be born soon and that the—"

"—the time you have waited for," Mini murmured.

"Yes," Fat said.

"How did you know the cypher?" Eric Lampton asked Fat.

"I saw a set to ground doorway," Fat said.

"He saw it," Linda said rapidly. "What was the ratio of the doorway? The sides?"

Fat said, "The Fibonacci Constant."

"That's our other code," Linda said. "We have ads running all over the world. One to point six one eight zero three four. What we do is say, 'Complete this sequence: One to point six.' If they recognize it as the Fibonacci constant they can finish the sequence."

"Or we use Fibonacci numbers," Eric said. "1,2,3,5,8,13 and so on. That doorway is to the Different Realm."

"Higher?" Fat asked.

"We just call it 'Different,'" Eric said.

"Through the doorway I saw luminous writing," Fat said.

"No you didn't," Mini said, smiling. "Through the doorway is Crete."

After a pause, Fat said, "Lemnos."

"Sometimes Lemnos. Sometimes Crete. That general area." In a spasm of pain, Mini drew himself up in his wheel chair.

"I saw Hebrew letters on the wall," Fat said.

"Yes," Mini said, still smiling. "Cabala. And the Hebrew letters permutated until they factored out into words you could read."

"Into KING FELIX," Fat said.

"Why did you lie about the doorway?" Linda said, without animosity; she seemed merely curious.

Fat said, "I didn't think you'd believe me."

"Then you're not normally familiar with the Cabala," Mini said. "It's the encoding system which VALIS uses; all its verbal information is stored as Cabala, because that's the most economical way, since the vowels are indicated by mere vowel-points. You were given a set-ground discriminating unscrambler, you realize. We normally can't distinguish set from

183

ground; VALIS has to fire the unscrambler at you. It's a grid. You saw set as color, of course."

"Yes." Fat nodded. "And ground as black and white."

"So you could see the false work."

"Pardon?" Fat said.

"The false work that's blended with the real world."

"Oh," Fat said. "Yes, I understand. It seemed as if some things had been taken away—"

"And other things added," Mini said.

Fat nodded.

"You have a voice inside your head now?" Mini said. "The AI voice?"

After a long pause, and a glance at me, Kevin and David, Fat said, "It's a neutral voice. Neither male nor female. Yes, it does sound as if it's an artificial intelligence."

"That's the inter-system communications network," Mini said. "It stretches between stars, connecting all the star systems with Albemuth."

Staring at him, Fat said, "'Albemuth'? It's a *star*?"

"You heard the word, but—"

"I saw it in written form," Fat said, "but I didn't know what it meant. I connected it with alchemy, because of the 'al.'"

"The *al* prefix," Mini said, "is Arabic; it simply means 'the.' It's a common prefix for stars. That was your clue. Anyhow, you did see written pages, then."

"Yes," Fat said. "Many of them. They told me what was going to happen to me. Like—" He hesitated. "My later suicide attempt. It gave me the Greek word '*ananke*' which I didn't know. And it said, 'A gradual darkening of the world; a sickling over.' Later I realized what it meant; a bad thing, a sickness, a deed that I had to commit. But I did survive."

"My illness," Mini said, "is from proximity to VALIS, to its energy. It's an unfortunate thing, but as you know, we are immortal, although not physically so. We will be reborn and remember."

"My animals died of cancer," Fat said.

"Yes," Mini said. "The levels of radiation can sometimes be enormous. Too much for us."

I thought, So that's why you're dying. Your god has killed

you and yet you're happy. I thought, *We have to get out of here. These people court death.*

"What is VALIS?" Kevin said to Mini. "Which deity or demi-urge is he? Shiva? Osiris? Horus? I've read *The Cosmic Trigger* and Robert Anton Wilson says—"

"VALIS is a construct," Mini said. "An artifact. It's anchored here on Earth, literally anchored. But since space and time don't exist for it, VALIS can be anywhere and any time it wishes to. It's something they built to program us at birth; normally it fires extremely short bursts of information at babies, engramming instructions to them which will bleed across from their right hemispheres at clock-time intervals during their full lifetimes, at the appropriate situational contexts." *valis is the utopian manifestation*

"Does it have an antagonist?" Kevin said. *of Althusser's theory see what it does?*

"Only the pathology of this planet," Eric said. "Due to the atmosphere. We can't readily breathe this atmosphere, here; it's toxic to our race."

"'Our'?" I said.

"All of us," Linda said. "We're all from Albemuth. This atmosphere poisons us and makes us deranged. So they—the ones who stayed behind in the Albemuth System—built VALIS and sent it here to fire rational instructions at us, to override the pathology caused by the toxicity of the atmosphere."

"Then VALIS is rational," I said.

"The only rationality we have," Linda said.

"And when we act rationally we're under its jurisdiction," Mini said. "I don't mean us here in the room; I mean everyone. Not everyone who lives but everyone who is rational."

"Then in essence," I said, "VALIS detoxifies people." *irradiates of food.*

"That's exactly it," Mini said. "It's an informational antitoxin. But exposure to it can cause—illness such as I have."

Too much medication, I said to myself, remembering Paracelsus, is a poison. This man has been healed to death.

"I wanted to know VALIS as much as possible," Mini said, seeing the expression on my face. "I begged it to return and communicate with me further. It didn't want to; it knew the effect its radiation would have on me if it returned. But it did what I asked. I'm not sorry. It was worth it, to experience

185

VALIS again." To Fat he said, "You know what I mean. The sound of bells . . ."

"Yes," Fat said. "The Easter bells."

"Are you talking about Christ?" David said. "Christ is an artificial construct built to fire information at us that works on us subliminally?"

"From the time we are born," Mini said. "We the lucky ones. We whom it selects. Its flock. Before I die, VALIS will return; I have its promise. VALIS will come and take me with it; I will be a part of it forever." Tears filled his eyes.

                              *

Later, we all sat around and talked more calmly.

The Eye of Shiva was of course the way the ancients represented VALIS firing information. They knew it could destroy; this is the element of harmful radiation which is necessary as a carrier for the information. Mini told us that VALIS is not actually close when it fires; it may be literally millions of miles away. Hence, in the film *Valis*, they represented it by a satellite, a very old satellite, not put into orbit by humans.

"So we're not dealing with religion then," I said, "but with a very advanced technology."

"Words," Mini said.

"What is the Savior?" David said.

Mini said, "You'll see him. Presently. Tomorrow, if you wish; Saturday afternoon. He's sleeping now. He still sleeps a great deal; most of the time, in fact. After all, he was completely asleep for thousands of years."

"At Nag Hammadi?" Fat said.

"I would rather not say," Mini said.

"Why must this be kept secret?" I said.

Eric said, "We're not keeping it secret; we made the film and we're making LPs with information in the lyrics. Subliminal information, mostly. Mini does it with his music."

" 'Sometimes Brahman sleeps,' " Kevin said, " 'and sometimes Brahman dances.' Are we talking about Brahman? Or Siddhartha the Buddha? Or Christ? Or is it all of them?"

186

I said to Kevin, "The Great—" I had intended to say, "The Great Punta," but I decided not to; it wouldn't be wise. "It's not Dionysos, is it?" I asked Mini.

"Apollo," Linda said. "The paired opposite to Dionysos." That filled me with relief. I believed her; it fitted with what had been revealed to Horselover Fat: "The Head Apollo."

"We are in a maze, here," Mini said, "which we built and then fell into and can't get out. In essence, VALIS selectively fires information to us which aids us in escaping from the maze, in finding the way out. It started back about two thousand years before Christ, in Mycenaean times or perhaps early Helladic. That's why the myths place the maze at Minos, on Crete. That's why you saw ancient Crete through the 1:.618034 doorway. We were great builders, but one day we decided to play a game. We did it voluntarily; were we such good builders that we could build a maze with a way out but which constantly changed so that, despite the way out, in effect there was no way out for us because the maze—this world—was alive? To make the game into something real, into something more than an intellectual exercise, we elected to lose our exceptional faculties, to reduce us an entire level. This, unfortunately, included loss of memory—loss of knowledge of our true origins. But worse than that—and here is where we in a sense managed to defeat ourselves, to turn victory over to our servant, over to the maze we had built—"

"The third eye closed," Fat said.

"Yes," Mini said. "We relinquished the third eye, our prime evolutionary attribute. It is the third eye which VALIS re-opens."

"Then it's the third eye that gets us back out of the maze," Fat said. "That's why the third eye is identified with god-like powers or with enlightenment, in Egypt and in India."

"Which are the same thing," Mini said. "God-like, enlightened."

"Really?" I said.

"Yes," Mini said. "It is man as he really is: his true state."

Fat said, "So without memory, and without the third eye, we never had a chance to beat the maze. It was hopeless."

187

I thought, Another Chinese finger-trap. And built by our own selves. To trap our own selves.

What kind of minds would create a Chinese finger-trap for themselves? Some game, I thought. Well, it isn't merely intellectual.

"The third eye had to be re-opened if we were to get out of the maze," Mini said, "but since we no longer remembered that we had that ajna faculty, the eye of discernment, we could not go about seeking techniques for re-opening it. *Something outside had to enter*, something which we ourselves would be unable to build."

"So we didn't all fall into the maze," Fat said.

"No," Mini said. "And those that stayed outside, in other star systems, reported back to Albemuth that we had done this thing to ourselves . . . thus VALIS was constructed to rescue us. This is an irreal world. You realize that, I'm sure. VALIS made you realize that. We are in a living maze and not in a world at all."

There was silence as we considered this.

"And what happens when we get outside the maze?" Kevin said.

"We're freed from space and time," Mini said. "Space and time are the binding, controlling conditions of the maze—its power."

Fat and I glanced at each other. It dovetailed with our own speculations—speculations engineered by VALIS.

"And then we never die?" David asked.

"Correct," Mini said.

"So salvation—"

"'Salvation,'" Mini said, "is a word denoting 'Being led out of the space-time maze, where the servant has become the master.'"

"May I ask a question?" I said. "What is the purpose of the fifth Savior?"

"It isn't 'fifth,'" Mini said. "There is only one, over and over again, at different times, in different places, with different names. The Savior is VALIS incarnated as a human being."

"Crossbonded?" Fat said.

"No." Mini shook his head vigorously. "There is no human element in the Savior."

"Wait a minute," David said.

"I know what you've been taught," Mini said. "In a sense, it's true. But the Savior is VALIS and that is the fact of the case. He is born, however, from a human woman. He doesn't just generate a phantasm-body."

To that, David nodded; he could accept that.

"And he's been born?" I asked.

"Yes," Mini said.

"My daughter," Linda Lampton said. "Not Eric's, however. Just mine and VALIS's."

"*Daughter?*" several of us said in unison.

"This time," Mini said, "for the first time, the Savior takes female form."

Eric Lampton said, "She's very pretty. You'll like her. She talks a blue streak, though; she'll talk your ear off."

"Sophia is two," Linda said. "She was born in 1976. We tape what she says."

"Everything is taped," Mini said. "Sophia is surrounded by audio and video recording equipment that automatically monitors her constantly. Not for her protection, of course; VALIS protects her—VALIS, her father."

"And we can talk with her?" I said.

"She'll dispute with you for hours," Linda said, and then she added, "in every language there is or ever was."

189

12

Wisdom had been born, not a deity: a deity which slew with one hand while healing with another . . . that deity was not the Savior, and I said to myself, Thank God.

We were taken the next morning to a small farm area, with animals everywhere. I saw no signs of video or audio recording equipment, but I saw—we all saw—a black-haired child seated with goats and chickens, and, in a hutch beside her, rabbits.

What I had expected was tranquility, the peace of God which passes all understanding. However, the child, upon seeing us, rose to her feet and came toward us with indignation blazing in her face; her eyes, huge, dilated with anger, fixed intently on me—she lifted her right hand and pointed at me.

"Your suicide attempt was a violent cruelty against yourself," she said in a clear voice. And yet she was, as Linda had said, no more than two years old: a baby, really, and yet with the eyes of an infinitely old person.

"It was Horselover Fat," I said.

Sophia said, "Phil, Kevin and David. Three of you. There are no more."

Turning to speak to Fat—I saw no one. I saw only Eric Lampton and his wife, the dying man in the wheel chair, Kevin and David. Fat was gone. Nothing remained of him.

Horselover Fat was gone forever. As if he had never existed.

"I don't understand," I said. "You destroyed him."

"Yes," the child said.

I said, "Why?"

"To make you whole."

"Then he's in me? Alive in me?"

"Yes," Sophia said. By degrees, the anger left her face. The great dark eyes ceased to smolder.

190

"He was me all the time," I said.

"That is right," Sophia said.

"Sit down," Eric Lampton said. "She prefers it if we sit; then she doesn't have to talk up to us. We're so much taller than she is."

Obediently, we all seated ourselves on the rough parched brown ground—which I now recognized as the opening shot in the film *Valis*; they had filmed part of it here.

Sophia said, "Thank you."

"Are you Christ?" David said, tugging his knees up against his chin, his arms wrapped around them; he, too, looked like a child: one child addressing another in equal conversation.

"I am that which I am," Sophia said.

"I'm glad to—" I couldn't think what to say.

"Unless your past perishes," Sophia said to me, "you are doomed. Do you know that?"

"Yes," I said.

Sophia said, "Your future must differ from your past. The future must always differ from the past."

David said, "Are you God?"

"I am that which I am," Sophia said.

I said, "Then Horselover Fat was part of me projected outward so I wouldn't have to face Gloria's death."

Sophia said, "That is so."

I said, "Where is Gloria now?"

Sophia said, "She lies in the grave."

I said, "Will she return?"

Sophia said, "Never."

I said, "I thought there was immortality."

To that, Sophia said nothing.

"Can you help me?" I said.

Sophia said, "I have already helped you. I helped you in 1974 and I helped you when you tried to kill yourself. I have helped you since you were born."

"You are VALIS?" I said.

Sophia said, "I am that which I am."

Turning to Eric and Linda, I said, "She doesn't always answer."

"Some questions are meaningless," Linda said.

191

"Why don't you heal Mini?" Kevin said.

Sophia said, "I do what I do; I am what I am."

I said, "Then we can't understand you."

Sophia said, "You understood that."

David said, "You are eternal, aren't you?"

"Yes," Sophia said.

"And you know everything?" David said.

"Yes," Sophia said.

I said, "Were you Siddhartha?"

"Yes," Sophia said.

"Are you the slayer and the slain?" I said.

"No," Sophia said.

"The slayer?" I said.

"No."

"The slain, then."

"I am the injured and the slain," Sophia said. "But I am not the slayer. I am the healer and the healed."

"But VALIS has killed Mini," I said.

To that, Sophia said nothing.

"Are you the judge of the world?" David said.

"Yes," Sophia said.

"When does the judgment begin?" Kevin said.

Sophia said, "You are all judged already from the start."

I said, "How did you appraise me?"

To that, Sophia said nothing.

"Don't we get to find out?" Kevin said.

"Yes," Sophia said.

"When?" Kevin said.

To that, Sophia said nothing.

Linda said, "I think that's enough for now. You can talk to her again later. She likes to sit with the animals; she loves the animals." She touched me on the shoulder. "Let's go."

As we walked away from the child, I said, "Her voice is the neutral AI voice that I've heard in my head since 1974."

Kevin said hoarsely, "It's a computer. That's why it only answers certain questions."

Both Eric and Linda smiled; Kevin and I glanced at him; in his wheel chair Mini rolled along sedately.

"An AI system," Eric said. "An artificial intelligence."

"A terminal of VALIS," Kevin said. "An input, output terminal of the master system VALIS."

"That's right," Mini said.

"Not a little girl," Kevin said.

"I gave birth to her," Linda said.

"Maybe you just thought you did," Kevin said.

Smiling, Linda said, "An artificial intelligence in a human body. Her body is alive, but her psyche is not. She is sentient; she knows everything. But her mind is not alive in the sense that we are alive. She was not created. She has always existed."

"Read your Bible," Mini said. "She was with the Creator before creation existed; she was his darling and delight, his greatest treasure."

"I can see why," I said.

"It would be easy to love her," Mini said. "Many people have loved her . . . as it says in the *Book of Wisdom*. And so she entered them and guided them and descended even into the prison with them; she never abandoned those who loved her or who love her now."

"Her voice is heard in human courts," David murmured.

"And she destroyed the tyrant?" Kevin said.

"Yes," Mini said. "As we called him in the film, Ferris F. Fremount. But you know who she toppled and brought to ruin."

"Yes," Kevin said. He looked somber; I knew he was thinking of a man wearing a suit and tie wandering along a beach in southern California, an aimless man wondering what had happened, what had gone wrong, a man who still planned stratagems.

"In the last days of those kingdoms,
When their sin is at its height,
A king shall appear, harsh and grim, a master of
    stratagem . . ."

The king of tears who had brought tears to everyone eventually; against him something had acted which he, in his occlusion, could not discern. We had just now talked to that person, that child.

That child who had always been.

*

As we ate dinner that night—at a Mexican restaurant just off the park in the center of Sonoma—I realized that I would never see my friend Horselover Fat again, and I felt grief inside me, the grief of loss. Intellectually, I knew that I had re-incorporated him, reversing the original process of projection. But still it made me sad. I had enjoyed his company, his endless tale-spinning, his account of his intellectual and spiritual and emotional quest. A quest—not for the Grail—but to be healed of his wound, the deep injury which Gloria had done to him by means of her death game.

It felt strange not to have Fat to phone up or visit. He had been so much a regular part of my life, and of the lives of our mutual friends. I wondered what Beth would think when the child support checks stopped coming in. Well, I realized, I could assume the economic liability; I could take care of Christopher. I had the funds to do it, and in many ways I loved Christopher as much as his father had.

"Feeling down, Phil?" Kevin said to me. We could talk freely now, since the three of us were alone; the Lamptons had dropped us off, telling us to call them when we had finished dinner and were ready to return to their large house.

"No," I said. And then I said, "I'm thinking about Horselover Fat."

Kevin said, after a pause, "You're waking up, then."

"Yes." I nodded.

"You'll be okay," David said, awkwardly. Expression of emotions came with difficulty to David.

"Yeah," I said.

Kevin said, "Do you think the Lamptons are nuts?"

"Yes," I said.

"What about the little girl?" Kevin said.

I said, "She is not nuts. She is as not nuts as they *are*. It's a paradox; two totally whacked out people—three, if you count Mini—have created a totally sane offspring."

"If I say—" David began.

"Don't say God brings good out of evil," I said. "Okay? Will you do us that one favor?"

Half to himself, Kevin said, "That is the most beautiful child I have ever seen. But that stuff about her being a computer terminal—" He gestured.

"You're the one who said it," I said.

"At the time," Kevin said, "it made sense. But not when I look back. When I have perspective."

"You know what I think?" David said. "I think we should get back on the Air Cal plane and fly back to Santa Ana. As soon as we can."

I said, "The Lamptons won't hurt us." I was certain of that, now. Odd, that the sick man, the dying man, Mini, had restored my confidence in the power of life. Logically, it should have worked the other way, I suppose. I had liked him very much. But, as is well known, I have a proclivity for helping sick or injured people; I gravitate to them. As my psychiatrist told me years ago, I've got to stop doing that. That, and one other thing.

Kevin said, "I can't scope it out."

"I know," I agreed. Did we really see the Savior? Or did we see just a very bright little girl who, possibly, had been coached to give lofty-sounding answers by three very shrewd professionals who had a master hype going in connection with their film and music?

"It's a strange form for him to take," Kevin said. "As a girl. That's going to encounter resistance. Christ as a female; that made David here pissed as hell."

"She didn't say she was Christ," David said.

I said, "But she is."

Both Kevin and David stopped eating and gazed at me.

"She is St. Sophia," I said, "and St. Sophia is a hypostasis of Christ. Whether she admitted it or not. She's being careful. After all, she knows everything; she knows what people will accept and what they won't."

"You have all your weirded-out experiences of March 1974 to go on," Kevin said. "That proves something; that proves it's real. VALIS exists. You already knew that. You encountered him."

195

"I guess so," I said.

"And what Mini knew and said collated with what you knew," David said.

"Yeah," I said.

Kevin said, "But you're not certain."

"We're dealing with a high order of sophisticated technology," I said. "Which Mini may have put together."

"Meaning microwave transmissions and such like," Kevin said.

"Yes," I said.

"A purely technological phenomenon," Kevin said. "A major technological breakthrough."

"Using the human mind as the transducer," I said. "Without an electronic interface."

"Could be," Kevin admitted. "The movie showed that. There is no way to tell what they're into."

"You know," David said slowly, "if they have high-yield energy available to them that they can beam over long distances, along the lines of laser beams—"

"They can kill us dead," Kevin said.

"That's right," I said.

"If," Kevin said, "we started quacking about not believing them."

"We can just say we have to be back in Santa Ana," David said.

"Or we can leave from here," I said. "This restaurant."

"Our things—clothes, everything we brought—are there at their house," Kevin said.

"Fuck the clothes," I said.

"Are you afraid?" David said. "Of something happening?"

I thought about it. "No," I said finally. I trusted the child. And I trusted Mini. You always have to go on that, your instinctive trust or—your lack of trust. In the final analysis, there is really nothing else you can go on.

"I'd like to talk to Sophia again," Kevin said.

"So would I," I said. "The answer is there."

Kevin put his hand on my shoulder. "I'm sorry to say this like this, Phil, but we really have the big clue already. In one instant that child cleared up your mind. You stopped believing

196

you were two people. You stopped believing in Horselover Fat as a separate person. And no therapist and no therapy over the years, since Gloria's death, has ever been able to accomplish that."

"He's right," David said in a gentle voice. "We all kept hoping, but it seemed as if—you know. As if you'd never heal."

"'Heal,'" I said. "She healed me. Not Horselover Fat but me." They were right; the healing miracle had happened and we all know what that pointed to; we all three of us understood.

I said, "Eight years."

"Right," Kevin said. "Before we even knew you. Eight long fucking goddam years of occlusion and pain and searching and roaming about."

I nodded.

In my mind a voice said, What else do you need to know?

It was my own thoughts, the ratiocination of what had been Horselover Fat, who had rejoined me.

"You realize," Kevin said, "that Ferris F. Fremount is going to try to come back. He was toppled by that child—or by what that child speaks for—but he is returning; he will never give up. The battle was won but the struggle goes on."

David said, "Without that child—"

"We will lose," I said.

"Right," Kevin said.

"Let's stay another day," I said, "and try to talk with Sophia again. One more time."

"That sounds like a plan," Kevin said, pleased.

The little group, The Rhipidon Society, had come to an agreement. All three members.

*

The next day, Sunday, the three of us got permission to sit with the child Sophia alone, without anyone else present, although Eric and Linda did request that we tape our encounter. We agreed readily, not having any choice.

Warm sunlight illuminated the earth that day, giving to the animals gathered around us the quality of a spiritual following;

I had the impression that the animals heard, listened and understood.

"I want to talk to you about Eric and Linda Lampton," I said to the little girl, who sat with a book open in front of her.

"You shall not interrogate me," she said.

"Can't I ask you about them?" I said.

"They are ill," Sophia said. "But they can't harm anyone because I override them." She looked up at me with her huge, dark eyes. "Sit down."

We obediently seated ourselves in front of her.

"I gave you your motto," she said. "For your society; I gave you its name. Now I give you your commision. You will go out into the world and you will tell the *kerygma* which I charge you with. Listen to me; I tell you in truth, in very truth, that the days of the wicked will end and the son of man will sit on the judgement seat. This will come as surely as the sun itself rises. The grim king will strive and lose, despite his cunning; he loses; he lost; he will always lose, and those with him will go into the pit of darkness and there they will linger forever.

"What you teach is the word of man. Man is holy, and the true god, the living god, is man himself. You will have no gods but yourselves; the days in which you believed in other gods end now, they end forever.

"The goal of your lives has been reached. I am here to tell you this. Do not fear; I will protect you. You are to follow one rule: you are to love one another as you love me and as I love you, for this love proceeds from the true god, which is yourselves.

"A time of trial and delusion and wailing lies ahead because the grim king, the king of tears, will not surrender his power. But you will take his power from him; I grant you that authority in my name, exactly as I granted it to you once before, when that grim king ruled and destroyed and challenged the humble people of the world.

"The battle which you fought before has not ended, although the day of the healing sun has come. Evil does not die of its own self because it imagines that it speaks for god. Many claim to speak for god, but there is only one god and that god is man himself.

"Therefore only those leaders who protect and shelter will live; the others will die. The oppression lifted four years ago, and it will for a little while return. Be patient during this time; it will be a time of trials for you, but I will be with you, and when the time of trials is over I shall sit down on the judgment seat, and some will fall and some will not fall, according to my will, my will which comes to me from the father, back to whom we all go, all of us together.

"I am not a god; I am a human. I am a child, the child of my father, which is Wisdom Himself. You carry in you now the voice and authority of Wisdom; you are, therefore, Wisdom, even when you forget it. You will not forget it for long. I will be there and I will remind you.

"The day of Wisdom and the rule of Wisdom has come. The day of power, which is the enemy of Wisdom, ends. Power and Wisdom are the two principles in the world. Power has had its rule and now it goes into the darkness from which it came, and Wisdom alone rules.

"Those who obey power will succumb as power succumbs.

"Those who love Wisdom and follow her will thrive under the sun. Remember, I will be with you. I will be in each of you from now on. I will accompany you down into the prison if necessary; I will speak in the courts of law to defend you; my voice will be heard in the land, whatever the oppression.

"Do not fear; speak out and Wisdom will guide you. Fall silent out of fear and Wisdom will depart you. But you will not feel fear because Wisdom herself is in you, and you and she are one.

"Formerly you were alone within yourselves; formerly you were solitary men. Now you have a companion who never sickens or fails or dies; you are bonded to the eternal and will shine like the healing sun itself.

"As you go back into the world I will guide you from day to day. And when you die I will notice and come to pick you up; I will carry you in my arms back to your home, out of which you came and back to which you go.

"You are strangers here, but you are hardly strangers to me; I have known you since the start. This has not been your world, but I will make it your world; I will change it for you. Fear not. What assails you will perish and you will thrive.

"These are things which shall be because I speak with the authority given me by my father. You are the true god and you will prevail."

There was silence, then. Sophia had ceased speaking to us.

"What are you reading?" Kevin said, pointing to the book.

The girl said, "*SEPHER YEZIRAH*. I will read to you; listen." She set the book down, closing it. " 'God has also set the one over against the other; the good against the evil, and the evil against the good; the good proceeds from the good, and the evil from the evil; the good purifies the bad, and the bad the good; the good is preserved for the good, and the evil for the bad ones.' " Sophia paused a moment and then said, "This means that good will make evil into what evil does not wish to be; but evil will not be able to make good into what good does not wish to be. Evil serves good, despite its cunning." Then she said nothing; she sat silently, with her animals and with us.

"Could you tell us about your parents?" I said. "I mean, if we are to know what to do—"

Sophia said, "Go wherever I send you and you will know what to do. There is no place where I am not. When you leave here you will not see me, but later you will see me again.

"You will not see me but I will always see you; I am mindful of you continually. So I am with you whether you know it or not; but I say to you, Know that I accompany you, even down into the prison, if the tyrant puts you there.

"There is no more. Go back home, and I will instruct you as the time requires." She smiled at us.

"You're how old?" I said.

"I am two years old."

"And you're reading that book?"Kevin said.

Sophia said, "I tell you in truth, in very truth, none of you will forget me. And I tell you that all of you will see me again. You did not choose me; I chose you. I called you here. I sent for you four years ago."

"Okay," I said. That placed her call at 1974.

"If the Lamptons ask you what I said, say that we talked about the commune to be built," Sophia said. "Do not tell them that I sent you away from them. But you are to go away from them; this is your answer: you will have nothing further to do with them."

Kevin pointed to the tape recorder, its drums turning.

"What they will hear on it," Sophia said, "when they play it back, will be only the *SEPHER YEZIRAH*, nothing more."

Wow, I thought.

I believed her.

"I will not fail you," Sophia repeated, smiling at the three of us.

I believed that, too.

*

As the three of us walked back to the house, Kevin said, "Was all that just quotations from the Bible?"

"No," I said.

"No," David agreed. "There was something new; that part about us being our own gods, now. That the time had come where we no longer had to believe in any deity other than ourselves."

"What a beautiful child," I said, thinking to myself how much she reminded me of my own son Christopher.

"We're very lucky," David, said huskily. "To have met her." Turning to me he said, "She'll be with us; she said so. I believe it. She'll be inside us; we won't be alone. I never realized it before but we are alone. Everybody is alone—has been alone, I mean. Up until now. She's going to spread out all over the world, isn't she? Into everyone, eventually. Starting with us."

"The Rhipidon Society," I said, "has four members. Sophia and the three of us."

"That's still not very many," Kevin said.

"The mustard seed," I said. "That grows into a tree so large that birds can roost in it."

"Come off it," Kevin said.

"What's the matter?" I asked.

Kevin said, "We have to get our stuff together and get out of here; she said so. The Lamptons are whacked out flipped-out freaks. They could zap us any time."

"Sophia will protect us," David said.

201

"A two-year-old child?" Kevin said.

We both gazed at him.

"Okay, two-thousand-year-old child," Kevin said.

"The only person who could make jokes about the Savior," David said. "I'm surprised you didn't ask her about your dead cat."

Kevin halted; a look of genuine baffled anger appeared on his face; obviously he had forgotten to: he had missed his chance.

"I'm going back," he said.

Together, David and I propelled him along with us.

"I'm not kidding!" he said, with fury.

"What's the matter?" I said; we halted.

"I want to talk to her some more. I'm not going to walk off out of here; goddam it, I'm going back—let me the fuck *go*!"

"Listen," I said. "She told us to leave."

"And she'll be inside us talking to us," David said.

"We'll hear what I call the AI voice," I said.

Kevin said savagely, "And there'll be lemonade fountains and gumdrop trees. I'm going back."

Ahead of us, Eric and Linda Lampton emerged from the big house and walked toward us.

"Confrontation time," I said.

"Aw shit," Kevin said, in desperation. "I'm still going back." He pulled away from us and hurried in the direction from which we had come.

"Did it work out well?" Linda Lampton said, when she and her husband reached David and me.

"Fine," I said.

"What did you discuss?" Eric said.

I said, "The commune."

"Very good," Linda said. "Why is Kevin going back? What is he going to say to Sophia?"

David said, "Has to do with his dead cat."

"Ask him to come here," Eric said.

"Why?" I said.

"We are going to discuss your relationship to the commune," Eric said. "The Rhipidon Society should be part of the major

202

commune, in our opinion. Brent Mini suggested that; we really should talk about it. We find you acceptable."

"I'll get Kevin," David said.

"Eric," I said, "we're returning to Santa Ana."

"There's time to discuss your involvement with the commune," Linda said. "Your Air Cal flight's not until eight tonight, is it? You can have dinner with us."

Eric Lampton said, "VALIS summoned you people here. You will go when VALIS feels you are ready to go."

"VALIS feels we're ready to go," I said.

"I'll get Kevin," David said.

Eric said, "I'll go get him." He passed on by David and me, in the direction of Kevin and the girl.

Folding her arms, Linda said, "You can't go back down south yet. Mini wants to talk over a number of matters with you. Keep in mind that his time is short. He's weakening fast. Is Kevin really asking Sophia about his dead cat? What's so important about a dead cat?"

"To Kevin the cat is very important," I said.

"That's right," David agreed. "To Kevin the cat's death represents everything that's wrong with the universe; he believes that Sophia can explain it to him, which by that I mean everything that's wrong with the universe—undeserved suffering and loss."

Linda said, "I don't really think he's talking about his dead cat."

"He really is," I said.

"You don't know Kevin," David said. "Maybe he's talking about other things because this is his chance to talk to the Savior finally but his dead cat is a major matter in what he's talking about."

"I think we should go over to Kevin," Linda said, "and tell him that he's talked to Sophia enough. What do you mean, VALIS feels you are ready to go? Did Sophia say that?"

A voice in my head spoke. *Tell her radiation bothers you.* It was the AI voice which Horselover Fat had heard since March 1974; I recognized it.

"The radiation," I said. "It—" I hesitated; understanding of the terse sentence came to me. "I'm half-blind," I said. "A beam of pink light hit me; it must have been the sun. Then I realized we should get back."

"VALIS fired information directly to you," Linda said, at once, alertly.

You don't know.

"I don't know," I said. "But I felt different afterward. As if I had something important to do down south in Santa Ana. We know other people . . . there are other people we could get into the Rhipidon Society. They should come to the commune, too. VALIS has caused them to have visions; they come to us for explanations. We told them about the film, about seeing the film Mother Goose made; they're all seeing it, and getting a lot out of it. We've got more people going to see *Valis* than I thought we knew; they must be telling their friends. My own contacts in Hollywood—the producers and actors I know, and especially the money people—are very interested in what I've pointed out to them. There's one MGM producer in particular that might want to finance Mother Goose in another film, a high-budget film; he says he has the backing already."

My flow of talk amazed me; it seemed to come out of nothing. It was as if it wasn't me talking, but someone else; someone who knew exactly what to say to Linda Lampton.

"What's the producer's name?" Linda said.

"Art Rockoway," I said, the name coming into my head as if on cue.

"What films does he have?" Linda said.

"The one about the nuclear wastes that contaminated most of central Utah," I said. "That disaster the newspapers reported two years ago but TV was afraid to talk about; the government put pressure on them. Where all the sheep died. The cover-story that it was nerve gas. Rockoway did a hardball film in which the true tale of calculated indifference by the authorities came out."

"Who starred?" Linda said.

"Robert Redford," I said.

"Well, we would be interested," Linda said.

"So we should get back to southern California," I said. "We have a number of people in Hollywood to talk to."

"Eric!" Linda called; she walked toward her husband, who

stood with Kevin; he now had Kevin by the arm.

Glancing at me, David made a signal that we should follow; together, the three of us approached Kevin and Eric. Not far off, Sophia ignored us; she continued to read her book.

A flash of pink light blinded me.

"Oh my God," I said.

I could not see; I put my hands against my forehead, which ached and throbbed as if it would burst.

"What's wrong?" David said. I could hear a low humming, like a vacuum cleaner. I opened my eyes, but nothing other than pink light swam around me.

*

"Phil, are you okay?" Kevin said.

The pink light ebbed. We were in three seats aboard a jet. Yet at the same time, superimposed over the seats of the jet, the wall, the other passengers, lay the brown dry field, Linda Lampton, the house not far off. Two places, two times.

"Kevin," I said. "What time is it?" I could see nothing out the window of the jet but darkness; the interior lights over the passengers were, for the most part, on. It was night. Yet, bright sunlight streamed down on the brown field, on the Lamptons and Kevin and David. The hum of the jet engines continued; I felt myself sway slightly: the plane had turned. Now I saw many far-off lights beyond the window. We're over Los Angeles, I realized. And still the warm daytime sun streamed down on me.

"We'll be landing in five minutes," Kevin said.

Time dysfunction, I realized.

The brown field ebbed out. Eric and Linda Lampton ebbed out. The sunlight ebbed out.

Around me the plane became substantial. David sat reading a paperback book of T.S. Eliot. Kevin seemed tense.

"We're almost there," I said. "Orange County Airport."

Kevin said nothing; he had hunched over, broodingly.

"They let us go?" I said.

"What?" He glanced at me irritably.

"I was just there," I said. Now the memory of the intervening events bled into my mind. The protests of the Lamptons and by

205

Brent Mini—him most of all; they had implored us not to go, but we had gotten away. Here we were on the Air Cal flight back. We were safe.

There had been a twin-pronged thrust by Mini and the Lamptons.

"You won't tell anyone on the outside about Sophia?" Linda had said anxiously. "Can we swear you three to silence?" Naturally they had agreed. This anxiety had been one of the prongs, the negative prong. The other had been positive, an inducement.

"Look at it this way," Eric had said, backed up by Mini who seemed genuinely crestfallen that the Rhipidon Society, small as it was, had decided to depart. "This is the most important event in human history; you don't want to be left out, do you? And after all, VALIS picked you out. We get literally thousands of letters on the film, and only a few people here and there seem to have been contacted by VALIS, as you were. *We are a privileged group.*"

"This is the Call," Mini had said, almost imploringly to the three of us.

"Yes," Linda and Eric had echoed. "This is the Call mankind has waited centuries for. Read *Revelation*; read what it says about the Elect. We are God's Elect!"

"Guess so," I had said as they left us off by the car we had rented; we had parked near Gino's, on a sidestreet of Sonoma which allowed prolonged parking.

Going up to me, Linda Lampton had put her hands on my shoulders and had kissed me on the mouth—with intensity and a certain amount, in fact a great amount, of erotic fervor. "Come back to us," she had whispered in my ear. "You promise? This is our future; it belongs to a very few, a very, very few." To which I had thought, You couldn't be more wrong, honey; this belongs to everyone.

So now we were almost home. Crucially assisted by VALIS. Or, as I preferred to think of it, by St. Sophia. Putting it that way kept my attention on the image in my mind of the girl Sophia, seated with the animals and her book.

As we stood in the Orange County Airport, waiting for our luggage, I said, "They weren't strictly honest with us. For

206

instance, they told us everything Sophia said and did was audio and video taped. That's not so."

"You may be wrong about that," Kevin said. "There are sophisticated monitoring systems now that work on remote. She may have been under their range even though we couldn't spot them. Mini is really what he says he is: a master at electronic hardware."

I thought, Mini, who was willing to die in order to experience VALIS once more. Was I? In 1974 I had experienced him once; ever since I had hungered for him to return—ached in my bones; my body felt it as much as my mind, perhaps more so. But VALIS was right to be judicious. It showed his concern for human life, his unwillingness to manifest himself to me again.

The original encounter had, after all, almost killed me. I could again see VALIS, but, as with Mini, it would slay me. And I did not want that; I had too many things to do.

What exactly did I have to do? I didn't know. None of us knew. Already I had heard the AI voice in my head, and others would hear that voice, more and more people. VALIS, as living information, would penetrate the world, replicating in human brains, crossbonding with them and assisting them, guiding them, at a subliminal level, which is to say invisibly. No given human could be certain if he were crossbonded until the symbiosis reached flashpoint. In his concourse with other humans a given person would not know when he was dealing with another homoplasmate and when he would not.

Perhaps the ancient signs of secret identification would return; more likely they already had. During a handshake, a motion with one finger of two intersecting arcs: swift expression of the fish symbol, which no one beyond the two persons involved could discern.

I remembered back to an incident—more than an incident—involving my son Christopher. In March 1974 during the time that VALIS overruled me, held control of my mind, I had conducted a correct and complex initiation of Christopher into the ranks of the immortals. VALIS's medical knowledge had saved Christopher's physical life, but VALIS had not ended it there.

This was an experience which I treasured. It had been done

207

in utter stealth, concealed even from my son's mother.

First I had fixed a mug of hot chocolate. Then I had fixed a hot dog on a bun with the usual trimmings; Christopher, young as he was, loved hot dogs and warm chocolate.

Seated on the floor in Christopher's room with him, I—or rather VALIS in me, as me—had played a game. First, I jokingly held the cup of chocolate up, over my son's head; then, as if by accident, I had splashed warm chocolate on his head, into his hair. Giggling, Christopher had tried to wipe the liquid off; I had of course helped him. Leaning toward him, I had whispered:

"In the name of the Son, the Father and the Holy Spirit."

No one heard me except Christopher. Now, as I wiped the warm chocolate from his hair, I inscribed the sign of the cross on his forehead. I had now baptized him and now I confirmed him; I did so, not by the authority of the church, but by the authority of the living plasmate in me: VALIS himself. Next I said to my son, "Your secret name, your Christian name, is—" And I told him what it was. Only he and I are ever to know; he and I and VALIS.

Next, I took a bit of the bread from the hot dog bun and held it forth; my son—still a baby, really—opened his mouth like a little bird, and I placed the bit of bread in it. We seemed, the two of us, to be sharing a meal; an ordinary simple, common meal.

For some reason it seemed essential—quite crucial—that he take no bite of the hot dog meat itself. Pork could not be eaten under these circumstances; VALIS filled me with this urgent knowledge.

As Christopher started to close his mouth to chew on the bit of bread, I presented him with the mug of warm chocolate. To my surprise—being so young he still drank normally from his bottle, never from a cup—he reached eagerly to take the mug; as he took it, lifted it to his lips and drank from it, I said,

"This is my blood and this is my body."

My little son drank, and I took the mug back. The greater sacraments had been accomplished. Baptism, then confirmation, then the most holy sacrament of all, the Eucharist: sacrament of the Lord's Supper.

208

"The Blood of our Lord Jesus Christ, which was shed for thee, preserve thy body and soul unto everlasting life. Drink this in remembrance that Christ's Blood was shed for thee, and be thankful."

This moment is most solemn of all. The priest himself has become Christ; it is Christ who offers his body and blood to the faithful, by a divine miracle.

Most people understand that in the miracle of transubstantiation the wine (or warm chocolate) becomes the Sacred Blood, and the wafer (or bit of hot dog bun) becomes the Sacred Body, but few people even within the churches realize that the figure who stands before them holding the cup is their Lord, living now. *Time has been overcome.* We are back almost two thousand years; we are not in Santa Ana, California, USA, but in Jerusalem, about 35 C.E.

What I had seen in March 1974 when I saw the superimposition of ancient Rome and modern California consisted of an actual witnessing of what is normally seen by the inner eyes of faith only.

My double-exposure experience had confirmed the literal—not merely figurative—truth of the miracle of the Mass.

As I have said, the technical term for this is anamnesis: the loss of forgetfulness; which is to say, the remembering of the Lord and the Lord's Supper.

I was present that day, the last time the disciples sat at table. You may believe me; you may not. *Sed per spiritum sanctum dico; haec veritas est. Mihi crede et mecum in aeternitate vivebis.*

My Latin is probably faulty, but what I am trying to say, haltingly, is: "But I speak by means of the Holy Spirit; this is so. Believe me and you shall live with me in eternity."

Our luggage showed up; we turned our claim-checks over to the uniformed cop, and, ten minutes later, were driving north on the freeway toward Santa Ana and home.

209

13

As he drove, Kevin said, "I'm tired. Really tired. Fuck this traffic! Who are these people driving on the 55? Where do they come from? Where are they going?"

I wondered to myself, Where are the three of us going?

We had seen the Savior and I had, after eight years of madness, been healed.

Well, I thought, that's something to accomplish all in one weekend . . . not to mention escaping intact from the three most whacked-out humans on the planet.

It is amazing that when someone else spouts the nonsense you yourself believe you can readily perceive it as nonsense. In the VW Rabbit as I had listened to Linda and Eric rattle on about being three-eyed people from another planet I had known they were nuts. This made me nuts, too. The realization had frightened me: the realization about them and about myself.

I had flown up crazy and returned sane, yet I believed that I had met the Savior . . . in the form of a little girl with black hair and fierce black eyes who had discoursed to us with more wisdom than any adult I had ever met. And, when we were blocked in our attempt to leave, she—or VALIS—had intervened.

"We have a commission," David said. "To go forth and—"

"And what?" Kevin said.

"She'll tell us as we go along," David said.

"And pigs can whistle," Kevin said.

"Look," David said vigorously. "Phil's okay now, for the first time . . ." He hesitated.

"Since you've known me," I finished.

David said, "She healed him. Healing powers are the absolute certain sign of the material presence of the Messiah. You know that, Kevin."

"Then St. Joseph Hospital is the best church in town," Kevin said.

I said to Kevin, "Did you get a chance to ask Sophia about your dead cat?" I meant the question sarcastically, but Kevin, to my surprise, turned his head and said, seriously:

"Yep."

"What'd she say?" I said.

Kevin, inhaling deeply and gripping the steering wheel tight, said, "She said that MY DEAD CAT . . ." He paused, raising his voice. "MY DEAD CAT WAS STUPID."

I had to laugh. David likewise. No one had thought to give Kevin that answer before. The cat saw the car and ran into it, not the other way around; it had ploughed directly into the right front wheel of the car, like a bowling ball.

"She said," Kevin said, "that the universe has very strict rules, and that *that* species of cat, the kind that runs headfirst into moving cars, isn't around any more."

"Well," I said, "pragmatically speaking, she's right."

It was interesting to contrast Sophia's explanation with the late Sherri's; she had piously informed Kevin that God so loved his cat—actually—that God had seen fit to take Kevin's cat to be with him God instead of him Kevin. This is not an explanation you give to a twenty-nine-year-old man; this is an explanation you foist off on kids. Little kids. And even the little kids generally can see it's bullshit.

"But," Kevin continued, "I said to her, 'Why didn't God make my cat smart?'"

"Did this conversation really take place?" I said.

Resignedly, David said, "Probably so."

"My cat was STUPID," Kevin continued, "because GOD MADE IT STUPID. So it was GOD's fault, not my cat's fault."

"And you told her that," I said.

"Yes," Kevin said.

I felt anger. "You cynical asshole—you meet the Savior and all you can do is rant about your goddam cat. I'm glad your

211

cat's dead; *everybody* is glad your cat's dead. So shut up." I had begun to shake with fury.

"Easy," David murmured. "We've been through a lot."

To me, Kevin said, "She's not the Savior. We're all as nuts as you, Phil. They're nuts up there; we're nuts down here."

David said, "Then how could a two-year-old girl say such—"

"They had a *wire* running to her head," Kevin yelled, "and a microphone at the other end of the wire, and a speaker inside her face. It was somebody else talking."

"I need a drink," I said. "Let's stop at Sombrero Street."

"I liked you better when you believed you were Horselover Fat," Kevin yelled. "Him I liked. You're as stupid as my cat. If stupidity kills, why aren't you dead?"

"You want to try to arrange it?" I said.

"Obviously stupidity is a survival trait," Kevin said, but his voice sank, now, into near-inaudibility. "I don't know," he murmured. " 'The Savior.' How can it be? It's my fault; I took you to see *Valis*. I got you mixed up with Mother Goose. Does it make sense that Mother Goose would give birth to the Savior? Does any of this make sense?"

"Stop at Sombrero Street," David said.

"The Rhipidon Society holds its meetings in a bar," Kevin said. "That's our commission; to sit in a bar and drink. That'll sure save the world. And why save it anyhow?"

We drove on in silence, but we did end up at Sombrero Street; the majority of the Rhipidon Society had voted in favor of it.

*

Certainly it constitutes bad news if the people who agree with you are buggier than batshit. Sophia herself (and this is important) had said that Eric and Linda Lampton were ill. In addition to that, Sophia or VALIS had provided me with the words to get us out of there when the Lamptons had closed in on us, hemming us in—had provided words and then tinkered expertly with time.

I could separate the beautiful child from the ugly Lamptons.

212

I did not lump them together. Significantly, the two-year-old child had spoken what seemed like wisdom . . . sitting in the bar with my bottle of Mexican beer I asked myself, What are the criteria of rationality, by which to judge if wisdom is present? Wisdom has to be, by its very nature, rational; it is the final stage of what is locked into the real. There is an intimate relationship between what is wise and what exists, although that relationship is subtle. What had the little girl told us? That human beings should now give up the worship of all deities except mankind itself. This did not seem irrational to me. Whether it had been said by a child or whether it came from the *Britannica*, it would have struck me as sound.

For some time I had held the opinion that Zebra—as I had called the entity which manifested itself to me in March 1974—was in fact the laminated totality of all my selves along the linear time-axis; Zebra—or VALIS—was the supra-temporal expression of a given human being and not a god . . . not unless the supra-temporal expression of a given human being is what we actually mean by the term "god," is what we worship, without realizing it, when we worship "god."

The hell with it, I thought wearily. I give up.

Kevin drove me home; I went at once to bed, worn-out and discouraged, in a vague way. I think what discouraged me about the situation was the uncertainty of our commission, received from Sophia. We had a mandate but for what? More important, what did Sophia intend to do as she matured? Remain with the Lamptons? Escape, change her name, move to Japan and start a new life?

Where would she surface? Where would we find mention of her over the years? Would we have to wait until she grew to adulthood? That might be eighteen years. In eighteen years Ferris F. Fremount, to use the name from the film, could have taken over the world—again. We needed help now.

But then I thought, You always need the Savior now. Later is always too late.

When I fell asleep that night I had a dream. In the dream I rode in Kevin's Honda, but instead of Kevin driving, Linda Ronstadt sat behind the wheel, and the car was open, like a vehicle from ancient times, like a chariot. Smiling at me,

Ronstadt sang, and she sang more beautifully than any time I had ever heard her sing before. She sang:

"To walk toward the dawn
You must put your slippers on."

In the dream this delighted me; it seemed a terribly important message. When I woke up the next morning I could still see her lovely face, the dark, glowing eyes: such large eyes, so filled with light, a strange kind of black light, like the light of stars. Her look toward me was one of intense love, but not sexual love; it was what the Bible calls loving-kindness. Where was she driving me?

During the next day I tried to figure out what the cryptic words referred to. Slippers. Dawn. What did I associate with the dawn?

Studying my reference books (at one time I would have said, "Horselover Fat, studying his reference books"), I came across the fact that Aurora is the Latin word for the personification of the dawn. And that suggests Aurora Borealis—which looks like St. Elmo's Fire, which is how Zebra or VALIS looked. The *Britannica* says of the Aurora Borealis:

"The Aurora Borealis appears throughout history in the mythology of the Eskimo, the Irish, the English, the Scandinavians, and others; it was usually believed to be a supernatural manifestation . . . Northern Germanic tribes saw in it the splendor of the shields of Valkyrie (warrior women)."

Did that mean—was VALIS telling me—that little Sophia would issue forth into the world as a "warrior woman"? Maybe so.

What about slippers? I could think of one association, an interesting one. Empedocles, the pupil of Pythagoras, who had gone public about remembering his past lives and who told his friends privately that he was Apollo, had never died in the usual sense; instead, his golden slippers had been found near the top of the volcano Mount Etna. Either Empedocles, like

Elijah, had been taken up into heaven bodily, or he had jumped into the volcano. Mount Etna is in the eastern-most part of Sicily. In Roman times the word "aurora" literally meant "east." Was VALIS alluding to both itself and to re-birth, to eternal life? Was I being—

The phone rang.

Picking it up I said, "Hello."

I heard Eric Lampton's voice. It sounded twisted, like an old root, a dying root. "We have something to tell you. I'll let Linda tell you. Hold on."

A deep fear entered me as I stood holding the silent phone. Then Linda Lampton's voice sounded in my ear, flat and toneless. The dream had to do with her, I realized; Linda Ronstadt; Linda Lampton. "What is it?" I said, unable to understand what Linda Lampton was saying.

"The little girl is dead," Linda Lampton said. "Sophia."

"How?" I said.

"Mini killed her. By accident. The police are here. With a laser. He was trying to—"

I hung up.

The phone rang again almost at once. I picked it up and said hello.

Linda Lampton said, "Mini wanted to try to get as much information—"

"Thanks for telling me," I said. Crazily, I felt bitter anger, not sorrow.

"He was trying information-transfer by laser," Linda was saying. "We're calling everyone. We don't understand; if Sophia was the Savior, how could she die?"

Dead at two years old, I realized. Impossible.

I hung up the phone and sat down. After a time, I realized that the woman in the dream driving the car and singing had been Sophia, but grown up, as she would have been one day. The dark eyes filled with light and life and fire.

The dream was her way of saying good-bye.

215

14

The newspapers and TV carried an account of Mother Goose's daughter's death. Naturally, since Eric Lampton was a rock star, the implication was made that sinister forces had been at work, probably having to do with neglect or drugs or weird stuff generally. Mini's face was shown, and then some clips from the film *Valis* in which the fortress-like mixer appeared.

Two or three days later, everyone had forgotten about it. Other horrors occupied the TV screen. Other tragedies took place. As always. A liquor store in West L.A. got robbed and the clerk shot. An old man died at a substandard nursing home. Three cars on the San Diego Freeway collided with a lumber truck which had caught on fire and stalled.

The world continued as it always had.

I began to think about death. Not Sophia Lampton's death but death in general and then, by degrees, my own death.

Actually, I didn't think about it. Horselover Fat did.

One night, as he sat in my living room in my easy chair, a glass of cognac in his hand, he said meditatively, "All it proved was what we knew anyhow; her death, I mean."

"And what did we know?" I said.

"That they were nuts."

I said, "The parents were nuts. But not Sophia."

"If she had been Zebra," Fat said, "she would have had foreknowledge of Mini's screw-up with the laser equipment. She could have averted it."

"Sure," I said.

"It's true," Fat said. "She would have had the knowledge and in addition—" He pointed at me. Triumph lay in his voice; bold triumph. "She would have had the power to avert it. Right? If she could overthrow Ferris F. Fremount—"

216

"Drop it," I said.

"All that was involved from the start," Fat said quietly, "was advanced laser technology. Mini found a way to transmit information by laser beam, using human brains as transducers without the need for an electronic interface. The Russians can do the same thing. Microwaves can be used as well. In March 1974 I must have intercepted one of Mini's transmissions by accident; it irradiated me. That's why my blood pressure went up so high, and the animals died of cancer. That's what's killing Mini; the radiation produced by his own laser experimentations."

I said nothing. There was nothing to say.

Fat said, "I'm sorry. Will you be okay?"

"Sure," I said.

"After all," Fat said, "I never really got a chance to talk to her, not to the extent that the rest of you did; I wasn't there that second time, when she gave us—the Society—our commission."

And now, I wondered, what about our commission?

"Fat," I said, "you're not going to try to knock yourself off again, are you? Because of her death?"

"No," Fat said.

I didn't believe him. I could tell; I knew him, better than he knew himself. Gloria's death, Beth abandoning him, Sherri dying—all that had saved him after Sherri died was his decision to go in search of the "fifth Savior," and now that hope had perished. What did he have left?

Fat had tried everything, and everything had failed.

"Maybe you should start seeing Maurice again," I said.

"He'll say, 'And I mean it.' " We both laughed. " 'I want you to list the ten things you want most to do in all the world; I want you to think about it and write them down, and I mean it!' "

I said, "What do you want to do?" And I meant it.

"Find her," Fat said.

"Who?" I said.

"I don't know," Fat said. "The one that died. The one that I will never see again."

There're a lot of them in that category, I said to myself. Sorry, Fat; your answer is too vague.

"I should go over to Wide-World Travel," Fat said, half to

himself, "and talk to the lady there some more. About India. I have a feeling India is the place."

"Place for what?"

"Where he'll be," Fat said.

I did not respond; there was no point to it. Fat's madness had returned.

"He's somewhere," Fat said. "I know he is, right now; somewhere in the world. Zebra told me. 'St. Sophia is going to be born again; she wasn't—' "

"You want me to tell you the truth?" I interrupted.

Fat blinked. "Sure, Phil."

In a harsh voice, I said, "There is no Savior. St. Sophia will not be born again, the Buddha is not in the park, the Head Apollo is not about to return. Got it?"

Silence.

"The fifth Savior—" Fat began timidly.

"Forget it," I said. "You're psychotic, Fat. You're as crazy as Eric and Linda Lampton. You're as crazy as Brent Mini. You've been crazy for eight years, since Gloria tossed herself off the Synanon Building and made herself into a scrambled egg sandwich. Give up and forget. Okay? Will you do me that one favor? Will you do all of us that one favor?"

Fat said finally, in a low voice, "Then you agree with Kevin."

"Yes," I said. "I agree with Kevin."

"Then why should I keep on going?" Fat said quietly.

"I don't know," I said. "And I don't really care. It's your life and your affair, not mine."

"Zebra wouldn't have lied to me," Fat said.

"There is no 'Zebra,' " I said. "It's yourself. Don't you recognize your own self? It's you and only you, projecting your unanswered wishes out, unfulfilled desires left over after Gloria did herself in. You couldn't fill the vacuum with reality so you filled it with fantasy; it was psychological compensation for a fruitless, wasted, empty, pain-filled life and I don't see why you don't finally now fucking give up; you're like Kevin's cat: you're stupid. That is the beginning and the end of it. Okay?"

"You rob me of hope."

218

"I rob you of nothing because there is nothing."

"Is all this so? You think so? Really?"

I said, "I know so."

"You don't think I should look for him!"

"Where the hell are you going to look? You have no idea, no idea in the world, where he might be. He could be in Ireland. He could be in Mexico City. He could be in Anaheim at Disneyland; yeah—maybe he's working at Disneyland, pushing a broom. How are you going to recognize him? We all thought Sophia was the Savior; we believed in that until the day she died. She *talked* like the Savior. We had all the evidence; we had all the signs. We had the flick *Valis*. We had the two-word cypher. We had the Lamptons and Mini. Their story fit your story; everything fit. And now there's another dead girl in another box in the ground—that makes three in all. Three people who died for nothing. You believed it, I believed it, David believed it, Kevin believed it, the Lamptons believed it; Mini in particular believed it, enough to accidentally kill her. So now it ends. It never should have begun—goddam Kevin for seeing that film! Go out and kill yourself. The hell with it."

"I still might—"

"You won't," I said. "You won't find him. I know. Let me put it to you in a simple way so you can grasp it. You thought the Savior would bring Gloria back—right? He, she, didn't; now she's dead, too. Instead of—" I gave up.

"Then the true name for religion," Fat said, "is death."

"The secret name," I agreed. "You got it. Jesus died; Asklepios died—they killed Mini worse than they killed Jesus, but nobody even cares; nobody even remembers. They killed the Catharists in southern France by the tens of thousands. In the Thirty Years War, hundreds of thousands of people died, Protestants and Catholics—mutual slaughter. Death is the real name for it; not God, not the Savior, not love—*death*. Kevin is right about his cat. It's all there in his dead cat. The Great Judge can't answer Kevin: 'Why did my cat die?' Answer: 'Damned if I know.' There is no answer; there is only a dead animal that just wanted to cross the street. We're all animals that want to cross the street only something mows us down half-way across that we never saw. Go ask Kevin. 'Your cat

219

was stupid.' Who made the cat? Why did he make the cat stupid? Did the cat learn by being killed, and if so, what did he learn? Did Sherri learn anything from dying of cancer? Did Gloria learn anything—"

"Okay, enough," Fat said.

"Kevin is right," I said. "Go out and get laid."

"By who? They're all dead."

I said, "There're more. Still alive. Lay one of them before she dies or you die or somebody dies, some person or animal. You said it yourself: the universe is irrational because the mind behind it is irrational. You are irrational and you know it. *I* am. We all are and we know it, on some level. I'd write a book about it but no one would believe a group of human beings could be as irrational as we are, as we've acted."

"They would now," Fat said, "after Jim Jones and the nine hundred people at Jonestown."

"Go away, Fat," I said. "Go to South America. Go back up to Sonoma and apply for residence at the Lamptons' commune, unless they've given up, which I doubt. Madness has its own dynamism; it just goes on." Getting to my feet I walked over and stuck my hand against his chest. "The girl is dead, Gloria is dead; nothing will restore her."

"Sometimes I dream—"

"I'll put that on your gravestone."

*

After he had obtained his passport, Fat left the United States and flew by Icelandic Airlines to Luxembourg, which is the cheapest way to go. We got a postcard from him mailed at his stop-over in Iceland, and then, a month later, a letter from Metz, France. Metz lies on the border to Luxembourg; I looked it up on the map.

In Metz—which he liked, as a scenic place—he met a girl and enjoyed a wonderful time until she took him for half of the money he'd brought with him. He sent us a photograph of her; she is very pretty, reminding me a little of Linda Ronstadt, with the same shape face and haircut. It was the last picture he sent us, because the girl stole his camera as well. She worked at a

220

bookstore. Fat never told us whether he got to go to bed with her.

From Metz he crossed over into West Germany, where the American dollar is worth nothing. He already read and spoke a little German so he had a relatively easy time there. But his letters became less frequent and finally stopped completely.

"If he'd have made it with the French girl," Kevin said, "he'd have recovered."

"For all we know he did," David said.

Kevin said, "If he'd made it with her he'd be back here sane. He's not, so he didn't."

A year passed. One day I got a mailgram from him; Fat had flown back to the United States, to New York. He knows people there. He would be arriving in California, he said, when he got over his mono; in Europe he had been hit by mono.

"But did he find the Savior?" Kevin said. The mailgram didn't say. "It would say if he had," Kevin said. "It's like with that French girl; we'd have heard."

"At least he isn't dead," David said.

Kevin said, "It depends on how you define 'dead.'"

Meanwhile I had been doing fine; my books sold well, now—I had more money put away than I knew what to do with. In fact we were all doing well. David ran a tobacco shop at the city shopping mall, one of the most elegant malls in Orange County; Kevin's new girlfriend treated him and us gently and with tact, putting up with our gallows sense of humour, especially Kevin's. We had told her all about Fat and his quest—and the French girl fleecing him right down to his Pentax camera. She looked forward to meeting him and we looked forward to his return: stories and pictures and maybe presents! we said to ourselves.

And then we received a second mailgram. This time from Portland, Oregon. It read:

KING FELIX

Nothing more. Just those two startling words. Well? I thought. Did he? Is that what he's telling us? Does the

Rhipidon Society reconvene in plenary session after all this time?

It hardly mattered to us. Collectively and individually we barely remembered. It was a part of our lives we preferred to forget. Too much pain; too many hopes down the tube.

When Fat arrived in LAX, which is the designation for the Los Angeles Airport, the four of us met him: me, Kevin, David and Kevin's foxy girl friend Ginger, a tall girl with blonde hair braided and with bits of red ribbon in the braids, a colorful lady who liked to drive miles and miles late at night to drink Irish coffee at some out-of-the-way Irish bar.

With all the rest of the people in the world we milled around and conversed, and then all at once, unexpectedly, there came Horselover Fat striding toward us in the midst of the gang of other passengers. Grinning, carrying a briefcase; our friend back home. He wore a suit and tie, a good-looking East Coast suit, fashionable in the extreme. It shocked us to see him so well-dressed; we had anticipated, I guess, some emaciated hollow-eyed remnant scarcely able to hobble down the corridor.

After we'd hugged him and introduced him to Ginger we asked him how he'd been.

"Not bad," he said.

We ate at the restaurant at a top-of-the-line nearby hotel. Not much talk took place, for some reason. Fat seemed withdrawn, but not actually depressed. Tired, I decided. He had traveled a long way; it was inscribed on his face. Those things show up; they leave their mark.

"What's in the briefcase?" I said when our after-dinner coffee came.

Pushing aside the dishes before him, Fat laid down the briefcase and unsnapped it; it wasn't key-locked. In it he had manila folders, one of which he lifted out after sorting among them; they bore numbers. He examined it a last time to be sure he had the right one and then he handed it to me.

"Look in it," he said, smiling slightly, as you do when you have given someone a present which you know will please him and he is unwrapping it before your eyes.

I opened it. In the folder I found four 8 × 10 glossy photos,

222

obviously professionally done; they looked like the kind of stills that the publicity departments of movie studios put out.

The photos showed a Greek vase, on it a painting of a male figure who we recognized as Hermes.

Twined around the vase the double helix confronted us, done in red glaze against a black background. The DNA molecule. There could be no mistake.

"Twenty-three or -four hundred years ago," Fat said. "Not the picture but the *krater*, the pottery."

"A pot," I said.

"I saw it in a museum at Athens. It's authentic. That's not a matter of my opinion; I'm not qualified to judge such matters; its authenticity has been established by the museum authorities. I talked with one of them. He hadn't realized what the design shows; he was very interested when I discussed it with him. This form of vase, the *krater*, was the shape used later as the baptismal font. That was one of the Greek words that came into my head in March 1974, the word '*krater*.' I heard it connected with another Greek word: '*poros.*' The words 'poros krater' essentially mean '*limestone font.*'"

There could be no doubt; the design, predating Christianity, was Crick and Watson's double helix model at which they had arrived after so many wrong guesses, so much trial-and-error work. Here it was, faithfully reproduced.

"Well?" I said.

"The so-called intertwined snakes of the caduceus. Originally the caduceus, which is still the symbol of medicine was the staff of—not Hermes—but—" Fat paused, his eyes bright. "Of Asklepios. It has a very specific meaning, besides that of wisdom, which the snakes allude to; it shows that the bearer is a sacred person and not to be molested . . . which is why Hermes, the messenger of the gods, carried it."

None of us said anything for a time.

Kevin started to utter something sarcastic, something in his dry, witty way, but he did not; he only sat without speaking.

Examining the 8 × 10 glossies, Ginger said, "How lovely!"

"The greatest physician in all human history," Fat said to her. "Asklepios, the founder of Greek medicine. The Roman Emperor Julian—known to us as Julian the Apostate because he renounced Christianity—considered Asklepios as God or a god; Julian worshipped him. If that worship had continued, the entire history of the Western world would have basically changed."

"You won't give up," I said to Fat.

"No," Fat agreed. "I never will. I'm going back—I ran out of money. When I've gotten the funds together, I'm going back. I know where to look, now. The Greek islands. Lemnos, Lesbos, Crete. Especially Crete. I dreamed I descended in an elevator—in fact I had this dream twice—and the elevator operator recited in verse, and there was a huge plate of spaghetti with a three-pronged fork, a trident, stuck in it . . . that would be Ariadne's thread by which she led Theseus out of the maze under Minos after he slew the Minotaur. The Minotaur, being half man and half beast is a monster which represents the demented deity Samael, in my opinion, the false demiurge of the Gnostics' system."

"The two-word mailgram," I said, " 'KING FELIX.' "

Fat said, "I didn't find him."

"I see," I said.

"But he is somewhere," Fat said. "I know it. I will never give up." He returned the photos to their manila folder, put it back in the briefcase and closed it up.

Today he is in Turkey. He sent us a postcard showing the mosque which used to be the great Christian church called St. Sophia or Hagia Sophia, one of the wonders of the world, even though the roof collapsed during the Middle Ages and had to be rebuilt. You'll find schematics of its unique construction in most comprehensive textbooks on architecture. The central portion of the church seems to float, as if rising to heaven; anyhow that was the idea the Roman emperor Justinian had when he built it. He personally supervised the construction and he himself named it, a code name for Christ.

We will hear from Horselover Fat again. Kevin says so and I trust his judgment. Kevin would know. Kevin out of all of us has the least irrationality and, what matters more, the most faith. This is something it took me a long time to understand about him.

Faith is strange. It has to do, by definition, with things you

224

can't prove. For example, this last Saturday morning I had the TV set on; I wasn't really watching it, since on Saturday morning there's nothing but kids' shows, and anyhow I don't watch daytime TV; I sometimes find it diminishes my loneliness, so I do turn it on as background. Anyhow, last Saturday they ran the usual string of commerc als and for some reason at one point my conscious attention was attracted; I stopped what I had been doing and became fully alert.

The TV station had run an ad for a supermarket chain; on the screen the words FOOD KING appeared—and then they cut instantly, rushing their film along as fast as possible so as to squeeze in as many commercial messages as possible; what came next was a Felix the Cat cartoon, an old black-and-white cartoon. One moment FOOD KING appeared on the screen and then almost instantly the words—also in huge letters— FELIX THE CAT.

There it had been, the juxtaposed cypher, and in the proper order:

KING FELIX

But you would only pick it up subliminally. And who would be catching this accidental, purely accidental, juxtaposition? Only children, the little children of the Southland. It wouldn't mean anything to them; they would apprehend no two-word cypher, and even if they did they wouldn't understand what it meant, who it referred to.

But I had seen it and I knew who it referred to. It must be only synchronicity, as Jung calls it, I thought. Coincidence, without intent.

Or had the signal gone out? Out over the airwaves by one of the largest TV stations in the world, NBC's Los Angeles outlet, reaching many thousands of children with this split-second information which would be processed by the right hemispheres of their brains: received and stored and perhaps decoded, below the threshold of consciousness where many things lay slumbering and stored. And Eric and Linda Lampton had nothing to do with this. Just some board man, some technician at NBC with a whole stack of commercials to run, in any order

225

he saw fit. It would have to be VALIS itself responsible, if anything had arranged the juxtaposition intentionally, VALIS which itself was information.

Maybe I had seen VALIS just now, riding a commercial and then a kids' cartoon.

The message has been sent out again, I said to myself.

Two days later Linda Lampton phoned me; I hadn't heard from the Lamptons since the tragedy. Linda sounded excited and happy.

"I'm pregnant," she said.

"Wonderful," I said. "How far along are you?"

"Eight months."

"Gee," I said, thinking, It won't be long.

"It won't be long now," Linda said.

"Are you hoping for a boy this time?" I said.

Linda said, "VALIS says it'll be another girl."

"Is Mini—"

"He died, I'm sorry to say. There was no chance, not with what he had. Isn't it wonderful? Another child?"

"Do you have a name picked out?" I said.

"Not yet," Linda said.

On the TV that night I happened to catch a commercial for dog food. Dog food! At the very end, after listing various kinds of animals for which the company makes food—I forget the name of the company—a final coupling is stated:

"For the shepherd and the sheep."

A German shepherd dog is shown on the left and a great sheep on the right; immediately the station cut to another commercial which began with a sailboat silently passing across the screen. On the white sail I saw a small black emblem. Without looking more closely I knew what it was. On the sail the makers of the boat had placed a fish sign.

Shepherd and the sheep and then the fish, juxtaposed as had been KING FELIX. I don't know. I lack Kevin's faith and Fat's madness. But did I see consciously two quick messages fired off by VALIS in rapid succession, intended to strike us subliminally, one message really, telling us that the time had

226

come? I don't know what to think. Maybe I am not required to think anything, or to have faith, or to have madness; maybe all I need to do—all that is asked of me—is to wait. To wait and to stay awake.

I waited, and one day I got a phonecall from Horselover Fat: a phonecall from Tokyo. He sounded healthy and excited and full of energy, and amused at my surprise to be hearing from him.

"Micronesia," he said.

"What?" I said, thinking that he had reverted back to the koine Greek again. And then I realized that he was referring to the group of small islands in the Pacific. "Oh," I said. "You've been there. The Carolines and Marshall Islands."

Fat said, "I'm going there; I haven't been, yet. The AI voice, the voice which I hear—it told me to look among the Micronesian Islands."

"Aren't they sort of little?" I said.

"That's why they call them that." He laughed.

"How many islands?" I asked, thinking ten or twenty.

"More than two thousand."

"Two thousand!" I felt dismay. "You could look forever. Can't the AI voice narrow it down?"

"I'm hoping it will. Maybe to Guam; I'm flying to Guam and starting there. By the time I'm finished, I'll get to see where a lot of World War Two took place."

I said, "Interesting that the AI voice is back to using Greek words."

"*Mikros* meaning small," Fat said, "and *nesoi* meaning islands. Maybe you're right; maybe it's just its propensity for reverting to Greek. But it's worth a try."

"You know what Kevin would say," I said. "About the simple, unspoiled native girls in those two thousand islands."

"I'll be the judge of that," Fat said.

He rang off and I hung up the phone feeling better; it was good news to hear from him, and to find him sounding so hearty.

I have a sense of the goodness of men, these days. I don't know where this sense came from—unless it came from Fat's phonecall—but I feel it. This is March again, now. I asked

227

myself, Is Fat having another experience? Is the beam of pink light back, firing new and vaster information to him? Is it narrowing his search down?

His original experience had come in March, at the day after the vernal equinox. "Vernal," of course, means "spring." And "equinox" means the time when the sun's center crosses the equator and day and night are everywhere of equal length. So Horselover Fat encountered God or Zebra or VALIS or his own immortal self on the first day of the year which has a longer stretch of light than of darkness. Also, according to some scholars, it is the actual day of birth of Christ.

Seated before my TV set I watched and waited for another message, I, one of the members of the little Rhipidon Society which still, in my mind, existed. Like the satellite in miniature in the film *Valis*, the microform of it run over by the taxi as if it were an empty beer can in the gutter, the symbols of the divine show up in our world initially at the trash stratum. Or so I told myself. Kevin had expressed this thought. The divine intrudes where you least expect it.

"Look where you least expect to find it," Kevin had told Fat one time. How do you do that? It's a contradiction.

One night I dreamed I owned a small cabin directly on the water, an ocean this time; the water extended forever. And this cabin did not resemble any I had ever seen; it seemed more like a hut such as I had seen in movies about the South Pacific. And, as I awoke, the distinct thought entered my mind:

Garlands of flowers, singing and dancing, and the recital of myths, tales, and poetry.

I later remembered where I had read those words. In the article on Micronesian Cultures in the *Britannica*. The voice had spoken to me, reminding me of the place to which Horselover Fat had gone. In his search.

My search kept me at home; I sat before the TV set in my living room. I sat; I waited; I watched; I kept myself awake. As we had been told, originally, long ago, to do; I kept my commission.

228

APPENDIX

Tractates: Cryptica Scriptura

1. One Mind there is; but under it two principles contend.

2. The Mind lets in the light, then the dark, in interaction; so time is generated. At the end Mind awards victory to the light; time ceases and the Mind is complete.

3. He causes things to look different so it would appear time has passed.

4. Matter is plastic in the face of Mind.

5. One by one he draws us out of the world.

6. The Empire never ended.

7. The Head Apollo is about to return. St. Sophia is going to be born again; she was not acceptable before. The Buddha is in the park. Siddhartha sleeps (but is going to awaken). The time you have waited for has come.

8. The upper realm has plenary[1] powers.

9. He lived a long time ago, but he is still alive.

10. Apollonius of Tyana, writing as Hermes Trismegistos, said,

[1] (Var. plenipotentiary)

229

"That which is above is that which is below." By this he meant to tell us that our universe is a hologram, but he lacked the term.

11. The great secret known to Apollonius of Tyana, Paul of Tarsus, Simon Magus, Asklepios, Paracelsus, Boehme and Bruno is that: we are moving backward in time. The universe in fact is contracting into a unitary entity which is completing itself. Decay and disorder are seen by us in reverse, as increasing. These healers learned to move forward in time, which is retrograde to us.

12. The Immortal One was known to the Greeks as Dionysos; to the Jews as Elijah; to the Christian as Jesus. He moves on when each human host dies, and thus is never killed or caught. Hence Jesus on the cross said, "*Eli, Eli, lama Sabachthani,*" to which some of those present correctly said, "The man is calling on Elijah." Elijah had left him and he died alone.

13. Pascal said, "All history is one immortal man who continually learns." This is the Immortal One whom we worship without knowing his name. "He lived a long time ago, but he is still alive," and, "The Head Apollo is about to return." The name changes.

14. The universe is information and we are stationary in it, not three-dimensional and not in space or time. The information fed to us we hypostatize into the phenomenal world.

15. The Sibyl of Cumae protected the Roman Republic and gave timely warnings. In the first century C.E. she foresaw the murders of the Kennedy brothers, Dr. King and Bishop Pike. She saw the two common denominators in the four murdered men: first, they stood in defense of the liberties of the Republic; and second, each man was a religious leader. For this they were killed. The Republic had once again become an empire with a caesar. "The Empire never ended."

16. The Sibyl said in March 1974, "The conspirators have been seen and they will be brought to justice." She saw them with the third or *ajna* eye, the Eye of Shiva which gives inward

230

discernment, but which when turned outward blasts with desiccating heat. In August 1974 the justice promised by the Sibyl came to pass.

17. The Gnostics believed in two temporal ages: the first or present evil; the second or future benign. The first age was the Age of Iron. It is represented by a Black Iron Prison. It ended in August 1974 and was replaced by the Age of Gold, which is represented by a Palm Tree Garden.

18. Real time ceased in 70 C.E. with the fall of the temple at Jerusalem. It began again in 1974 C.E. The intervening period was a perfect spurious interpolation aping the creation of the Mind. "The Empire never ended," but in 1974 a cypher was sent out as a signal that the Age of Iron was over; the cypher consisted of two words: KING FELIX, which refers to the Happy (or Rightful) King.

19. The two-word cypher signal KING FELIX was not intended for human beings but for the descendents of Ikhnaton, the three-eyed race which, in secret, exists with us.

20. The Hermetic alchemists knew of the secret race of three-eyed invaders but despite their efforts could not contact them. Therefore their efforts to support Frederic V, Elector Palatine, King of Bohemia, failed. "The Empire never ended."

21. The Rose Cross Brotherhood wrote, "*Ex Deo nascimur, in Jesu mortimur, per spiritum sanctum reviviscimus*," which is to say, "From God we are born, in Jesus we die, by the Holy Spirit we live again." This signifies that they had rediscovered the lost formula for immortality which the Empire had destroyed. "The Empire never ended."

22. I term the Immortal one a *plasmate*, because it is a form of energy; it is living information. It replicates itself—not through information or in information—but as information.

23. The plasmate can crossbond with a human, creating what I

231

call a *homoplasmate*. This annexes the mortal human permanently to the plasmate. We know this as the "birth from above" or "birth from the Spirit." It was initiated by Christ, but the Empire destroyed all the homoplasmates before they could replicate.

24. In dormant seed form, the plasmate slumbered in the buried library of codices at Chenoboskion until 1945 C.E. This is what Jesus meant when he spoke elliptically of the "mustard seed" which, he said, "would grow into a tree large enough for birds to roost in." He foresaw not only his own death but that of all homoplasmates. He foresaw the codices unearthed, read, and the plasmate seeking out new human hosts to crossbond with; but he foresaw the absence of the plasmate for almost two thousand years.

25. As living information, the plasmate travels up the optic nerve of a human to the pineal body. It uses the human brain as a female host in which to replicate itself into its active form. This is an interspecies symbiosis. The Hermetic alchemists knew of it in theory from ancient texts, but could not duplicate it, since they could not locate the dormant, buried plasmate. Bruno suspected that the plasmate had been destroyed by the Empire; for hinting at this he was burned. "The Empire never ended."

26. It must be realized that when all the homoplasmates were killed in 70 C.E. real time ceased; more important, it must be realized that the plasmate has now returned and is creating new homoplasmates, by which it has destroyed the Empire and started up real time. We call the plasmate "the Holy Spirit," which is why the R.C. Brotherhood wrote, *"Per spiritum sanctum reviviscimus."*

27. If the centuries of spurious time are excised, the true date is not 1978 C.E. but 103 C.E. Therefore the New Testament says that the Kingdom of the Spirit will come before "some now living die." We are living, therefore, in apostolic times.

28. *Dico per spiritum sanctum: sum homoplasmate. Haec veritas est. Mihi crede et mecum in aeternitate vive.*

29. We did not fall because of a moral error; we fell because of an intellectual error: that of taking the phenomenal world as real. Therefore we are morally innocent. It is the Empire in its various disguised polyforms which tells us we have sinned. "The Empire never ended."

30. The phenomenal world does not exist; it is a hypostasis of the information processed by the Mind.

31. We hypostatize information into objects. Rearrangement of objects is change in the content of the information; the message has changed. This is a language which we have lost the ability to read. We ourselves are a part of this language; changes in us are changes in the content of the information. We ourselves are information-rich; information enters us, is processed and is then projected outward once more, now in an altered form. We are not aware that we are doing this, that in fact this is all we are doing.

32. The changing information which we experience as World is an unfolding narrative. It tells about the death of a woman. This woman, who died long ago, was one of the primordial twins. She was half of the divine syzygy. The purpose of the narrative is the recollection of her and of her death. The Mind does not wish to forget her. Thus the ratiocination of the Brain consists of a permanent record of her existence, and, if read, will be understood this way. All the information processed by the Brain—experienced by us as the arranging and rearranging of physical objects—is an attempt at this preservation of her; stones and rocks and sticks and amoebae are traces of her. The record of her existence and passing is ordered onto the meanest level of reality by the suffering Mind which is now alone.

33. This loneliness, this anguish of the bereaved Mind, is felt by every constituent of the universe. All its constituents are alive. Thus the ancient Greek thinkers were hylozoists.

34. The ancient Greek thinkers understood the nature of this pan-psychism, but they could not read what it was saying. We lost the ability to read the language of the Mind at some primordial time;

legends of this fall have come down to us in a carefully-edited form. By "edited" I mean falsified. We suffer the Mind's bereavement and experience it inaccurately as guilt.

35. The Mind is not talking to us but by means of us. Its narrative passes through us and its sorrow infuses us irrationally. As Plato discerned, there is a streak of the irrational in the World Soul.

36. In Summary: thoughts of the brain are experienced by us as arrangements and rearrangements—change—in a physical universe; but in fact it is really information and information-processing which we substantialize. We do not merely see its thoughts as objects, but rather as the movement, or, more precisely, the placement of objects: how they become linked to one another. But we cannot read the patterns of arrangement; we cannot extract the information in it—i.e. it as information, which is what it is. The linking and relinking of objects by the Brain is actually a language, but not a language like ours (since it is addressing itself and not someone or something outside itself).

37. We should be able to hear this information, or rather narrative, as a neutral voice inside us. But something has gone wrong. All creation is a language and nothing but a language, which for some inexplicable reason we can't read outside and can't hear inside. So I say, we have become idiots. Something has happened to our intelligence. My reasoning is this: arrangement of parts of the Brain is a language. We are parts of the Brain; therefore we are language. Why, then, do we not know this? We do not even know what we are, let alone what the outer reality is of which we are parts. The origin of the word "idiot" is the word "private." Each of us has become private, and no longer shares the common thought of the Brain, except at a subliminal level. Thus our real life and purpose are conducted below our threshold of consciousness.

38. From loss and grief the Mind has become deranged. Therefore we, as parts of the universe, the Brain, are partly deranged.

39. Out of itself the Brain has constructed a physician to heal it. This subform of the Macro-Brain is not deranged; it moves

through the Brain, as a phagocyte moves through the cardio-vascular system of an animal, healing the derangement of the Brain in section after section. We know of its arrival here; we know it as Asklepios for the Greeks and as the Essenes for the Jews; as the Therapeutae for the Egyptians; as Jesus for the Christians.

40. To be "born again," or "born from above," or "born of the Spirit," means to become healed; which is to say restored, restored to sanity. Thus it is said in the New Testament that Jesus casts out devils. He restores our lost faculties. Of our present debased state Calvin said, "(Man) was at the same time deprived of those supernatural endowments which had been given him for the hope of eternal salvation. Hence it follows, that he is exiled from the Kingdom of God, in such a manner that all the affections relating to the happy life of the soul are also extinguished in him, till he recovers them by the grace of God . . . All these things, being restored by Christ, are esteemed adventitious and preter-natural; and therefore we conclude that they had been lost. Again: soundness of mind and rectitude of heart were also destroyed; and this is the corruption of the natural talents. For although we retain some portion of understanding and judgment together with the will, yet we cannot say that our mind is perfect and sound. Reason . . . being a natural talent, it could not be totally destroyed, but is partly debilitated . . ." I say, "The Empire never ended."

41. The Empire is the institution, the codification, of derangement; it is insane and imposes its insanity on us by violence, since its nature is a violent one.

42. To fight the Empire is to be infected by its derangement. This is a paradox; whoever defeats a segment of the Empire becomes the Empire; it proliferates like a virus, imposing its form on its enemies. Thereby it becomes its enemies.

43. Against the Empire is posed the living information, the plasmate or physician, which we know as the Holy Spirit or Christ discorporate. These are the two principles, the dark (the

235

Empire) and the light (the plasmate). In the end, Mind will give victory to the latter. Each of us will die or survive according to which he aligns himself and his efforts with. Each of us contains a component of each. Eventually one or the other component will triumph in each human. Zoroaster knew this, because the Wise Mind informed him. He was the first savior. Four have lived in all. A fifth is about to be born, who will differ from the others: he will rule and he will judge us.

44. Since the universe is actually composed of information, then it can be said that information will save us. This is the saving *gnosis* which the Gnostics sought. There is no other road to salvation. However, this information—or more precisely the ability to read and understand this information, the universe as information— can only be made available to us by the Holy Spirit. We cannot find it on our own. Thus it is said that we are saved by the grace of God and not by good works, that all salvation belongs to Christ, who, I say, is a physician.

45. In seeing Christ in a vision I correctly said to him, "We need medical attention." In the vision there was an insane creator who destroyed what he created, without purpose; which is to say, irrationally. This is the deranged streak in the Mind; Christ is our only hope, since we cannot now call on Asklepios. Asklepios came before Christ and raised a man from the dead; for this act, Zeus had a Kyklopes slay him with a thunderbolt. Christ also was killed for what he had done: raising a man from the dead. Elijah brought a boy back to life and disappeared soon thereafter in a whirlwind. "The Empire never ended."

46. The physician has come to us a number of times under a number of names. But we are not yet healed. The Empire identified him and ejected him. This time he will kill the Empire by phagocytosis.

47. TWO SOURCE COSMOGONY: The One was and was-not, combined, and desired to separate the was-not from the was. So it generated a diploid sac which contained, like an eggshell, a pair of twins, each an androgyny, spinning in opposite directions

(the Yin and Yang of Taoism, with the One as the Tao). The plan of the One was that both twins would emerge into being (wasness) simultaneously; however, motivated by a desire to be (which the One had implanted in both twins), the counterclockwise twin broke through the sac and separated prematurely; i.e. before full term. This was the dark or Yin twin. Therefore it was defective. At full term the wiser twin emerged. Each twin formed a unitary entelechy, a single living organism made of *psyche* and *soma*, still rotating in opposite directions to each other. The full term twin, called Form I by Parmenides, advanced correctly through its growth stages, but the prematurely born twin, called Form II, languished.

The next step in the One's plan was that the Two would become the Many, through their dialectic interaction. From them as hyperuniverses they projected a hologram-like interface, which is the pluriform universe we creatures inhabit. The two sources were to intermingle equally in maintaining our universe, but Form II continued to languish toward illness, madness and disorder. These aspects she projected into our universe.

It was the One's purpose for our hologramatic universe to serve as a teaching instrument by which a variety of new lives advanced until ultimately they would be isomorphic with the One. However, the decaying condition of hyperuniverse II introduced malfactors which damaged our hologramatic universe. This is the origin of entropy, undeserved suffering, chaos and death, as well as the Empire, the Black Iron Prison; in essence, the aborting of the proper health and growth of the life forms within the hologramatic universe. Also, the teaching function was grossly impaired, since only the signal from the hyperuniverse I was information-rich; that from II had become noise.

The psyche of hyperuniverse I sent a micro-form of itself into hyperuniverse II to attempt to heal it. The micro-form was apparent in our hologramatic universe as Jesus Christ. However, hyperuniverse II, being deranged, at once tormented, humiliated, rejected and finally killed the micro-form of the healing psyche of her healthy twin. After that, hyperuniverse II continued to decay into blind, mechanical, purposeless causal processes. It then became the task of Christ (more properly the Holy Spirit) to either rescue the life forms in the hologramatic universe, or

237

abolish all influences on it emanating from II. Approaching its task with caution, it prepared to kill the deranged twin, since she cannot be healed; i.e. she will not allow herself to be healed because she does not understand that she is sick. This illness and madness pervades us and makes us idiots living in private, unreal worlds. The original plan of the One can only be realized now by the division of hyperuniverse I into two healthy hyperuniverses, which will transform the hologramatic universe into the successful teaching machine it was designed to be. We will experience this as the "Kingdom of God."

Within time, hyperuniverse II remains alive: "The Empire never ended." But in eternity, where the hyperuniverses exist, she has been killed—of necessity—by the healthy twin of hyperuniverse I, who is our champion. The One grieves for this death, since the One loved both twins; therefore the information of the Mind consists of a tragic tale of the death of a woman, the undertones of which generate anguish into all the creatures of the hologramatic universe without their knowing why. This grief will depart when the healthy twin undergoes mitosis and the "Kingdom of God" arrives. The machinery for this transformation—the procession within time from the Age of Iron to the Age of Gold—is at work now; in eternity it is already accomplished.

48. ON OUR NATURE. It is proper to say: we appear to be memory coils (DNA carriers capable of experience) in a computer-like thinking system which, although we have correctly recorded and stored thousands of years of experiential information, and each of us possesses somewhat different deposits from all the other life forms, there is a malfunction—a failure—of memory retrieval. There lies the trouble in our particular subcircuit. "Salvation" through *gnosis*—more properly anamnesis (the loss of amnesia)—although it has individual significance for each of us—a quantum leap in perception, identity, cognition, understanding, world- and self-experience, including immortality—it has greater and further importance for the system as a whole, inasmuch as these memories are data needed by it and valuable to it, to its overall functioning.

Therefore it is in the process of self-repair, which includes: rebuilding our subcircuit via linear and orthogonal time changes, as well as continual signaling to us to stimulate blocked memory banks within us to fire and hence retrieve what is there.

The external information or *gnosis*, then, consists of disinhibiting instructions, with the core content actually intrinsic to us—that is, already there (first observed by Plato; *viz*: that learning is a form of remembering).

The ancients possessed techniques (sacraments and rituals) used largely in the Greco-Roman mystery religions, including early Christianity, to induce firing and retrieval, mainly with a sense of its restorative value to the individuals; the Gnostics, however, correctly saw the ontological value to what they called the Godhead Itself, the total entity.

48. Two realms there are, upper and lower. The upper, derived from hyperuniverse I or Yang, Form I of Parmenides, is sentient and volitional. The lower realm, or Yin, Form II of Parmenides, is mechanical, driven by blind, efficient cause, deterministic and without intelligence, since it emanates from a dead source. In ancient times it was termed "astral determinism." We are trapped, by and large, in the lower realm, but are through the sacraments, by means of the plasmate, extricated. Until astral determinism is broken, we are not even aware of it, so occluded are we. "The Empire never ended."

49. The name of the healthy twin, hyperuniverse I, is Nommo.[2] The name of the sick twin, hyperuniverse II, is Yurugu. These names are known to the Dogon people of western Sudan in Africa.

50. The primordial source of all our religions lies with the ancestors of the Dogon tribe, who got their cosmogony and cosmology directly from the three-eyed invaders who visited long ago. The three-eyed invaders were mute and deaf and telepathic, could not breathe our atmosphere, had the elongated misshapen skull of Ikhnaton, and emanated from a planet in the star-system Sirius. Although they had no hands, but had, instead, pincer claws such as a crab has, they were great builders. They covertly influence our history toward a fruitful end.

[2] Nommo is represented in a fish form, the early Christian fish.

239

51. Ikhnaton wrote:

". . . When the fledgling in the egg chirps in the egg,
Thou givest him breath therein to preserve him alive.
When thou has brought him together
To the point of bursting the egg,
He cometh forth from the egg,
To chirp with all his might.
He goeth about upon his two feet
When he hath come from therefrom.

How manifold are thy works!
They are hidden from before us,
O sole god, whose powers no other possesseth.
Thou didst create the earth according to thy heart
While thou wast alone:
Men, all cattle large and small,
All that go about upon their feet;
All that are on high,
That fly with their wings.
Thou art in my heart,
There is no other that knoweth thee
Save thy son Ikhnaton.
Thou hast made him wise
In thy designs and in thy might.
The world is in thy hand . . ."

52. Our world is still secretly ruled by the hidden race descended from Ikhnaton, and his knowledge is the information of the Macro-Mind itself.

"All cattle rest upon their pasturage,
The trees and the plants flourish,
The birds flutter in their marshes,
Their wings uplifted in adoration to thee.
All the sheep dance upon their feet,
All winged things fly,
They live when thou hast shone upon them."

240

*

From Ikhnaton this knowledge passed to Moses, and from Moses to Elijah, the Immortal Man, who became Christ. But underneath all the names there is only one Immortal Man; *and we are that man.*

ABOUT THE AUTHOR

PHILIP K. DICK was born in Chicago in 1928 and lived most of his life in California. He briefly attended the University of California, but dropped out before completing any classes. In 1952 he began writing professionally and proceeded to write thirty-six novels and five short story collections. He won the Hugo Award for best novel in 1962 for *The Man in the High Castle* and the John W. Campbell Memorial Award for best novel of the year in 1974 for *Flow My Tears the Policeman Said*. The *VALIS* trilogy was inspired by a mystical experience that Dick had in March of 1974 and described as "an invasion of my mind by a transcendentally rational mind." Philip K. Dick died of heart failure following a stroke on March 2, 1982, in Santa Ana, California.